'Turnham Malpas rectory. Anna Sanderson speaking.'

'Anna! Good morning. Craddock Fitch here. I've just heard some gossip about you and I think you ought to know. They're saying in the village that Paddy Cleary is living with you. I mean really living, as in live-in lover.' He left a pause, didn't get an answer, so continued, 'It needs scotching straight away, it's very damaging gossip. Don't know how, but scotch it otherwise it'll be at the Abbey before nightfall, and the balloon will go up.' Still no reply. 'It's not true, obviously, but it still needs dealing with, as of now. Good morning to you. Sorry to be giving you such bad news.'

Anna put down the receiver, sick at heart.

Educated at a co-educational Quaker boarding school, Rebecca Shaw went on to qualify as a teacher of deaf children. After her marriage, she spent the ensuing years enjoying bringing up her family. The departure of the last of her four children to university has given her the time and opportunity to write. *Whispers in the Village* is the latest in the highly popular Tales from Turnham Malpas series. Visit her website at www.rebeccashaw.co.uk.

By Rebecca Shaw

Whispers in the Village

Rebecca Shaw

ORION

An Orion paperback

First published in Great Britain in 2005
by Orion
This paperback edition published in 2005
by Orion Books Ltd,
Orion House, 5 Upper St Martin's Lane,
London WC2H 9EA

The Orion Publishing Group's policy is to use papers that
are natural, renewable and recyclable products and
made from wood grown in sustainable forests. The logging
and manufacturing processes are expected to conform to
the environmental regulations of the country of origin.

A CIP catalogue record for this book is available
from the British Library.

Typeset by Deltatype Ltd, Birkenhead, Merseyside

Printed and bound in Great Britain by
Clays Ltd, St Ives plc

www.orionbooks.co.uk

INHABITANTS OF TURNHAM MALPAS

Willie Biggs	Retired verger
Sylvia Biggs	His wife and housekeeper at the Rectory
Sir Ronald Bissett	Retired Trade Union leader
Lady Sheila Bissett	His wife
James (Jimbo) Charter-Plackett	Owner of the Village Store
Harriet Charter-Plackett	His wife
Fergus, Finlay, Flick and Fran	Their children
Katherine Charter-Plackett	Jimbo's mother
Alan Crimble	Barman at the Royal Oak
Linda Crimble	His wife
Lewis Crimble	Their son
H. Craddock Fitch	Owner of Turnham House
Kate Fitch	Village school headteacher
Maggie Dobbs	School caretaker
Jimmy Glover	Taxi driver
Mrs Jones	A village gossip
Vince Jones	Her husband
Barry Jones	Her son and estate carpenter
Pat Jones	Barry's wife
Dean and Michelle	Barry and Pat's children

Revd Peter Harris MA (Oxon)	Rector of the parish
Dr Caroline Harris	His wife
Alex and Beth	Their children
Jeremy Mayer	Manager at Turnham House
Venetia Mayer	His wife
Neville Neal	Accountant and church treasurer
Liz Neal	His wife
Guy and Hugh	Their children
Tom Nicholls	Assistant in the Store
Evie Nicholls	His wife
Anne Parkin	Retired secretary
Jenny Sweetapple	Complementary medicine practitioner
Sir Ralph Templeton	Retired from the diplomatic service
Lady Muriel Templeton	His wife
Andy Moorhouse	Social Worker
Dicky & Georgie Tutt	Licensees at the Royal Oak
Bel Tutt	Assistant in the Village Store
Don Wright	Maintenance engineer (now retired)
Vera Wright	Cleaner at the nursing home in Penny Fawcett
Rhett Wright	Their grandson

Whispers in the Village

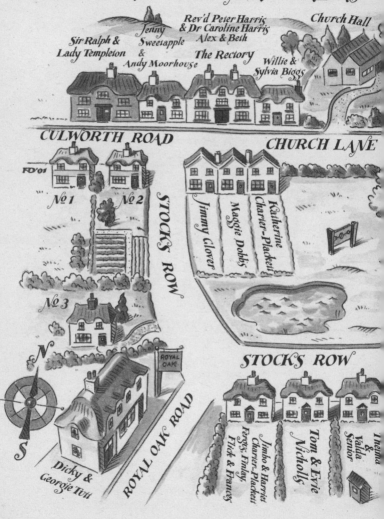

THE VILLAGE OF TURNHAM MALPAS

Sir Ralph & Lady Templeton

Jenny Sweetapple & Andy Moorhouse

Rev'd Peter Harris & Dr Caroline Harris
Alex & Beth

The Rectory

Church Hall

Willie & Sylvia Biggs

FD'01

CULWORTH ROAD

CHURCH LANE

No 1

No 2

STOCKS ROW

Jimmy Glover

Maggie Dobbs

Katherine Charter-Plackett

No 3

N

S

ROYAL OAK

STOCKS ROW

Dicky & Georgie Tutt

ROYAL OAK ROAD

Jimbo & Harriet Charter-Plackett
Fergus, Finlay, Flick & Franey

Tom & Evie Nicholls

Thelma & Valda Senior

Chapter 1

So, now they'd all got over saying *au revoir* to Peter, Caroline and the twins, and the rectory had stood empty and abandoned for a week, there were lights on once more. Some of the villagers had caught a glimpse now and then of her emptying the van she'd hired to transport her belongings and they had introduced themselves, but tonight everyone was going to a 'get-to-know-you' party in the church hall.

It had been a serious shock when they found out their locum rector was a woman. A *woman*! They'd narrowly escaped having their own railway station, tolerated the coming of the wireless, then the telephone poles and TV, they'd embraced computers, mobile phones – and a blessed nuisance they were on the Saturday shopping bus – and digital this and DVD that, but a woman rector! This was one step too far.

'She'll have to be blinking good to replace Peter,' someone could be overheard saying in the pub, at the table nearest the bar.

But then someone else added, 'No one living could replace Peter. He was one in a million. And so was Caroline.'

Sylvia Biggs dabbed at her eyes and sniffed loudly. 'Well, there's one thing certain: I shall miss them. I've worked at the rectory since the twins first came home from the hospital; they're like my own grandchildren, and I'm worried to death. All that heat and them nasty crawly things. They could catch anything in a blasted hot place like Africa.'

'They'll be all right, kids is resilient.' Willie patted her arm comfortingly. 'Don't fret yourself.'

'They're not any old kids, they're *children*, Willie, *my children*, and very sensitive. I shan't need to make their favourite for twelve whole months.' Sylvia dabbed her eyes again.

'What is their favourite?'

'Pecan pie now. It used to be Farmhouse Delight and then it was Crunchie.'

'Well, make it for me instead if things get desperate.' By now Willie had an arm around her shoulder, because he could feel his Sylvia was about to cry. 'Now, come on, love, there's worse things at sea.'

'Not much. When they come back they'll have grown, and they won't be mine any more.'

'Of course they will. I bet they'll be asking for pecan pie as they walk in the door.'

'As for missing the rector and Doctor Harris . . .' Sylvia gulped. 'It doesn't bear thinking about.'

Vera Wright, squeezed on the settle between her Don and Sylvia, said, 'Still, you'll be able to keep an eye on things, won't you, while they're away? Dust Doctor Harris's ornaments and such?'

Sylvia shook her head. 'Says she couldn't dream of having someone to clean when she's perfectly capable of doing it herself. So, I'm out of a job.'

'You'll miss the money.'

Sylvia drew herself up tall. 'Actually it's not the money

I'm missing, it's them. And dusting the flatback Staffordshire pottery Doctor Harris collects. Lovely, it is. We wash 'em together, her and me. They won't get that kind of attention, not now.'

'Never mind, you can always give 'em a good do when they get back. Well, if we're to get something to eat at this get-to-know-you party, we'd better be off.' Vera picked up her bag and said to Don, 'Come on, love.' Don stood up, then forgot why he had and sat down again. 'Don, we're off to the party. Get up.'

'Yes, that's right.' The two of them, thinking Willie and Sylvia were following them, set off for the door.

But Sylvia remained there, staring into space. Willie began to worry; she'd sat staring into space far too often these last few days.

'We've got to face it, love, they've gone, but if we keep busy, they'll be back before we know it. It's only for a year and, like you said yourself, all four of them need a complete change. Young Alex and Beth especially. They seemed to grow up overnight after—'

Sylvia turned on him, eyes blazing and fists clenched. 'Don't mention *her* name in my presence. She might have given birth to them, but she isn't and never will be their mother. She needed horse-whipping, turning up like she did to meet the twins. It upset Doctor Harris something terrible. It's all because of her they left and this party's on tonight. Damn her. And damn and blast this Anna whatever-she's-called. If you think I'm going to speak to her you've another think coming, because I'm not.'

'Now see here, my Sylvia, it's not her fault she's been sent to look after us all. She didn't ask to, she was *sent* from the Abbey, so you've to put a good face on it and smile. Maybe she's dreading this evening as much as you.'

3

Sylvia didn't answer. Her hurt was far too deep to speak about. No one, not even Willie, knew how crushingly sad she felt. When your whole world has crashed about your ears, when you feel as though you've a raw, open wound inside yourself, it's hard to carry on as though your world is hunky-dory. She got to her feet and led the way out, waving here and there to friends, hoping none of them could see the gaping hole inside her.

The church hall was agog when she and Willie arrived. The new rector was standing at the door greeting everyone, with Sir Ralph at the side of her, introducing them all. So there was to be no avoiding her.

'The rector and I've already met, Sir Ralph.' There was a finality in Sylvia's voice, which left nothing for anyone else to say.

Ralph came to the rescue. 'Of course you must have. You know, Anna, the rectory has relied on Sylvia since the twins first came home from the hospital. She was Caroline's right-hand woman, weren't you, Sylvia?'

'I was. And proud to be, too.'

Anna's grip on Sylvia's hand was firm, which instantly gave the impression she was a force to be reckoned with. 'Delighted to see you again, Sylvia. And you, Willie.'

Willie shook hands. 'You've a good memory for names.'

'One needs it in this game.'

Willie was captivated by Anna's green eyes; they looked so directly at him, giving the clear-cut impression she had nothing to hide. He liked that. Her dark hair and flawless complexion were very attractive, though she wasn't beautiful at all. Then she really smiled at him and in a split second had won him over.

'There's tea and refreshments in the small hall, and they look delicious. Help yourselves.'

'Thank you, we will. We both of us is looking forward to enjoying your time with us. See you soon.' Willie shook hands with her again and turned to allow Sylvia to do the same, but she'd already left his side and was heading for the refreshments. As he went after her he thought he'd better play his cards close to his chest. He wouldn't tell her how wholesomely good the new rector appeared to be to him.

Anna Sanderson ran a finger around her clerical collar as though it felt tight. 'I'm afraid Sylvia is upset about me. But I can't help it. I'm one of those people who needs their own space to retreat to, and Sylvia cleaning for me wouldn't help to make the rectory my own.'

'Don't worry, please. A year off won't harm.'

'There'd always be comparisons, you know.'

'Of course.' Ralph introduced the people who'd just arrived. 'This is Sir Ronald and Lady Bissett.'

Anna only just stopped herself from commenting on Lady Bissett's outfit. It was startling to say the least; a leopard-skin fur coat (Was it real?), leopard-patterned dress (more suitable for a cocktail party), and a pair of faux leopard-skin shoes, which Anna was sure she'd last seen on TV at one of the party conferences.

'Delighted to meet you, Lady Bissett, and you, Sir Ronald. So pleased you could come.'

Sheila Bissett gushed her greetings. 'We wouldn't have missed it for the world, so looked forward to meeting you. A pleasure to see a lady in a clerical collar. I'm all for it.' She glanced sideways at Ron and saw the sickly grin on his face. Well, really!

5

Ron said, holding Anna's hand for longer than was necessary, 'Pleased to meet you I'm sure.' And when he let go of her hand he stood there, speechless, looking an idiot.

'Everyone calls me Sheila and I'd be pleased if you did the same.' She nudged Ron into action. 'We'll head for the refreshments, if you don't mind. Don't want to hold up the queue.' Ron trudged after her, noting from her back view that she was furious with him.

While they stood queueing for the gateaux and coffee, Sheila said, 'Well?'

'What?'

'What do you think of her?'

'Seems OK to me.'

'There was no need to gawk. Made yourself look a right fool, you did. I knew you were impressed, but I think she's very ordinary. Not a patch on Peter for charisma.' She dwelt silently on Peter's good looks and magnetism, and remembered the time when her heart had gone head over heels as he'd held her hand while appealing to her better nature. He'd truly brought out the best in her. Well, this Anna wouldn't be bringing out the best in her, because she wouldn't give her the chance. Not likely. 'She'll have to earn her Brownie points as far as I'm concerned. But at least her eyes are not as perceptive as Peter's. He knew my every thought, I'm sure.'

Ron said, 'Look, there's Don.'

'So there is. Vera's determined to make it look as though everything's all right, but it isn't. How he drives that car I don't know, I'm sure it's illegal, him as he is.'

'Wonder he survived, falling from that height.'

'You're right there. I feel sorry for Vera; she's not quite in our class but she means well. For heaven's sake, shove up, Ron, you're holding the queue up. And you've

6

chosen the creamiest, richest cake on the table. Will you never learn sense? No wonder your gut is like it is.'

Ron ignored her bullying as he always did. It was no good her pretending the two of them were from the higher echelons. He was a pragmatist and knew he only had his title because it was the easiest way to get rid of him from his union, 'for services rendered, thirty years a union man, a champion of the underdog, always the peacemaker, his valued contributions . . .' And so it went on. He knew exactly where he stood, very close to the bottom of the pile, but if it pleased Sheila to think otherwise then why not let her? Kept her off his back. He glanced at her and decided she wasn't such a bad old thing, although she hardly ever got her clothes right.

Relieved, Ron spotted his son-in-law. 'Gilbert!' Now here was someone who called a spade a spade and never pretended anything else. 'Gilbert!' He waved furiously and at last Gilbert saw them. He strode across, another one who didn't know how to dress. Here was he, Ron, in his countryman's ginger tweed suit, itched to death by the roughness of it, and strangled by his collar and tie, all worn to please Sheila. But Gilbert pleased himself and he was dressed casually as he always was except on Sundays when he wore his choirmaster's outfit. Tonight it was a brick-red shirt, open almost to his navel, with a pair of black cord trousers, fitting where they touched and his everyday open sandals without socks. But he had presence, had Gilbert.

Holding his cup and saucer and the plate well away from his mother-in-law, he kissed her on both cheeks and would have hugged her if he could.

'Mother-in-law, lovely to see you! How's things?'

'Fine. How's Louise? She's not with you?'

'No. Young Gilbert has a temperature. Nothing serious, but she didn't want the babysitter having to cope.'

'She doesn't get out enough.'

'I know but it is difficult with five children so young.'

'Mmm. I don't know where she gets it from.'

'What?'

'Having all these children. All Ron and I managed was two, with difficulty, and that felt like two too many.'

'In that case, I won't tell you our news.' Gilbert's dark eyes shone with amusement.

She'd seen that look on his face before and had grown to dread it. Sheila's hand trembled, her coffee threatened to spill over. Her throat felt about to close up. All she could find to say was, 'Not again.'

Gilbert nodded.

'But that'll be six.'

Smiling, Gilbert counted on his fingers. 'Yes. It will. It'll be six and then we're stopping.'

Sheila was reduced to silence. She was damned if she was going to be enthusiastic about it. That'd be six children and the eldest only just seven. It was disgusting. Ron, who liked Gilbert and was deeply envious of his ability to father beautiful children in such rapid succession, clapped him on the shoulder and said, 'Wonderful news! Wonderful! You make me very proud.'

'Louise is thrilled to bits.'

Ron answered, 'I'm sure she is. You've worked miracles with that daughter of ours. Miracles. She's a different woman since she met you.'

'Thanks.' Gilbert bowed slightly in acknowledgement of Ron's praise, adding, 'And you, Sheila, how do you feel?'

'How do I feel? You ask me that? Three was quite

enough, but six! It's indecent of you. Absolutely disgusting! You're worse than rabbits.'

Taken aback by the comparison Gilbert replied with a sharp edge to his voice, 'I don't care a damn what people think and neither does Louise.'

Sheila, speaking before she had engaged her mind, almost shouted, 'She used to care what people thought before you charmed her into your bed. Well, there's one thing for certain: I shan't be rushing to tell people, and I shan't know where to look when they all find out. They'll be sniggering, all of them, behind our backs. It's so embarrassing.' Sheila downed the rest of her coffee, slapped the cup and the remains of her gateaux on a table, and stalked off, avoiding people's eyes in case they'd heard her outburst.

Ron remarked, 'She'll get over it. I'm pleased, but I really think six is enough, if only from the money point of view. They all have to be fed and clothed, you know.'

'I agree. We just love our family life. Love it. I was an only one and very, very, lonely, and when I see our boys playing together I realize what I missed. Being one of a large family rounds off the corners, makes one more able to fit in, if you know what I mean. Louise keeps everything so well organized, but then she always has been good at organization, hasn't she? What do you think to our new rector?'

Ron's eyes swivelled round the room, searching for Anna and found her standing in the doorway to the large hall, deep in conversation with Lady Templeton. Well, Muriel, as they all knew her. No edge to Muriel but sometimes she innocently spoke the truth when it wasn't altogether the moment to do so, but what she said was without any malice. From the look on Anna's face he thought she might be doing that very thing right now.

'. . . You see, my dear, and I say this with trepidation but it has to be said, Peter was an angel sent from heaven. Shock waves went through the village when we heard they were going to Africa. We were all devastated. So all I'm saying is tread carefully; they're all very touchy about him and guard very jealously all the things he did for us when he came. And Caroline and the twins. Very touchy.'

'From what I've heard, he isn't the angel everyone might think he is.'

'I beg your pardon!'

'Well, is he?'

Eyes wide with surprise, Muriel didn't have to think even for a moment. 'Yes, he is. I can't fault him on anything at all.'

'At the Abbey they always spoke of him as the Turnham Malpas Casanova.'

'Casanova!' Muriel was shocked to the core. 'He was no such thing! He couldn't help being handsome and attractive; if anyone did the running it certainly wasn't him.'

'The Village Show secretary? The sports organizer up at the Big House? They all laughed about him and his harem.'

Trembling with indignation, Muriel retorted, '*They* were running after *him*. He didn't do a thing to encourage them. He and Caroline were the happiest couple one could ever meet. And I shall be glad if you did not bring up this matter again. Casanova indeed. It's shameful of you. Listening to gossip, and you a member of the clergy.'

'Not gossip, Muriel, stark fact. Sorry to have upset you. I shan't mention it again.'

'Indeed not. Because it isn't true. Though—'

'Yes?'

Muriel changed her mind about what she was going to say. Instead she decided to retire gracefully. 'I'd better circulate, I have people to meet.' She patted Anna's arm by way of an apology and retired to contemplate the impression those at the Abbey had of Peter. What a scandalmongering lot of cassocks they were. How cruel. She felt so angry and wished Ralph were free to calm her nerves, but he was organizing the chairs with Dean Jones, ready for Anna to address them all.

When they were all seated, Anna gave a perfectly splendid speech, full of promise and energy, which went a long way to relieving the anxiety and resentment some of them had. While various members of the church were getting up in their turn to welcome her, Muriel's mind wandered and her eyes alighted on Dean Jones. Cambridge had certainly altered him. He had so much more poise and confidence now, a far cry from the mumbling, embarrassed teenager he had been. She could see him almost full face from where she sat and she saw then that he was gazing raptly at Anna, his face alight. What with, though? Muriel's mind shied away from the truth; she lit on the word 'fascination' and left it at that, though a blush tinted her cheeks and took a while to subside.

Anna stood up to speak again so Muriel pulled herself back from where she'd been and listened.

'Thank you everyone for such a splendid welcome. I know I shall be making changes, to the services perhaps or to the societies and clubs belonging to the church, but please believe me when I say this, anything I do will be for the good of the church as a whole and not to satisfy my ego. The church is patently a vibrant living part of this community and that's how I shall keep it. Goodnight and God bless you all. See you in the morning. Goodnight.'

They found out what she meant at the ten o'clock service, and Ralph was livid.

Chapter 2

Dean lay in bed the morning after the get-to-know-you party and thought about Anna. Her lovely dark hair, and the way it wasn't quite wavy but almost, and it was the colour of a raven's wing, no, not quite, more the colour of a Scottish river in full spate, dark and deep and a shining peat colour. The grey cassock she wore, well, somehow it made her sexy when it wasn't at all, because you couldn't see a single curve. He'd been ages getting to sleep last night, his head full of Anna and what she'd said and how she'd acted. Had he time to get ready and drive to church? His clock said nine exactly. He had time, if the bathroom was free.

It was. He scrubbed himself raw under the shower, slapped on his body lotion, which he kept hidden behind the lavatory cistern in case they all thought he was a wimp, used matching aftershave liberally, and then got into his dark suit. The shirt could have been better ironed but, as his mother said, if he wasn't satisfied with her handiwork he knew what to do. But he hadn't time to re-iron it now.

Breakfast. He could have eaten a horse.

Barry said with a grin, 'You're in a hurry. Got somewhere to go?'

Dean nodded, his mouth full of muesli. He sensed his

mother warning Barry off with a shake of her head. 'I'm off to church.'

Barry didn't express his surprise, but kind of skirted round the issue. 'Well, I can't complain about that. In fact, Dean, you lead such a blameless life I can't complain about anything you do.'

Dean looked up. He wasn't bad, wasn't Barry, for a stepfather, there were a lot worse. 'Got the habit in college.'

Barry nodded. 'Ah! Bring a Sunday paper back. I'm helping your mother with getting the sitting room ready for decorating. Your grandad's got a friend of his starting it tomorrow, so as he'll be supervising it all, I've got to make a fist of getting it ready. You know what he's like.'

'Don't throw any of my books out, will you?'

'Course not. Wouldn't dream of it. Glad you love books, seems an admirable trait to me.'

'Toast, Mum? You make me sound a right goody-goody. One day I shall break out.'

'Good. I'm glad. Time you did.'

His mother squeezed his shoulder as she put the toast on his plate. 'Take no notice, do as you want. You're doing fine as you are. There's no one more proud than Barry and me. No one. I never thought I'd live to see the day when a child of mine went to Cambridge. When I was your age I didn't even know what it was.'

Barry protested. 'I'm proud, of course I am, but it would do no harm for you to kick over the traces once in a while.'

Dean was tempted to say that, given half a chance, that was just what he was going to do, but held his own counsel.

He arrived at church with five minutes to spare. To his

amazement, the church was packed to the doors and he had to sit on a bench Zack always brought in from the church boiler house when they ran short of seats. It was low and Dean's long legs felt awkward scrunched up almost under his chin. He'd hoped for a seat closer to the front where he could scrutinize her every move to prove to himself he was still as captivated with her as he had been last night.

Mrs Peel concluded her organ recital with a tremendous flourish from one end of the keyboard to the other, and then began the processional hymn.

There came Gilbert with his choirboys. They looked so angelic, but he spotted the two who'd been caught stealing from the fruit trees in Glebe House garden. Now they looked as though their eyes were on the heavens and they'd be staying there throughout the service. He remembered those red cassocks they wore from his brief sojourn – was it two weeks? – in the choir when he was about ten. He'd felt angelic, too, but it didn't last because Gilbert very sensitively told him he hadn't the capacity to improve his singing and he'd do better putting his talents to more earthly matters.

Then Anna came in. She'd looked ravishing last night in her cassock, but today, in the full panoply of her surplice and cassock and the heavy gold cross she wore, she looked . . . well, she looked heavenly. Almost ethereal.

Heavens above! They were singing the hymn to the tune of 'Yellow Submarine'. Wow! Mrs Peel was putting everything she'd got into it. The rafters were ringing, people began beating time with their heads or their hands, and thoroughly enjoying themselves. How utterly, utterly splendid of her to do this. Mrs Peel, getting quite carried away, played the last verse twice and, after a hesitant start, they all followed suit and sang it again.

Dean sat down breathless with wonder. Anna was transforming church into something jolly and wonderful. Her voice, without any amplification, carried way back as far as Dean, seated as he was right at the back in front of the font. Who could believe that such a slim, almost, to his eyes, fragile woman could have such a powerful voice? Conviction, that was what it was, total conviction in her beliefs. Dean admired her more than ever.

He followed the crowd out into the sunshine and slipped away round the back of the church. He couldn't face shaking hands with her. Not in front of all these people. He sat on a convenient grave stone and thought about her: the tone of her voice, the humility she displayed when she knelt to pray, the joy of her singing, the deep pleasure she took in giving her sermon the exact amount of passion needed to drive her message home. What was her message? He couldn't remember, he'd been so absorbed in watching her. She was superb. A splash of cold water fell on his emotions when he realized she must be at least ten years older than him. Still, did it matter? Mr Fitch was more than twenty years older than Kate-Pascoe-as-was, and it didn't appear to matter at all. Deep in thought, he didn't hear Rhett Wright approaching.

Rhett had never been the brightest star in the firma-ment but he was very attractive to girls. He knew all the latest chat-up lines and, with working outside all day, was tanned and muscled. Dean wouldn't have wanted to garden anywhere at all, but Rhett loved it.

'Hi!'

'Hi.' Dean shifted up to make room for Rhett to sit beside him.

'Been to church?'

Dean nodded.

'That's a first, then.'

'Yes.'

'Just taking a short cut to the pub. I don't know why but Little Derehams seems to get further away. Still, Gran will be retiring soon and then we can move back to Turnham Malpas. Fancy coming?'

Dean shook his head.

'Oh, come on. Can't spend the rest of your life living like a monk. Can't be much fun working in that Neville Neal's office. He's a stuffed shirt, if ever there was one. I do his garden weekends, and he's so prissy about what I'm allowed to do. I like casual country gardens, with lush, herbacious borders and climbing roses, honeysuckle, clematis and stuff, not stiff French marigolds marching in regimental rows. But no, old Neville wants ornamental flowerbeds with every plant measured with a ruler, and I reckon that's just how he is. Inhibited. Watch yourself; you might grow like him, you working in his office.' Rhett looked at Dean and laughed.

'OK, OK. We'll go for a pint and then I'm off home. Mum makes a thing of Sunday lunch and I don't want to ruin it for her.'

'Time you left home.'

'You haven't.'

'No, well, my gran needs a hand with . . . well, anyway, I owe them a lot. Off your backside then. Chop-chop!' Rhett stood up.

The Royal Oak was already filling up with Sunday morning drinkers. Dicky and Georgie had begun opening as soon as the morning service was over, instead of waiting until twelve noon when anyone fancying a drink after church had already gone elsewhere.

Being a fine morning, the windows were all open and the main door into the bar was propped wide to welcome customers inside. If you were hesitant, the joyful sound of voices was a temptation in itself. Dean didn't often frequent the bar, partly because of shyness and partly because there was no one of his age group nor any who shared his interests, for he'd been educated out of his own strata in village life and he hadn't yet learned how to bridge the gap.

To his surprise there was Anna, leaning against the bar with a drink in her hand talking to Dicky. As they approached the bar to order their drinks, Anna saw them and waved. Dean flushed all over; Rhett nodded and smiled, then ordered a lager for himself and a shandy for Dean.

'Hi, there. Introduce yourselves. I'm Anna, the locum rector. I saw you squatting on the bench by the font. You are?'

'Dean Jones.'

'And this is?'

'I work in the gardens at the Big House. My name's Rhett Wright.'

She turned to look at Dean. 'What do you do?'

'I'm training to be an accountant in Neville Neal's office in Culworth. He's the church treasurer.'

'Of course. Yes. So, do you have a degree?'

'Yes. Mathematics.'

'Where?'

'Cambridge.'

Anna's lovely green eyes opened wide. 'Cambridge! My word.'

Rhett put down his lager and said to fill the silence, 'He's the clever one amongst us. Me, I'm just a gardener. His sister's in charge of me.'

'Your sister?'

Dean opened his mouth to answer her but as usual Rhett was there first. 'She's head gardener, following in her grandad's footsteps.'

'That's wonderful, isn't it? You must be proud of her.'

Dean nodded. 'Yes, I am. She's totally devoted to gardening, and she does a good job, doesn't she, Rhett?'

'Well, if doing a good job means knowing when to put the boot in, then yes. There's no sneaking off to the hot houses when there's work to be done.'

'She's a tartar. I have to admit she's blo . . . blinking good, she is, Michelle.'

'I'd like to meet her.'

Dean had to confess that Michelle wasn't much of a one for church.

'And you are?'

Rhett snorted his amusement at the question. 'This could be interesting.'

Dean looked her straight in the eye and said quietly, 'Not much, until just recently.' He took refuge in his shandy, intensely aware of Anna watching him. 'Rhett's in the scouts, but I left when I was doing A-Levels. Working hard, you know how it is.' He found the courage to meet her eyes but she was looking at Rhett now.

Rhett answered. 'Dicky here is the leader and I'm one of his little helpers. He's great.'

Anna looked at Dicky, who was busy serving, and raised her glass to him. 'So, it'll only be a small group? Ten, twelve boys?'

Rhett became indignant at the hint of derision he heard

in her voice. 'Ten or twelve? Come on, there's at least forty boys, and then another twelve in Venture Scouts, and about forty in the cubs. Contrary to the general trend nowadays we've a waiting list as long as your arm. They come from all around: Penny Fawcett, Little Derehams, Turnham Malpas. They'd come from Culworth except we draw the line at that. Poaching, you know. Not fair. Best and most successful scout troop in the county. We've even got our own band. You should hear us.'

Anna smiled at Rhett and asked what instrument he played.

'Big drum, given the chance.'

'And you, Dean, what do you play?'

'I don't. Like I said, I'm not involved.'

Dean felt his isolation again, but before he could do anything about it, Rhett was asking Anna if he could buy her another drink.

'Thank you, yes, I'd like that. Mine's a gin and orange.'

Rhett asked Dean if he wanted another and got out his wallet ready to pay, but Dean pushed him away. 'It's my round.'

As Dean passed Anna's drink to her there was something in his manner, a kind of reverence that was disconcerting. But then he deliberately turned his back and engaged himself in a conversation with Rhett and she decided she'd been mistaken.

She turned to survey the bar. So, here apparently was a cross-section of her flock for the next twelve months. What a mixture! What a challenge! From sons-of-the-soil to sons-of-the-soil elevated out of their true element by education.

Anna knew from Peter's notes that there were those

with whom she'd have to tread very carefully. She'd noted the looks of disapproval on some of their faces when they'd sung the first hymn to The Beatles' tune. But in her opinion they needed shaking up. Peter's rather orthodox, old-fashioned way of doing things was all right in its way but how could they expect young people like these two beside her to respond to such outdated ways? Gloriously dignified and solemnly reverent, and certainly no less devout, but not for the twenty-first century. Oh no. What would they say when she introduced some of the old slave hymns that she learned when she was in Alabama? She smiled to herself, not realizing that Dean was looking at her and was clearly mistaking her smile as being personal to him. He flushed and returned her smile.

Anna said, 'Must be going. Work to do. Nice to have met you, Rhett. See you again no doubt?'

'It's Dean.'

'Sorry, yes, of course, Dean. Bye, Rhett, looking forward to seeing you on the big drum.'

As Anna reached the door, knowing they were all watching her, she raised both her arms without turning round and waved, calling out loudly. 'Bye, everyone. Be seeing you.'

Her reply was a general chorus of 'goodbyes' and a silence fell until they thought she was out of earshot. Then a babel of talk broke out, which she could hear as she passed the side window of the bar on her way home. Mentally she shrugged. Only what could be expected: lots to say when she'd gone, but very little to say to her face.

The rectory still smelled of Peter and Caroline. It was there in every cushion, every plate, every chair, the angle of every picture, the colour of the tablecloth, the newness of Peter's state-of-the-art computer, the sweep of the pelmet in the sitting room, even the sheets on her bed, which had been Beth's. Her pictures and maps and posters still adorned the walls. It would never be hers, but it was better than that dreadful flat in the Abbey precincts, which had been her home for two years. The tiny kitchen scarcely bigger than a cupboard, the dreary living room with its tiny windows, no space for a washing machine, no wiring for a TV. It was a living hell and she spent as little time there as she could.

Here at least she had space, all Peter's books to go at and, best of all, a woodburning stove in the sitting room, which, in the oncoming winter, would be sheer bliss. A washing machine, an Aga, a microwave – more bliss. She was back in the twenty-first century with every amenity for modern living.

Was she though? Anna settled herself at the kitchen table with her lunch. This village was so ancient she could feel history constantly dogging her footsteps as she walked about. The plague pit, the oak tree on the green, that tomb in the church, haunted or so they said. People from generations back seemed never to have left the village, because she felt that their presence still filled the streets.

As she bit into her Scotch egg, Anna decided to read Peter's 'Parish Notes'. She put down the egg and went to the study, picked up the file from his desk and carried it back into the kitchen. She wouldn't read straight through from the very beginning right now; she'd open it up at random and find an interesting piece.

The piece she found was about the discovery of the church silver hidden at the Big House in 1940 because of the fear of invasion. Peter had recorded how outraged the villagers were and of their hate campaign when they realized that Mr Fitch, having bought the estate, considered that everything in it was his to dispose of as he chose. Hate campaign? An *organized* hate campaign? It was positively medieval. Hanging an effigy from a tree on his drive? Cutting off the heating at the Big House? That they succeeded in getting the silver back in the church where it belonged amazed Anna. She shuddered. The whole episode felt to have a hint of evil about it, which she didn't care for at all. Was it all these ancestors she was so acutely aware of who had motivated the campaign? Now she really was being ridiculous.

A good walk in the autumn air to prepare herself for evensong would be much better than sitting here getting all goosepimpled. Having made the decision, she quickly cleared away her lunch, found a sweater, checked she had her keys, closed the front door and stood out in Church Lane, deciding which way to go. She caught sight of huge trees behind the roof of the Village Store and headed for them.

A breeze had got up and Anna revelled in it. She loved the wind. It stirred her emotions in a way that a hot summer day could never do. She'd been born during a gale and her mother had always said she'd loved the wind from her first day. Being Sunday, her hair was in a French pleat, but in moments she had released it, stuffed the hairpins in her pocket and shaken her hair free to blow in the wind. She paused to admire the display in the window of the Store and then she arrived at the wood, huge beech trees guarding the narrow entrance. Then, suddenly, there she was standing beside Turnham Beck. The water was gurgling along at a good pace, and briefly she spotted a kingfisher flitting along above the surface of the water.

Anna chose to cross the little bridge and then strode off along the footpath towards the woods.

She heard their voices long before she saw them. Twinkling, happy sounds interrupted by the deeper, well-rounded voice of a man.

Anna came upon the voices in a clearing. It was Gilbert Johns, the choirmaster, and four children. 'Hi, Gilbert.' She couldn't keep the surprise out of her voice. 'Are all of these yours?'

Gilbert had been brushing someone down who'd obviously taken a fall on the wettest part of the ground. He looked up. 'Hello there. Yes, I lay claim to them all.'

Standing in the clearing, with the sun finding its way between the branches, Gilbert smiled. He wasn't dressed as choirmasters ought to be. He wore navy shorts with a turquoise short-sleeved shirt open, displaying his manly hairy chest. His brown hair, suddenly teased by a gust of wind, blew over his eyes and he had to push it away with his spare hand, the other still holding the boy who'd fallen in the mud. His brown eyes looked amused. 'More washing!'

'You must have mountains of washing.'

'Thank heavens that's Louise's domain. She's gone home with the baby and I'm keeping them healthy and busy while she sees to lunch. Music OK this morning? Mrs Peel told me she enjoyed "Yellow Submarine".'

'Oh! Fine, absolutely fine. How are you with "Swing Low, Sweet Chariot?"'

Gilbert looked startled. 'OK. Are you thinking of trying it?'

'Why not?'

'No reason at all.' Gilbert kept his own feelings under wraps. He was a great believer in 'let's wait and see'. 'If you keep going on this path you eventually come out into Shepherd's Hill and opposite you is the stile to Sykes Wood. Go through there and you come out in a while into Church Lane; turn left and you'll soon be back in the village.'

'Thanks. Is that where you're going?'

'No. Too far. We've already been a long way. We're on our way back to the car. Enjoy.' Gilbert gathered his four children together, waved cheerfully, told the children to say bye-bye to the rector and went on his way. She watched them disappear through the wood. He was a giant of a man, not because of his height, though he was tall, but because of his aura. There was something very attractive about him. Earthy, kind of. Right down to his manly sandals.

Anna carried on walking, crossed the lane and then climbed over the ancient style and into Sykes Wood. Here the trees were different, closer and more huddled, with none of the sunlit openness of the first wood where she'd enjoyed lingering. She heard rustling in the trees, sounds of animals moving about, but what would they be? Not rabbits, nor badgers, nor foxes, not in the daytime; maybe squirrels, but there were none to be seen. It was the wind, she decided, which didn't just ruffle the twigs but tossed them about so they thrashed against each other. The path wound on and on, and she wished it went straight as an arrow to the other side of the wood. Then she came to a clearing, a big clearing, with the remains of old fires here and there, and logs laid as though they'd been used for sitting round the fires.

Anna wasn't a person who believed in ghosts but briefly she did wonder again about ancestors and it caused her to hasten along. Before she knew it she was jogging and then running along the path. She tripped on a tree root, fell, picked herself up and ran on.

Then, wham! She was out in the road, the sun on her face at last.

She panted with relief, hands on thighs, pulling in the fresh, unthreatening air as rapidly as she could.

A car pulled up. 'Anna! Want a lift?'

It was someone from church but she couldn't recollect the name. She'd seen him only this morning.

'Thanks, but no. I'm fine.'

'Been in Sykes Wood?'

'Yes. Found it a bit oppressive.'

'Well, that's one way to describe it. Most of us avoid it completely. If I can't give you a lift I'll be on my way. Bye.'

'Bye.'

The Rolls purred away. Now who was that? Not Sir Ralph. As she set off for home, Gilbert's navy shorts and turquoise shirt kept filtering into her mind.

On the mat she found a note inviting her for coffee the following morning, and mentioning there were a few things that needed to be discussed. It was signed Ralph Templeton and put all thoughts of Gilbert Johns out of her mind. She'd seen Sir Ralph's pursed lips and his refusal to sing in the morning service and guessed trouble was brewing.

Chapter 3

'I will not put up with it! I simply will not and don't think I'm the only one in the village to object.' Ralph wagged his finger at her to emphasize his point.

Anna answered quietly; nevertheless, she sounded adamant. 'It's not a matter of "putting up with it", it's a matter of embracing it with open arms and welcoming change. This is the way I want things to go.'

'You are undoing, what, thirteen, fourteen years and more of Peter's work. He's built this parish from virtually nothing and I will not stand by and see it demolished brick by brick.'

'No one is asking you to. But he's gone for a whole year and I'm standing in for him and this is how I want things to be. You wait and see, we'll have more young people coming to the services than ever before. I know. It's worked for me in Culworth and it'll work here.'

'You'll be having us dancing in the aisles soon.'

'It's funny you should say that. I had been wondering about removing some of the pews so we have room to move about or sit in a circle when there's only a few of us.'

Ralph went white with shock. He gripped the edge of his desk to steady himself. 'Remove some of the pews! We definitely cannot, most definitely not. Those pews are antiques.'

'Exactly. Just because they've been there hundreds of years does not mean to say they can't be moved, now does it? Added to which, they are blasted uncomfortable, as you must know. A few less will not be a matter for international consternation.'

Ralph took in a deep breath and endeavoured to control his temper. This damned upstart! He'd die first before allowing this happy-clappy modern young thing to ruin his village. Yes, he would. Then he caught Muriel's eye and knew he'd gone a step too far for her liking. He heard the tremble in her voice as she said, 'Would you care for a cup of tea, Anna?'

'Thank you, Lady Templeton, but no. I'm more a mineral water person. Thanks all the same.'

'Mineral water! I have some. Sit down and I'll bring it for you. Still or bubbly?'

'Bubbly, please!'

Muriel rushed off into the kitchen, delighted to have struck the right note with her.

Another damned modern innovation, thought Ralph. Next she'll be going round with a bottle of the stuff hooked on the belt of her cassock. That was another thing. Why couldn't she wear ordinary clothes *and* a clerical collar instead of this dove-grey cassock thing. It was ridiculous. He saw her as someone masquerading in fancy dress.

Anna saw an elderly man holding back the march of time as long as he could, but a very elegant elderly man, with his silver, well-groomed hair, his sparkling blue eyes and his very noble, distinguished nose. He had that aristocratic bearing, which, so far as he was concerned, meant he always got his own way.

Well, matey, that isn't going to happen, not to this smart cookie. Anna graciously thanked Muriel for her glass of water and, after drinking it all down in one go, set about cooling the atmosphere as only she could.

'I love the hanging baskets at your door, Lady Templeton. I think hanging lobelia looks so good and seems to get better and better as the summer goes by. The rectory garden is absolutely to my taste, I'm positively revelling in it. Caroline obviously has a real gardener's touch.'

'Oh, she has! She and I have such interesting talks. She didn't know one flower from another when she first came, but before they left she was winning prizes at the village show. We swapped cuttings, you know.'

'Do you do your own garden then?'

'Well, mostly. But Willie Biggs, the old verger, gives me a hand from time to time. He's got green fingers, too. But then you can see that for yourself from looking at the churchyard. The new chap . . . whatsisname, Ralph? I can never remember.'

Ralph muttered, 'Zack.'

'That's it, Zack. He's green-fingered as well. Except he's gone modern and all his colours clash. It makes Willie Biggs wince. He puts bright orange with dark purple and it looks quite nauseating.'

'What's wrong with going modern? They're still flowers, modern or not, and really, nothing in nature clashes, does it? At least they do make people look at the church, even if they don't come in.'

'But it's the colour schemes he uses.' Muriel's still-attractive face screwed up with disdain. 'I used to think—'

Ralph groaned inside. If Muriel got on about flowers he'd never get his view across. He interrupted her rather forcefully. 'More to the point, what on earth is Peter going to say when he gets back from Africa? Tambourines and castanets and guitars in *his* church, is that what's coming next?'

'Sir Ralph! It isn't *his*, it belongs to us all. But perhaps Peter might see the broader picture, like more young people in the church? Had you thought of it that way? What's wrong with that?'

'But all they'd be coming for is the music. If it can be called that. I thought you positively murdered that first hymn on Sunday. Murdered it. I've never sung it to "Yellow Submarine" before. Couldn't get the hang of it at all, so I stopped singing.'

'I noticed.'

Ralph's eyebrows shot up. 'Ah! Right.'

Muriel threw an anxious glance at him. 'Ralph, dear . . .'

The gentle remonstration in Muriel's voice set Ralph boiling with temper all over again. 'It was disgraceful, Anna, absolutely disgraceful.'

'I'm sorry, Sir Ralph, but that's how it's going to be. Now, I must leave. It's the Penny Fawcett mini-market on Monday morning. A chance to off-load what they didn't sell in Culworth Market on Saturday, but there we are.' With a wicked grin, Anna handed back her glass to Muriel. 'Most kind. Now, where did I put my car keys?'

Ralph picked them up from his desk and handed them to her. She took the opportunity to capture his hand and hold on to it. 'Please, Sir Ralph, please understand what I'm trying to do. With you on my side miracles could occur. All I ask is the chance to achieve it. I'll say good morning and God bless. I'll let myself out.'

As she left the study she smiled at them both and Muriel responded but Ralph had nothing to say.

'Ralph, how could you? To the rector. It really was not right, my dear.'

'She's going to ruin everything. When I said about dancing in the aisles I was joking but she meant it. Remove the pews? Absolutely not. I won't have it.'

He stormed about his study, his face growing redder by the minute, and Muriel feared for his heart. He wouldn't withstand another attack like the last one.

'Muriel, I'm going out.'

'Very well, dear, a walk might be soothing. Give you time to think.'

'I may not be back for lunch.'

Muriel knew this wasn't the moment for questioning him about where he was going; it would only wind him up even more. But in minutes she heard his car starting up. Muriel raced to see if he'd taken his tablets this morning, but when she looked in the box she couldn't decide if he had or he hadn't. If he was taking the car, that most likely meant Culworth and the Abbey and more aggravation. She must remain calm. As he'd said when he'd had his first heart attack, he couldn't live the rest of his life wrapped in cotton wool.

Milk. That's right, she needed some milk. Since the milkman had given up his round, Jimbo had stocked every possible kind of milk anyone could ask for. How he'd found space for it all she couldn't imagine; the Store was already so full of tempting goodies. She set off to walk round the Green, purse in hand, pushing all thought of Ralph and his heart right out of her mind.

She thought about the service and about the singing of that first hymn, how people had enjoyed it, and how much she'd thrown herself into singing it. Anna was right; you couldn't hold back the centuries. One had to move forward and take hold of the future.

The initial rush of mothers shopping on their way back home after seeing the children to school had disappeared. There were just two of them standing gossiping by the coffee machine, Tom behind the Post Office grille and the Senior sisters, Thelma and Valda, discussing a purchase from the frozen meal freezer in soft undertones. Out of the corner of her eye Muriel thought she saw Thelma slip a packet into her shopping bag, while Valda made a show of placing another boxed meal in her wire basket, saying, 'We'll take this one then.'

Muriel's face flooded with colour and burned with embarrassment. She hated things like this. To speak or not to speak, that was the question. Take pity on them, she thought. They existed on their pensions while she and Ralph had Ralph's investments to live on. Should she speak up? No, she wouldn't. She'd have a word with Jimbo.

But, as she waited behind them at the till, Muriel found the courage to point at Thelma's bag. 'Thelma! You'd be losing your head if it was loose, you've forgotten you put a meal from the freezer in your bag by mistake.'

It was Thelma's turn to blush. 'I haven't. Are you accusing me of shoplifting?'

'Well, no, more a senior moment.'

'Senior moment? Are you being funny? You mean we pinch stuff from here regularly?'

'No. I'm not saying you steal things, when I said "senior moment" I meant you were having a memory lapse.'

'Then why call it a Senior moment?'

'Well, that's what they say, isn't it?'

'Who says we Seniors steal?'

'Well . . . I haven't said you steal, it's just that—'

'You've just said we'd had a Senior moment, which means it's general knowledge that we steal and people say a Senior moment, meaning us.'

'Well, no, it's just a saying.'

'We don't steal, see.' Thelma prodded Muriel's lapel. 'We wouldn't dream of stealing from Jimbo, Huh! As if we would.' The two of them paid for their one meal and departed, leaving Muriel feeling the victim.

'I'm so sorry, Bel, to cause trouble. But I was sure—'

Bel beamed her usual loving smile. 'Don't worry, Lady Templeton, you're probably quite right. They're a slippy pair of customers. I'll keep an eye out. Jimbo is thinking of putting a mirror over the frozen food counters so we can see right from here at the till what's going on over there. Don't let yourself get upset about it. They're not worth it.'

'But I am. I feel quite dreadful.' Muriel paid for the milk and went out, but not before she'd overheard one of the mothers gossiping by the coffee machine say, 'This new Anna disagrees with Scouts. All uniformed organizations, in fact. Says it smacks of Hitler Youth.'

'Don't care what it smacks of, it gives me two hours of peace on a Scout night. And do I deserve two hours of peace? Yes, I do. So I'm all for it. What's Hitler Youth anyway?'

'Don't know, but it sounds like no good to me.'

Muriel paused to put her change away safely and heard Maggie Dobbs from the school say, 'She's got someone coming to stay. A vagabond or someone, what's got no home and's just off drugs. That's what I heard on the bus Saturday.'

Muriel dallied no longer. Surely they couldn't be talking about Anna? Not a drug addict in the rectory? Surely not. She wouldn't, would she? When she thought about those green eyes of hers and how direct they were, she had a nasty sneaking feeling that taking in a waif and stray would be just what she'd do. She wouldn't tell Ralph. He'd say she was listening to dangerous gossip and dismiss it. But it was surprising how many times gossip turned out to be true. A tramp in Caroline's lovely house. It didn't bear thinking about.

Ralph didn't come home for lunch and she wished he would. It was four o'clock before she heard him coming in through the back door. It occurred to her they'd need to lock their doors twenty-four/seven, as the Americans would say, if Anna brought a down-and-out to the village.

She called out as brightly as she could, 'Tea, Ralph?'

'Yes, please.'

As she put the tea tray down, Muriel looked at Ralph and decided he was a better colour, not that kind of puce shade his cheeks went when he got too angry. 'Where have you been, dear? If I might ask?'

'You may, of course. I've been in Culworth to the Abbey and were told that we'd got Anna allocated and there was no one else available. The number of ordinands being what it is.'

'I see.'

'What does that mean, Muriel, my dear?'

'Nothing. I was thinking, that's all.'

'Mmm.'

Muriel poured his tea for him, and kept the biscuits well

away because of his diet. She bit into her fruity shortbread and chewed it, there was nothing quite like a shortb—

'They were implacable. I told them what she was planning. I said, is this the way we have to go?'

'And?'

'All I got was a nod.'

'Right, then. We must put a brave face on it and let her get on with it.'

'I think we'll go abroad. Somewhere warm for the winter, for several months.'

Muriel swallowed the last of her biscuit, drank a few sips of her tea and said, a mite challengingly, 'I didn't know Templetons ran away from trouble. I wouldn't have married you if I'd known that.'

'Muriel! No one can accuse me of running away from anything. Ever.'

'You are now.'

'I am not. I am merely thinking of you and the winter weather.'

'And I'm thinking of missing lovely frosty mornings, when the trees are silver all over, and the children make a slide of that water-leak on the Green, which they never manage to cure. And the days when the pond is frozen over and the silly geese are sliding all over the ice, wondering why they can't swim as they usually do. And snuggling down in my nice warm bed with the curtains drawn and lying against your warm back and warming my cold feet on your legs.'

'Muriel! Stop it. If I want to run away I shall.'

'In that case you'll have to go on your own, because I'm not going. Most emphatically. Do you hear? I'm not going. Someone has to stay here and fight. If you're not ready for a fight, well, I am. Where shall you go?' Calmly she poured herself another cup of tea, popped a drop more milk in it and waited for her bombshell to land.

Ralph was aghast. He placed his hands on the arms of his leather chair, straightened his back and looked at her. He was devastated, she could see that. It was the very first time in their married life together that she had stood firm and refused to do what he proposed. He couldn't believe it. What on earth had happened to his world today? The village that he loved was about to be strung up and put out to die, and his wife, his beloved wife, his childhood sweetheart, was refusing to go to sunnier climes to avoid watching from the sidelines as their village was ruined. Not Muriel, she wouldn't do any such thing now, would she? A bit of persuasion, a bit of flattery and hey presto!

'My dear, you know I couldn't manage without you on a long trip. Who'd remember to look in the drawers before we checked out? Who'd know where we'd put our passports?'

'You.'

'Where we should go? What ruin we needed to visit? Which restaurant we should eat at? I couldn't manage without you. Think of the sun glittering on the sea, the delight of silvery sand trickling between your toes—'

'You don't like silvery sand getting between your toes. You hate it.'

'I do. I do. But please, Muriel. It wouldn't be the same pleasure without you and your wonderfully innocent outlook on the world.'

'I'm sorry, Ralph, but that's it. Absolutely not. The whole winter. No.'

Ralph placed his cup and saucer very firmly on the tray. 'Why are you being so awkward? So difficult? I'm offering you the whole winter in New Zealand or South America, or . . . wherever, think about it.'

'I shan't. Because I'm not going and no amount of persuasion will make me go. We're needed here. She's not a dragon, simply someone with a mind of her own, but somehow maybe we can mould it, if we stay. If we go, then we can't. Anna's not all bad. She's a lovely girl. Her eyes and her hair are very striking.'

Ralph didn't answer her. He saw those candid green eyes of hers again and remembered how he'd felt when she'd held his hand and pleaded so directly to him to give her a chance.

Neither of them was completely honest with the other. He didn't tell her how he felt about Anna and Muriel didn't tell him what she'd overheard in the Store.

Chapter 4

In the Store that morning Jimbo was finding space on his Village Voice noticeboard for an email from Peter and Caroline. When he'd found it on his computer first thing that morning he'd been delighted.

'Harriet! Harriet! Guess what? There's an email from Peter.'

'Coming.'

Together they read his message, relieved to realize that things appeared to be going well in Africa.

'Jimbo, let's put it on display then everyone can read it. They'll be thrilled.'

'Good idea. We'll do it immediately!'

So there it was in the middle of the board, and Jimbo had put a big notice on the door so that as people came in they were aware it was there for them to read. Quite a crowd from the morning bus queue was huddled around it.

To: Everyone at Turnham Malpas
From: New Hope Mission

We all send our greetings to everyone in Turnham Malpas. Finally, after a week's briefing at headquarters and a two-day journey in a 4×4 vehicle, sleeping under the stars and followed by two small trucks with our belongings and equipment for the medical centre we are at last at our destination.

The weather is hot but still tolerable and the building where we shall make our home does have fans to help keep us cool in the worst of the heat. It is one huge room, more like an aircraft hangar than a home, with the kitchen at one end, a big space for a sitting room in the middle and two bedrooms sectioned off by curtains and ditto a very primitive shower room at the bedroom end.

We have two local women to help us, one with nursing experience but no qualifications, and one to help with the church side of things. The church itself is virtually completed now. Made from local materials, it is airy, without proper walls, just matting hanging from horizontal poles, and everyone squats on the floor for the sermon.

Caroline's clinic is more sturdy and has much better facilities than she had expected, though they are very basic by English standards. She has already held her first session, a clinic for expectant mothers, and has found their knowledge of pregnancy and childbirth more Middle Ages than twenty-first century.

Alex and Beth begin at the International School next week. It is a forty-five-mile round trip so they will be weekly boarders.

The village is large, with more inhabitants than Turnham Malpas. We have plans for it; however, money is short. But we have great hopes for our work here.

God bless every one of you.

Your brother in Christ,

Peter Harris

P.S. It is lovely here and everyone is so friendly. We're

going out to a house in the village for our meal tonight. We
wonder what we shall get to eat!

Love, Beth and Alex xxxxxxx

Someone shouted. 'The bus is 'ere!' and everyone
crowding round the noticeboard stampeded for the door.
'He won't wait, he never does. Hurry up.'

The only customer left in the Store was Sheila Bissett.
She went to read the email as the others left. She could feel
the miles between her and them, and was saddened. Peter
would understand how she was feeling this morning, and
she wished, how she wished she could knock on the
rectory door and find him in his study, that lovely
welcoming room with its gold-coloured walls, the delicate
watercolours and the rough-hewn wooden cross over the
old fireplace. She'd be able to sit in one of his big squashy
chairs, Sylvia would bring them coffee and they'd talk
openly about her worries and he'd straighten things out for
her. Such a haven it was. She'd tell him how she felt about
this new baby of Louise and Gilbert's. She'd scarcely slept
all night, nor the previous one. What she really wanted
was for them to get rid of it. Five! And then number six!
Surely God wouldn't want her to go through it all over
again.

In that little cottage, too. It was a dear place, and lovely
for two or three but not eight! What really angered her
was there was no need nowadays to have all these children.
There were ways and means. She'd never needed to use
anything at all, because – she hoped no one could read her
thoughts – she'd never needed to use anything to stop
conception. How Louise had come to be so fertile, she
really couldn't think.

Sheila blushed at the thought. How on earth could she

discuss things like abortion or contraception with a daughter she'd lost real contact with years ago? She couldn't bring herself to. Honestly couldn't bring herself to. She could have talked to Peter about it but not Louise. But someone needed to say something. Though since Louise had met Gilbert she had been much easier to talk to. Maybe . . . she might manage to say something. After all, they had both of them given birth, even if they had little else in common.

Then she thought of how Gilbert would be dead against getting rid of the baby. He'd be appalled. She really wouldn't be able to talk to him about babies because . . . he intimidated her. He was so very clever, with his doctorate in archaeology and his musical talents. It was just the matter of his brainpower which frightened her, mainly because she knew she didn't possess anywhere near his kind of intelligence. She'd left school at sixteen and had hardly opened a book since. Though Gilbert never, ever, set out to make her feel as thick as a plank. Never. But she, right inside herself, knew she was.

She thought then about Peter's new church being poor. Surely something could be done. In comparison Turnham Malpas was rolling in money. Of course. Yes! The W.I. They could organize things. And as she was president this year, why not? Why ever not? She'd go round and see Anna this afternoon and suggest the W.I. spearheaded a fundraising effort for the New Hope Mission.

Anna opened the door in response to Sheila's knock and invited her in. The moment she walked in, she knew that, for her at least, that glorious feeling of being able to unburden herself had vanished. Peter and Caroline still lingered but the real essence of the two of them was gone.

'Hello, Sheila. How nice of you to call.'

'I've had an inspiration,' said Sheila.

'Then you'd better come in and find a chair.'

Anna led the way into the sitting room and Sheila felt choked when she remembered the coffee and gateaux evenings they'd had in there to raise funds for this and that. So she wasn't to be allowed in Anna's study. Well, perhaps it was for the best, because she couldn't talk to a young unmarried woman about what was troubling her heart.

Anna spoke first. 'Might as well cut to the chase.'

'Pardon?'

'I mean, what is it you need to talk to me about?'

'Right. First thing. I'm president of the W.I. this year and I wondered if you would like to speak to us about something or anything at all, one afternoon. Seeing as you're new. We've a fairly broad range of subjects so you needn't be afraid to choose something which interests you. The only date . . .' She rushed on, trying to shut out Louise and her troubles. Anything rather than that.

They both got out their diaries.

'I'm not very well up on W.I.s. They always seem to me to be entrenched in the past. Peg dolls and lace doyley competitions and such.'

Sheila was appalled. 'In the past! Most certainly not. We tackle all kinds of subjects and activities. Anything except politics, they are taboo. And our embroidery ventures are under the strict supervision of Evie Nicholls, who is very gifted. The millennium tapestry in the church was executed by us. In the past! Certainly not. We're right out there in the front leading the troops, we are. Believe me. We meet the first Monday afternoon in the month, at two o'clock. Our speaker for November has had to go into hospital and doesn't know when she'll be fit enough to speak so would that be suitable? November?'

Secretly amused by Sheila's stout defence, Anna agreed that her diary hadn't yet filled up and November would be fine. 'Anything else?'

'Have you read Peter's email thingy in the Store? No, of course you haven't, it only went up this morning. Well, his church in Africa is very poor and I wondered if the W.I. and the church could join together and do something for them. I'm not sure what. How do you feel about that?'

'I haven't read it yet but in Penny Fawcett this morning someone had been in the Store and seen the email, and they were all agog about it, so yes, I know they're short of money. I'd like to do something about that and yes, I think the church should make a contribution. Couldn't think of anything more worthwhile and let's face it, at least we would know the money will be going directly to those who need it and not towards vast rents and salaries for state-of-the-art headquarters. I think it's a good idea.'

'Thanks. At our next committee meeting we'll have a discussion and see what we come up with.' Sheila got to her feet, thankful not to have fallen to the temptation of unburdening herself.

Anna smiled at her. 'Perhaps next time when you come to see me you might feel able to tell me what's troubling you. I'm not a dragon, you know.'

Sheila visibly jumped.

'I might even be able to help.'

'Yes, maybe. But not today.'

Sheila all but rushed out of the rectory. What a narrow escape she'd had! Ron, she'd go home to Ron and tell him.

Ron was deeply involved with his stamp collection

when she got in, and not really in the mood for Sheila firing broadsides at him. But he gently pushed his albums aside and made room for her elbows on the table.

'Well, what is it?'

'It's like this . . .' She hesitated.

'It's Louise and Gilbert, isn't it?'

Sheila nodded.

'People can think what they like because it's nothing to do with them. They're all beautiful children, well behaved, you can take them anywhere at all and they come up trumps. If they were hooligans it would be a different matter.'

'I know. But six. It's disgusting.'

Ron baulked at that. 'No, it isn't. They're married, the children are happy. There's nothing disgusting in it.'

'Well, embarrassing, then.'

'Not even that. Gilbert's a great chap and I like him very much. There's no pretence with Gilbert, he's as frank and open as anyone could be. I like that in a man.'

Sheila, experiencing one of her rare perceptive moments, heard the envy in his voice and blurted out, 'Why, Ron, you're jealous of him. You wish you could have fathered children like he does.'

Ron didn't agree outright but he did say, 'Man to man, they'll all admire him for it.'

'I'm sorry I let you down. Though I wouldn't have wanted as many as she's going to have. I wouldn't have coped.'

'It's amazing what you can cope with when you need to. You'd have been just as well organized as Louise.'

'Not ever, believe me. I'd have sunk without trace under all that washing she has.'

Ron patted her forearm. 'You underestimate yourself.

Go lay on the sofa and I'll make you a cup of tea and you can watch *Countdown*. Challenge the old grey cells for a while.'

Sheila did as she was told, tucked her feet under a cushion to keep them warm, switched on the remote and prepared to relax. After *Countdown* she'd tell him that Anna had agreed to help raise money for Africa. But by the time Ron came back with the tea tray, she'd fallen asleep, dreaming of a positive hoard of children and losing one in the park and searching hysterically for it. She woke with a jerk but with the child still missing. The commercials were on and her tea was cold. After the dream she was even more bruised and concerned and in more of a puzzle than ever. Why dream of a missing child?

The W.I. committee meeting was that same week and Sheila thrust them all into a frenzied discussion about raising money for Africa.

'Ideas, ideas, let's have a brainstorming session, come on, come on.'

She was met with complete silence. So it was up to her to start them off.

'A cakebake? A gigantic raffle. A sponsored swim. An autumn fair. A fifty-pence mile in Culworth. Fancy dress party.'

'We've done all those things before,' someone stated despairingly.

Suddenly Sheila burst out with, 'How about a sponsored . . . midnight . . . *naked* swim in Jimbo's pool?' Then wondered where on earth that had come from.

There were gasps all round. Only Muriel protested outright. 'I don't think so. Whatever would people say?'

'A naked calendar then. Like that other W.I. did.' suggested Angie Turner.

'I don't think so either,' said Muriel. 'My word no. Whatever next. Surely a sponsored sew would be more in keeping?'

'Boring. Boring. I go for the naked swim.' When she'd said this, Sheila went bright red. What had possessed her to pursue such an incredibly bold idea?

'How about a sponsored hair-dyeing competition, too?'

'That sounds rather more acceptable.' This from Greta Jones, newly elected to the committee. 'I've always wanted red hair. I'd do that. And Vince could always dye the bit he's got left just for a laugh.'

'We couldn't have *two* sponsored events, now could we?'

'Why ever not? What about a pyjama party at Jimbo's house? Or at the Big House. Ten pounds a nob. I bet Kate Pascoe-that-was would go for that.'

'Better still, how about the naked swim at the Big House as well? Lovely big pool there.'

'Oh no. Definitely not. In the dark in Jimbo's garden, yes, but not that great pool.'

'You could be right. More mystical and attractive. At least the dark would hide the blushes. That could be really wild. How about it, Harriet? We'd get the youngsters to that.'

Harriet thought for a moment and reminded them that the funds were for helping a church not a gambling saloon.

'Gambling! Now that's an idea. What could we gamble on?'

Angie Turner shouted, 'I know! Guess the date when Gilbert and Louise announce they're expecting again. It's about time there was another announcement, they're running late.' A scandalized silence met this comment, and no one dared to look at Sheila, because they knew, definitely knew, she'd be scarlet all over.

Harriet intervened before Sheila got a chance to lose her temper. 'I don't think that is quite the kind of thing Peter would approve of.'

'Peter isn't here and it's money for his church and he won't be any wiser, will he, all those thousands of miles away?' said Angie Turner.

'It's not the gambling, it's what you're gambling on; it has to be in good taste,' Harriet remarked. 'How about gambling on the French Prix de L'Arc de Triomphe . . . That's in October, isn't it?'

Angie Turner, her mind working furiously, asked, 'You mean gamble, like in real gambling?'

Harriet nodded. 'I haven't thought out how it would work but something could be organized, couldn't it? Just think, we might win thousands.'

Angie said, 'My Colin's good at betting on horses. He studies form by the hour. The bookmakers always come off worst; we'd never manage on his wages if he didn't.'

'We don't need to settle on just one thing. We could do several.'

'Penny Fawcett and Little Derehams will be so jealous. I'd love that. They're so dull and boring, they never do anything out of the ordinary.'

General conversation started in which they recalled times when Turnham Malpas had scandalized the other two villages with one incident after another. Most of the stories began with 'remember that time when . . .'

Sheila had to call them to order. 'Thank you, ladies. Thank you. We must press on. I suggest Harriet looks into the possibility of a naked swim, Angie is in charge of the gambling, and we'll ask Rhett Wright and Dean Jones to organize the pyjama party, because that sounds like a youth thing and they'd be better at attracting young people. Greta, would you investigate the possibility of a hair-dyeing competition? Two pounds to enter and a cash prize for the most weird colour, or most flattering, or most outrageous, whatever. We mustn't undercharge. One pound is nothing nowadays. Then they've to get sponsor-ship. Anyone who wants to hold a coffee morning or something, please do, but report to me what you've planned. All agreed?'

Everyone agreed. They hadn't had a unanimous vote since anyone could remember. This surely must be a milestone in the annals of the Turnham Malpas W.I.

'Well, I never.'

'Would you believe it! Unanimous.'

It took a while for the enormity of what they had decided to sink in.

Harriet suggested they needed a name for the fund. 'What's the name of the village Peter's at?'

'It's unpronounceable, lots of m's and n's next to each other,' said Sheila, 'but the church is called the New Hope Mission. We could call it the New Hope Mission Fund. Or the New Hope Fund.'

'I think the New Hope Fund is more slick. And we are hoping to give them new hope, aren't we?' This from Harriet who specialized in smart, easily remembered slogans for the Store.

The vote for New Hope Fund was also unanimous.

Then Sheila asked for a volunteer to do the publicity. Not a single hand went up.

'Very well. I'll think about that. I suggest posters and flyers with the same artwork but advertising the different events. We'll reconvene next week, same place, same time. OK? Thanks and goodnight.'

Sheila arrived home shattered. Firstly because Louise and Gilbert had been mocked just as she knew they would be, given time, and she'd died a thousand deaths with a flushed face and a fast, beating heart. Thankfully no one had taken up the idea. Secondly she'd presided over a meeting that had never been equalled for the dozens of ideas they'd come up with and for sheer audacity.

'Ron! I need a gin and tonic. Don't ask why, just get it.' She flung her bag on the floor and fell in a heap on the sofa. The gin and tonic went down in one gulp, and she held out the glass for a refill.

'What the blazes has happened at the meeting? Have you resigned?'

Sheila sat up. 'Resigned? Of course not. Anybody would think I'm always resigning. I've just attended the most . . . the most . . . most . . .'

'Yes? Go on.'

'The most audacious W.I. meeting ever.'

'Audacious? What d'yer mean?'

'We've decided to raise money for Peter's church in Africa.'

Feeling thoroughly let down, Ron said, 'Oh! Is that all?'

'All? You should have been there.' The second gin went down a treat, and she asked for a third.

'No. That's enough. You'll be giggling soon, and you know I don't like that.'

Sheila began to laugh and couldn't stop. Tears of laughter ran down her face. 'Oh, Ron! We'll never live it down.' She dabbed her eyes, pulled herself together and said, 'Listen to this. A sponsored midnight *naked swim* in Jimbo's pool. I think we'll call that a sponsored midnight skinny-dipping. That's right. Yes. That's it. Skinny dipping, that's the buzz word of the moment for it. Then we're having a sponsored hair-dyeing competition, the most outrageous colours they can think of. A pyjama party at Harriet's for the teens and twenties, though Jimbo doesn't know yet and he might say no. A gamble on the race in Paris, you know the whatever it is . . . L'Arc de something . . .'

Ron couldn't believe he was hearing correctly. Had they had a drunken orgy at the meeting or had they started smoking pot? He was flabbergasted. 'What will they think at county headquarters?'

Sheila had begun laughing again, but she managed to say between gasps, 'They'll be hopping mad they never thought of it first. That's what.'

Ron woke in the night to hear Sheila still laughing. He grumbled at having his sleep disturbed. 'I bet if Peter were still here you wouldn't have gone along with this. He wouldn't like it at all.'

She sobered up. 'No, he wouldn't. I know that. But I'm determined. We've got to raise money for this church of his. I can't bear to think of him not able to do things because there's no money. It's going to be brilliant!'

'Did Grandmama Charter-Plackett agree?'

'Well, she couldn't be there, could she, because of that dreadful cold she's got.'

'You wait till she hears what you've planned. There'll be hell to pay.'

Sheila got a nasty feeling right at the pit of her stomach. He was right. What would she say? Hard cheese, they always did things by majority voting, so she'd be the only objector.

★

The shopping bus into Culworth on Saturdays was well worth catching if you wanted to hear the latest gossip. And the Saturday morning after the Friday evening W.I. meeting lived up to its reputation.

They'd begun by learning of the midnight skinny-dipping.

'Who's going to swim naked, midnight or not? Not me for one.'

'You'll get no one volunteering.'

'Won't we just. There's me for a start,' said Greta Jones defiantly.

A roar of laughter went up.

Maggie Dobbs from the school shouted, 'Well, I'm safe because I'm not a member of the W.I.'

'That doesn't matter. It's for everyone.'

Maggie shrunk into herself when she heard that.

'You'd have to lose some weight, Maggie, before you dared.'

'Less of your cheek, I'm not that fat.'

'I'd sponsor you if you'd do it.'

'You're on.' Maggie secretly agreed to herself that she'd volunteer as an incentive to lose weight. She squeezed the fat on her upper arms and thought, yes, this is it. What better incentive than swimming naked? In public?

A great hoot of laughter ran the length of the bus.

'Look at yourself in the mirror tonight in that posh bathroom of yours. See what you think then.'

A lot of sniggering went on and the conversation became general until Angie Turner got them back on track by saying she was also thinking of putting her name down for the sponsored swim.

'You'd be all right. Them kids of yours keeps you thin.'

Angie declared to one and all, 'I reckon there should be

a test before yer put yer name down. Stand in front of a mirror naked for two minutes and if you can still stand the sight of yourself you can put yer name down.'

'You would think of something like that. It doesn't matter what yer look like so long as yer brave enough to do it. Just imagine old Jimmy Glover doing it. That'd be a sight for sore eyes.'

'Or Sheila Bisset.'

'What about Ronald Bisset?'

Another burst of laughter greeted this suggestion. 'The pool'ud empty when he jumped in.'

'Still, doing it in the dark would make it sort of kinder, wouldn't it? Not the impact of broad daylight.'

'I'd give a lot to see Gilbert Johns in the nuddy. Cor, that'd be good.'

'Oh, yes! Three cheers for Gilbert.'

Three lusty cheers went up, followed by speculation as to who would cut the best figure among the men.

Thinking things were getting out of hand, if not downright rude, Greta Jones called out, 'There's a hair-dyeing competition, too. I'm dyeing mine scarlet. Always wanted red hair.'

Before they knew it the bus was pulling up in the Culworth bus station and they all had to dismount. The sophisticated inhabitants of Culworth were surprised by the passengers alighting from it, every single one of whom was grinning like a Cheshire Cat. Honestly, what were those yokels from the villages up to now?

Chapter 5

The news of the outrageous decisions made at the meeting was out. There was even a piece in the *Culworth Gazette*, though who'd leaked it to them was anybody's guess. (Sheila had her suspicions.)

When Anna heard, her heart sank. Before she'd taken time to weigh up her feelings and come to a balanced decision, she went round to see Sheila.

Slightly out of breath, she knocked on the door and then rang the chime bell. Before it had finished peeling, the door had opened and Sheila was standing there, dressed to kill at that time in the morning.

'Why, Anna! Do come in.'

Anna soon found herself sitting in a room that was decorated and furnished like a house in a country style magazine. This tickled her to death, but not enough to override her anger about the W.I. schemes.

'How can I help?'

'Frankly, I am appalled by the fundraising ideas that I've been hearing about. Thought I'd come to the fountain head. Is it all true?'

Sheila nodded.

'When I said the church would be glad to join forces with the W.I., I hadn't any idea it would mean naked swims and pyjama parties. How on earth did it come about?'

'Because someone suggested the ideas and we all agreed.'

'Unanimously?'

'Oh yes. For once. Never been known before.'

'Well, I'm not too sure I can allow it.'

'You're not too sure you can allow it? What do you mean?'

'I don't think it's suitable for a church activity.'

'Now look here,' Sheila couldn't bear the thought of their magnificent ideas being squashed at birth. In fact she wasn't going to allow it. 'None of these activities is being held on church premises so there's no need for you to approve or disapprove. For once in our lives we're being completely outrageous and, believe you me, those people Peter's looking after are going to gain so much from all our efforts that I won't let anyone stand in our way.' Sheila stood up to intimate that the discussion was concluded.

Anna stood up, too, her eyes on a level with Sheila's. 'I shall do my utmost to stop this ridiculous idea.'

'And there was I thinking that you were a bright, up-to-the-minute person who would fall in with our plans without batting an eyelid. Obviously I'm very wrong. If you'd been a dried-up old faggot I could understand it, but someone your age, well really! All it is is fun. Fun, in capital letters. It won't be rude, not anywhere near it. Just good fun.'

'Well, I'm sorry but I shall do my utmost to put a stop to it. It's simply not suitable. I'm going now for a word with Jimbo, as all the events appear to be taking place on his home ground. It's not personal, Sheila, don't take it that way, please, but I . . . however, I'll go and see him right now.'

Sheila raged about the house after Anna had left. The cat came in for a good slap when she found her in the kitchen sink and poor Tootles fled into the garden to find that warm place in the sun behind the lupins where she wouldn't be disturbed. Sheila no longer had a dog so she couldn't storm out to take him for a walk and let off steam; all she could do was drown in a sea of disappointment. Her heart would break if it didn't come off. It was all so fantastic, such a great opportunity to put Turnham Malpas on the map, so out of this world, and at least it kept her mind off Louise and the new baby for a while. Sheila stopped feeling sorry for herself and took time to wonder what Jimbo's reaction would be. If he was persuaded by Anna, that would be the end of the W.I.'s audacious plans.

Sitting in his storeroom, his boater placed on top of a case of top-quality mincemeat in stock for what he hoped would be his best Christmas ever, Jimbo was listening to Anna's arguments for cancelling the fundraising efforts.

' . . . And I'm surprised at you holding the events on your own property. Not really what I would have expected of you.'

'Have you quite finished?'

Disconcerted by his abruptness, Anna nodded. 'Yes, I have.'

'Good. Well, I can see your point, but it's all going to be very innocent. Everyone you speak to is terribly keen, and it's a long time since I've seen the village so enthusiastic about anything. My mother who's on the committee, but wasn't able to attend on Friday due to her bad cold, has laughed herself to a standstill about it and thinks it's a brilliant idea. As for the pyjama party, that's going to be held at Glebe House. So all I'm responsible for is selling tickets and holding the swim in my pool behind the Store.'

'Glebe House? Who lives there?'

'Neville Neal.'

'Neville Neal? As in Church Treasurer?'

'The very same.'

'I am appalled. He doesn't seem like that kind of person at all.'

'I think his boys, Hugh and Guy, must've persuaded him.'

'But that would mean that the church would appear to be supporting it.'

'What the blazes is wrong with a pyjama party? All good clean fun.'

'I remember pyjama parties from when I was at university. Good clean fun was not exactly the aim.'

Jimbo grinned. 'Well, it will be here, believe me. Neville, and certainly Liz, wouldn't tolerate anything else.'

'I still can't agree to it all. It's just not on.'

Jimbo leaned confidentially towards her. 'See here, we all want you to be accepted here. It came as a terrible blow when Peter said they were going to Africa for a year, terrible blow, because we love all four of them and we're trying so hard to accept you, so please, for your own sake, don't object. All it will do is alienate you, and I'm sure you won't want that.'

'I see.'

'They've been known in the past to do strange things, collectively, when matters are not going right for the village. Harriet and I have lived here fifteen years – or is it sixteen? – so we don't get these weird feelings, not like the real villagers do. I'm warning you to keep a low profile about this, well, if you've any sense, that is.'

'I'll think about it. My reputation will be in tatters if anything sensational occurs.'

'Believe me, it will be a nine-day wonder and then forgotten.' Jimbo didn't entirely believe this but he had to say something to persuade her to leave the matter alone.

'Your mother. Which house does she live in?'

'There's three cottages actually on the Green and she lives in the one nearest the school. Are you going to see her?'

Anna nodded. 'Yes. She's well enough?'

Jimbo said cautiously, 'Almost better.' Anna had no idea how formidable his mother could be. He grinned.

When Anna got to Grandmama Charter-Plackett's, she rang the bell on the smartly glowing bright yellow front door. It was a straightforward buzzing bell with none of the fancy ding-dongs of Sheila's, and briefly Anna wondered if that was significant. Did one subconsciously choose the doorbell that matched one's personality?

The door opened and there stood Mrs Charter-Plackett senior. 'Good morning, Anna.' She went instantly on the attack. 'If you've come about the Women's Institute plans, I'm all for it.'

Meekly Anna said, 'I've come for a talk.' She weighed up this tall, well-built woman who had great dignity – even though she was still wearing her impressive dressing gown at half past eleven in the morning – and decided that softly, softly was the best approach. 'Thought I would like to hear your opinions about the plans.'

'Come in. I've got Sylvia giving me a hand till I'm properly better.'

Sylvia emerged from the kitchen, china cup and saucer in her hand. 'Good morning, Anna. Here's your coffee, Katherine.'

'Thank you. Would you be so kind as to make one for the rector, Sylvia?'

Sylvia smiled sweetly but, without the slightest hint of apology in her voice, answered, 'I'm sorry, I haven't time. Got to go. Same time tomorrow?'

'Yes, please.' Mrs Charter-Plackett watched Sylvia go out through the front door and made a note to speak to her about her reasons for acting so out of character. 'Please sit down. Can *I* get you a coffee?'

Anna checked her watch. 'No thanks. Got things to do and I've someone to pick up in Culworth within the hour. It's about these bold, if not downright raunchy plans the W.I. have cooked up. I think they've gone a mite too far.'

'For heaven's sake! A "mite too far" nowadays? In my opinion there's nothing wrong with their plans at all. I'm delighted. And think of Peter with money to spend on his church. Hymn books, equipment for the Sunday School, altar furniture, a piano or possibly an organ – my good lord, Peter'll be delighted. We're millionaires in comparison with those poor people. Millionaires!'

'I know,' Anna could feel her opposition melting away, 'but it just doesn't seem right somehow.'

'And there was I thinking you were "cool", as my grandchildren would say.'

'I am but—'

'Then fall in with their plans, my dear. It's by far the safest thing to do if you want to survive.'

The doorbell buzzed again and they heard Muriel open the door and call out, 'Are you ready for visitors?'

'Come in, Muriel.'

Muriel appeared, carrying a cake well wrapped in greaseproof paper. 'I've brought you a cake, Katherine. So handy for filling a little corner when your appetite isn't up to par. Good morning, Anna, and how are you?'

'I'm fine, thanks. We're just discussing these ideas the W.I. have come up with. Have you heard about them?'

'Oh yes. I was there.'

Anna said she thought the vote was unanimous.

'It was.'

'So you agree?'

Muriel nodded. 'Yes. I thought it was just what was needed. Something daring, you know. Otherwise fund-raising gets tedious, doesn't it? The same familiar things and you begin to lose heart before you've even started. Yes, I agreed wholeheartedly.'

'And Sir Ralph?'

Muriel hesitated for a moment and then said, 'Oh! yes, he's all right about it.'

Mrs Charter-Plackett said, 'Muriel, is that true?'

'Of course. I wouldn't say so if he didn't agree. I'll be going now. Glad you're feeling better, Katherine.'

'Thank you for the cake, Muriel, most kind. I will very easily be tempted to eat a slice at lunchtime.'

When Muriel had closed the door, Grandmama Charter-Plackett said to Anna, 'There we are, then, there's your answer: Ralph agrees.'

'Must go. Thanks for talking to me. Be seeing you. God bless.'

'And you.'

Mrs Charter-Plackett sat down to enjoy her coffee in peace, luxuriating in the knowledge that this morning her home seemed to be the hub of everything. Three visitors and it wasn't even lunchtime yet; she was doing well. In fact, she was feeling much better than she had done for over a week. She hated being ill, it made her feel old, when she wasn't, well, not really. You're as old as you feel, that's right. The phone rang.

'Katherine Charter-Plackett speaking.'

'Craddock Fitch here. Good morning to you. Feeling better? I understand you've been ill, there's a lot of it about.'

'Much better, thank you. And you?'

'In the pink, thanks. About these amazing fundraising activities the W.I. have got themselves involved in — you're on the committee, aren't you?'

'Yes. Are you interested in the pyjama party, the midnight skinny-dipping or the hair-dyeing? Don't tell me you're putting your name down for dyeing that beautiful white hair of yours?'

'No, I am not. I've had an idea though.'

'Fire away.'

'This business of gambling on the L'Arc de Triomphe race in October. How about if I hire a big screen and we all watch it up here at the Big House? Make it a champagne party? I haven't worked out the details of the gambling side, but Kate suggested everyone dress up in black and white, like that race meeting in *My Fair Lady*, remember? Add a bit of distinction, wouldn't it?'

'There are times, Craddock, when I thoroughly approve of you and this is one of them. Excellent idea.' She heard Mr Fitch chuckle his approval of her.

'It is, isn't it. We'll have amplifiers as well as the big screen. Can I rely on you to inform the committee? Off to Sweden tonight, but Kate knows the details, she'll fill you in. I understand Colin Turner down Shepherd's Hill is a bit of a whizz with studying form. He might need to have a hand in this. Checking the date and runners and such, placing the bets. Speak to you soon.'

Mrs Charter-Plackett, despite her ill-health, danced around her sofa she was so excited. Yes, indeed. Things got better by the hour. She disliked the man, but there were times when he really did come up trumps. She'd ring Harriet and let her know.

Breathless, she dialled her number, but she wasn't in, so she rang Sheila instead.

Sheila listened spellbound to Mr Fitch's plans. 'I do not like the man, but this is perfect,' she said. 'Absolutely perfect. Isn't it exciting? I never imagined it would take off like this. We are going to have to be so well organized otherwise it will spiral out of control. Will you be at the committee meeting on Friday? . . . Oh good! Glad you're feeling better.'

Sheila leaped to her feet, trod on the cat's tail and, ignoring Tootles's cries, flung the French windows open and shouted, 'There's to be a champagne party at the Big House, Ron. Come in, come in and I'll tell you all about it. Come on!'

Ron shook off his wellington boots on the terrace, as Sheila called it, padded inside and dropped gratefully into a chair. 'Well?'

The news was round the village and all outlying districts long before Mr Fitch had boarded his plane for Sweden. By the following morning Sheila was getting phone calls asking for tickets.

'We don't know the price and we don't know the date

yet. You'll have to watch out for the publicity campaign,' she said each time.

At four o'clock, they stopped answering the phone and Ron put a new message on the answermachine saying just that.

'We can't go on like this, Ron. I'm exhausted. What's it going to be like nearer the day? What have I started?'

'Something enormous, that's what, old girl. Enormous. You'll really be on the map after this.'

Sheila smiled. 'I will, won't I?' She dropped off to sleep, when she'd really intended getting their supper ready, and dreamed of popularity and being the centre of things and having a clipboard to refer to, but then, out of the blue, she was back in that park hunting hysterically for that missing child, the child Louise had asked her to care for. She'd let her down badly. Which brought Louise to mind when she woke. Organization? Who better to ask?

'Soon as I've had supper I'm going to see Louise about all this. She'll show me how to organize it all.'

'Wait till she's got them to bed, you know what it's like. Total Bedlam.'

'I could help her to get them to bed, you know. It's not beyond me.'

'Very well, you go; I can't stand it.'

Due to her excitement and the supper going wrong and having to start all over again, instead of getting to Louise's early to help get the children to bed, she arrived at the cottage just as young Gilbert was saying goodnight.

'Goodnight, young man, sleep tight.'

'Say the other bit, Nana.' A big grin spread over his face and Sheila thought, 'There's no wondering who his father is, that's for sure.'

'Mind the bugs don't bite.'

He skipped off to bed, leaving Sheila's eyes wet with tears. Such a lovely boy, such a happy nature, just like his father.

Louise came downstairs and began ironing.

'I've come for help.'

'What with?'

'Where's Gilbert?'

'Just gone to a meeting in Culworth.'

'Doesn't he work long enough hours as it is?'

'Yes. He'll be back soon. Couldn't avoid it. So, what do you want help with? As if I didn't know.'

'You've heard then, about what we've planned?'

'It's difficult not to. They were all on about it at playgroup. I've an idea you'll have more swimmers than you ever imagined and I wouldn't be surprised if the membership of the W.I. rockets. Who suggested this midnight swim?'

'Me. Midnight skinny-dipping we're calling it.'

'Mother! Who'd believe it? So what do you want me to do?'

Sheila had been watching her banging her way through the ironing and wondered if really she had any right to ask her to do anything at all, apart from keeping her head above water. Then she thought of number six and instead of what she really meant to say she blurted, 'This new baby, are you pleased?'

'Gilbert and I both wanted six children, and this is it.'

'But how will you cope? I mean, six children all to be fed and clothed, in this tiny cottage, too.'

'Well, you know old Miss Gotobed, she was telling me the other day that she remembers there being ten children in this cottage when she was small.'

'But they'd no standards then, had they, not like we have today. We all—'

'I knew you weren't pleased. But don't make any suggestions about getting rid of it. I can't. For me it already exists and it would be murder if I did, so don't let's mention it again.'

'When is it due?'

'Not quite sure. What with feeding the baby for such a long time, and being so busy, I never really noticed I was pregnant.'

'It will be the last, will it? I don't want you getting depressed and doing something silly.'

'Silly? Is that a euphemism for killing myself?'

Sheila hesitated. 'Well, yes, that's what I mean. Yes.'

Louise looked up from the ironing. 'Gilbert and I know what we are doing. He and I have complete understanding, he's my rock. Believe me.'

'I know I've never been very good at being frank with you, but I just have the feeling you're not absolutely all right—'

'That's enough. It's early days and I'm having morning sickness like I've never had it before, so I'm not into food at the moment and it's a bit exhausting, but it will pass.'

'You've never had that before, have you?'

Louise tut-tutted in exasperation. 'What was it you came to see me about?'

'Oh yes. How shall I set about organizing all these sponsorship things?'

'When I've finished this ironing, I'll have a think.'

'Here, let me finish it and you sit down and think. I can iron where as I can't think.'

They changed places and Sheila noticed how relieved Louise appeared to have the opportunity to sit down. She can't pull the wool over my eyes, Sheila thought. She's worried. She ironed away, admiring the little shirts and frocks, unravelling a bundle of tights, pressing the baby's pram blanket, which had come out of the tumbler dryer looking too creased to use. She took a great pile of the boys' socks and paired them up, and when she'd neatly lined them up on top of the pile of ironing, and admired yet again the little frocks on their tiny hangers, she looked up and saw Louise had gone to sleep.

The cup of tea she'd made for her had gone cold before she woke. When she did wake, Sheila made a fresh pot and they sat chatting over organization, lists, codes, coloured stickers and files until Sheila's mind was awash with confusion.

'I'll think about it tomorrow. I'll go home and you go to bed. It's almost ten; Gilbert won't be long. Or would you like me to stay till he gets home?'

Rather too hastily, Louise said no she needn't. He would be home soon.

For once in her life Sheila said, 'If there's anything you need to confide, I shan't tell Gilbert or your dad. Just between you and me, you know.' She stood on tiptoe and kissed Louise's cheek. 'Don't forget.'

As Sheila drove down Little Derehams High Street, she spotted Gilbert driving home. They both pulled up and wound down their windows.

Gilbert called out anxiously, 'Everything all right, Sheila?'

'Of course. I've been getting Louise to show me how to organize these events for the W.I.'

'Right! They'll be a success, I'm sure.'

'Can I put your name down for the midnight skinny-dipping?'

'Certainly,' Gilbert laughed. 'They'll sponsor me at work, I'm sure.'

'Good! Be seeing you. I'll give you a sponsorship form very soon. Goodnight!'

'Goodnight to you, Sheila. Ron OK?'

'He's fine.'

There, she proved she could keep a secret by not telling Gilbert she was worried about Louise. So, her first official volunteer for skinny-dipping. They'd made a start.

Chapter 6

The very next name to go on the skinny-dipping list was Dean Jones. He'd met up with Sheila in the Store and asked her to include him. That was his first major decision about his change of lifestyle. Since his initial visit to church, when he'd attended simply to see Anna, he'd made a few more decisions, but these were to remain secret.

One: he couldn't get her out of his mind.

Two: he might come from peasant stock, as his tutor would have said, but he had been to Cambridge and that meant something in this world; he couldn't be kicked into touch as easily as a farm labourer could be.

Three: he needed another suit and some smart casual clothes.

Four: he had to find ways of being in touch with her without making his feelings too obvious. He'd no actual experience in the ways of a lover but if he was in touch with her then surely opportunities would arise.

The final decision he had made was that neither his mother, nor Barry, should know how he was feeling. They would be horrified. So was he, come to that. But immediately the sensation was obliterated by his overwhelming fascination with her. He had always been one who could face the consequences of his actions, and he knew there would be serious consequences, if not downright scandal. The thought of it filled him with elation and terror all at the same time. Consequently Dean was either full of himself or wallowing in despair, and his swinging moods did not go unnoticed by his mother.

This particular Saturday he drove to Culworth. His mission? New clothes. Michelle had begged a lift but he'd refused; he did not want his bossy sister dictating what he should buy. Still less did he want her to have one of her renowned intuitive moments and realize he had a woman in mind.

His allowance from Mr Fitch's education fund, paid to him while he was at Cambridge, had always been in excess of his requirements so besides his salary from Neville Neal he had a nest egg into which he would dip. The smartest man's shop in Culworth was A.J.P. Tindales. Dean looked in the window for a while then opened the door and entered the hushed portals.

In a whirlwind buying frenzy in which purchases were made at the snap of a finger, he emerged an hour and a half later with two new business suits and several casual clothes. The cost was astronomical. But if he was to succeed he had to look the part. He raced for the multistorey car park as fast as he could without appearing ridiculous, because meeting anyone he knew from Turnham Malpas would be a disaster. His clothes safely locked in his car boot, he sauntered off to find a coffee shop that would appeal to his new image.

There it was, the new one tucked alongside the cathedral. It was extremely busy, it being Saturday, and Dean had to squeeze his way between the tables to reach the only empty one right at the back. Café latte ordered, he sat back and waited its arrival. He glanced round and spent a few moments studying everyone. They were all quite heedless of his state of mind; how could they not know? He looked up at the waitress to thank her for his coffee and as she turned away to serve other people her space was filled by . . . Anna.

'Hello, Rhett. May I join you? There doesn't seem anywhere else free.'

'Absolutely.' He leaped to his feet and pulled out a chair for her. 'It's Dean, by the way.'

'Of course, sorry. What do you recommend? Cappuccino? Latte? Espresso? Instant? Or maybe they don't sell instant in here.'

Dean had to smile. 'I don't think they would. They consider themselves above a quick instant.' He caught the waitress's eye and she came across. 'What would you like? The latte is good.'

'Latte it shall be.' Anna put down her bag, her elbows on the table, her head to one side and smiled at him. Her teeth were perfectly white and even. 'So, Dean, why are you in Culworth on your own?'

'Been shopping, then I'm going to the library.'

'Do you know, I haven't found the library. Where is it?'

'You know the circular building at the far end of Kirkgate? It's so big you can't miss it. The one everyone says should never have been built? Well, there's shops and the library in there, a health centre and a cinema; they've called it the Rotunda.'

'Why don't they like it?'

'Too modern, too round, too big and the shops all sell things one could well do without.'

'I see. Oh good, here's my coffee. Thank you.' She stirred it, took a sip, nodded her approval and then said,

'I've been thinking: you know the Youth Club that Kate from the school and Venetia from the Big House run in the church hall?'

Dean nodded.

'Well, I'm thinking of taking a larger role than Peter took. I've been to visit it and it occurred to me we need young men to help run it. How would you feel about that?'

'Don't know.'

'I support it because it isn't uniformed, you see, and I intend building up the numbers.'

'Don't you approve of uniforms then?'

'Frankly, no, I don't. Too regimented, too much like an army, and I'm a pacifist.'

'So am I, but Dicky does a brilliant job with the cubs and scouts. Best pack in the county. They're always winning cups and things, top of this, top of that. I don't think the uniforms matter one jot. The boys love it.'

Anna completely ignored his support of the Scouts and carried on speaking as though she hadn't heard a word. 'The Youth Club needs a young man or two about. Good for role models, you see. And you're a role model and a half.' She smiled again and Dean thought his heart must be out there pinned to his sleeve.

To give himself time to think, Dean sipped his coffee, offered her the sugar bowl and when she refused it he had nothing else with which to fill the silence, so he said, 'I could help, I suppose. But I haven't any particular talent to bring to it.'

'That doesn't matter, it's you being there that counts. Think about it. The church needs people like you. Young, educated, full of ideas, confident, gregarious. Am I pleading my cause well?'

Again those beautiful teeth of hers, and he noted the very delicate pink lipstick that gleamed on her lips. 'You are, none better. I might give it a whirl. Not done anything like it before so I shan't know how to begin.'

'Just be there. Friday. Seven-thirty. Great bunch of people.'

Dean agreed, feeling as though her proposal was the answer to a prayer. The rest of the café was a blur, except for Anna sitting opposite him offering him the chance to have contact with her. He was filled with joy, great heaps of it, and felt like springing up from his chair and dancing. Such bliss.

'There you are, couldn't see you at first, tucked away here at the back.'

The accent he couldn't fix, but the blur had disappeared and, pulling out a chair and sitting down between Anna and himself, was a very tall thin man, meanly dressed, bearded, slightly unkempt. Anna introduced him. 'This is Paddy. Friend of mine. Paddy, this is Rhett. No, sorry, Dean, from the church.'

Dean offered to shake hands but Paddy ignored his outstretched hand, so after a moment, Dean said, 'Pleasure to meet you.'

Pleasure? A pleasure? Who was this man? Friend? Fellow priest? Lover? Dean cringed from head to foot. Surely not. He needed to know. 'Are you in the church? You know, a member of the clergy?'

A wry smile crossed Paddy's face. 'Nothing. That's what I am, nothing. Never met someone who's nothing, have you?'

That seemed to be the end of the matter, and Paddy began to roll a cigarette.

'Not in here. They don't allow smoking.' Dean was

glad of an opportunity to put him down but it didn't appear to affect Paddy in any way. He simply closed up his little tin box and stowed it away in his trouser pocket.

Anna asked, 'Coffee, Paddy?'

Paddy nodded and, as Dean was facing the café and could catch the eye of the waitress, it was left to him to draw her attention.

'What can I get you?'

Paddy replied, 'Coffee regular, black as night.'

Anna explained. 'I've known Paddy a long time. He's staying with me at the rectory for a while.'

That gave nothing away at all. Dean finished his coffee and got to his feet. 'I'll leave you to it, then. Friday, seven-thirty. OK?'

'Thanks, Dean, I do appreciate you deciding to help.' She took his hand and gave it a squeeze, they smiled at one another, and Dean left, his heart racing, his face flushed with delight. As he strode away from the table he heard Paddy say, in an unpleasant, sneering tone, 'What's that little pipsqueak going to help you with?'

Boiling over with humiliation, Dean went out of the café door and bumped straight into Michelle as she was coming in. 'What are you doing here?' He stooped to pick up a carrier she'd dropped.

'Coming in for a coffee. You've had yours, I assume? You look as if you've lost your wallet. Whatever's up?'

Dean shook his head. 'Nothing. Nothing at all.'

'So, you've no shopping with you.' She peered at him suspiciously. 'Did you come to meet someone and she hasn't turned up? That's it, isn't it?'

'Leave it. Leave it. How did you get here?'

'Bus, seeing as my darling brother wouldn't give me a

lift in. I wouldn't have spoiled your assignation. You only needed to say.'

'I didn't have an *assignation*. I'm going home now. Want a lift?'

'No, thanks. I've still got Grandad's birthday present to buy, though I can't think what to get him. What have you got him?'

'Nothing.' Dean studied the thronging High Street, rattling his small change in his pocket. 'I'll get something during the week at lunchtime. I'll be off, then.'

Before she could stop him he'd disappeared into the mêlée. Too late he realized he'd left Anna to pay for his coffee. What an idiot he was. That loathsome Paddy wouldn't pay, oh! no not he. He had sponger written all over him. And now he, Dean Jones, had foolishly volunteered to help with the youth club. He must be mad.

As he swung through the main gates of Turnham House, and up the drive to the Head Gardeners House, he had to smile. He'd got what he wanted, a chance to make contact with Anna, and his new clothes. So altogether it had been a successful morning.

Then he remembered Paddy. Just who was he? He couldn't believe he was her lover. Heavens above, he knew she had better taste than to fall for such a loser. It puzzled him and the more he dwelt on the matter, the more mysterious Paddy became.

Paddy, of course, hadn't given him a single thought once Dean had vacated the café. No, Paddy had more important matters on his mind, like where was he going to get some money. 'Nice house you've got, Anna. I reckon we've fallen on our feet here. Well, in Turnham Malpas, that is. Nice little village and the kind of people I like. Generous, easy-going—'

'I wouldn't be too sure about that; they can be damned stubborn when they want, I understand. Now I've got to get back to the rectory. Are you coming with me? Is there anything you need? Look, let me give you this,' she had a £20 note in her hand. 'Toothbrush, whatever; you'll be needing something, I'm sure.'

Paddy almost kissed that note in triumph, but he didn't, not when he was trying to look grateful. 'Thanks, Anna, that's very kind of you. I just hope your parishioners appreciate what a kind heart you have. You're a true friend. I'll come back on the bus.'

They left together, Paddy hanging back to retie his shoe until Anna had paid the bill. She set off for the car park and Paddy to the shops.

The market in the main street was thronging with people laden with carriers or just simply browsing, and he was hustled from time to time as he tried to get close to the stalls. Once or twice he pushed them back and gave them a glare. He was good at glares, was Paddy, even better at looking appreciative and better still at looking in need of buckets of TLC. He decided to try his luck on the corner at the end of the market.

Paddy dug out his stock-in-trade, a fold-up ancient panama, put it down on the pavement with an inviting two or three coins in it, and dug in his pocket for his mouth organ. He ran up and down a few scales to get himself in the mood and then began to play some well-known tunes: 'Abide With Me', 'Fast Falls the Eventide', 'The Lord's My Shepherd' and 'Ave Maria'. After all, you had to play according to your clientele.

He could get really soulful with 'Ave', he could and,

low and behold, he could hear coins dropping into his hat. By the time he'd rendered it twice with plenty of heart-rending *vibrato*, he'd made himself feel really sad so he decided to play 'Abide With Me' once more, then pack up and count what he'd collected, which was £1.82. Not bad. They were generous, like he'd said to Anna. It bought him a drink in a local hostelry and after that he wandered off to find the bus station. He'd have a kip when he got in, and would wake up just in time to eat the nice meal Anna would have ready for them both, then he could visit the Royal Oak this evening and establish himself with the locals. Tonight would be his chance to make them feel sorry for him.

In his bedroom at the rectory he emptied his pockets. Bar of soap, toothbrush, bar of chocolate, three pairs of socks, cheap shampoo and the £20 note still intact – oh, and three white handkerchiefs. That was the way to shop. The stallholders in Culworth market hadn't enough eyes in their heads to catch Paddy Cleary. Not nearly enough.

Saturday night was the big night of the week for the Royal Oak, if you wanted to meet someone. Take a perch in the bar and you'd meet most of the villagers and then some, because they came in from the outlying villages on Saturdays for their night out. Dean was there with Rhett, having a swift half before going into Culworth to the late-night film at the new multi-screen in the Rotunda. Dean had come in for some teasing about his new casual clothes, especially from Rhett. 'What's this, then? I reckon you've got a girl.'

'I have not got a girl, as you so politely put it, just decided to improve my image.'

'Oh yes, I've heard that one. I say, who's that chap sitting with Jimmy? Haven't seen him before.'

Dean turned . . . and saw Paddy. 'He's staying at the rectory.'

'Yer what? Are you sure?'

'Absolutely. I saw him with her in the new coffee shop in Culworth this morning.'

'Looks the wrong kind of chap for the rectory. Is it her brother or something?'

'No, an old friend.' Dean could have rushed across, dragged him to his feet and booted him out of the door and into the road, like he'd seen Bryn do with a disruptive punter in the old days. Willingly, gladly, with pleasure. But there was nothing disruptive about Paddy. He was quietly drinking his pint and talking animatedly to Jimmy, who was only half listening by the looks of it.

'Well, I don't reckon much to her friends if he's a sample. Looks like a sponger to me. Well, he'd better not try to get a pint out of me, because he won't.'

'Nor me.' Dean turned his back so Paddy wasn't in full view and wouldn't anger him quite so much. But his image was still there in his mind and Rhett wouldn't let the matter drop.

'He's the sort who thinks the world owes him a living. He'll think that I'm obliged to treat him because I'm in employment, even though I earn peanuts. He doesn't look too ill to work, does he?'

Dean didn't answer.

'Does he? Have you gone deaf?'

'No, just thinking. I don't believe Anna would give him shelter if he wasn't a worthwhile person.' Out of the corner of his mouth Dean muttered, 'Aye! He's coming across for another pint. Drink up, let's be off.'

They skidaddled out as fast as they could, leaving Dicky to serve Paddy with no one available to pay for his second pint.

He asked for the same again, complimenting Dicky on the quality of his special brew. 'Absolutely excellent, best pint I've had in years. Ah! Just a minute, would you believe it? I've left my wallet at home. Paid you with small change for the first one, didn't realize I hadn't picked up my wallet. Can you put it on the slate and I'll pay what I owe next time I'm in?'

'Of course. What name shall I put?'

'Put it down to the rectory. That's where I'm staying at the moment. I'm so sorry, really very sorry.'

'Oh, that's all right, easy done,' said Dicky. 'The rectory is as good a reference as any. There we are.' He pointed at Paddy's glass of beer. 'We call it Georgie's Special Brew after my dear wife.'

'What a tribute! She's called Georgina, is she?'

'That's right. 'cept she always gets Georgie.'

'Pretty name. Pretty village, too, you know. Lovely people.'

'Some is and some ain't, as you might say.'

Paddy raised a surprised eyebrow. 'Oh?'

Dicky laughed. 'No names, no packdrill.'

Paddy shifted a little and put a foot comfortably on the footrail, resting his forearms on the bar. 'Any casual work going anywhere, do you think?'

Dicky shook his head. 'Not that I know of, though sometimes there's casual work at the Big House, picking peaches, I shouldn't wonder, this time of year. You could try there Monday. You'll need to ask Michelle Jones — she's head gardener now. But she won't stand any nonsense. Nice as pie in here, but once she gets her overalls on and them secter things in her hand she's a different woman, and she's only a slip of a girl really.'

Paddy grinned. 'Sounds too much like hard work for me. Anyway, I might give it a whirl. That chap I've been talking to sitting on the settle – what does he do for a living?'

'Jimmy? He's a taxi driver. Sorry, someone to serve.' Dicky turned away, glad not to be free to give this chap a general run-down on the village and its inhabitants. He wondered why he didn't quite take to him.

Someone sitting the far side of the bar beyond the fireplace was whispering very quietly, 'See that chap at the bar? I saw him begging in the market this afternoon.'

'Begging? You never. You must be mistaken.'

'I'm not. It's him. I'm certain. Playing a mouth organ and a hat down on the ground for your money. I wonder what he's doing in here?'

That casual remark was overheard and it was round the bar in a moment. Several people patted their pockets or checked their bags to make sure they were still in possession of their money. A beggar, was he? At the rectory? Come on. It must have been someone else begging in the market, not him. Anna wouldn't have a beggar living with her, well, not *living* with her in that sense, but living in the same house. What would Peter say? What indeed. All Caroline's lovely things in there, too.

Ron and Sheila came in then, Sheila armed with her clipboard, hoping to get some more names down on her lists. Just the right night for it, Sheila had said, and had dragged Ron out on the pretext that a real lady didn't enter a bar unaccompanied, even in these enlightened times. They both went to order their drinks and found themselves innocently standing beside the subject of everyone's conversation.

Paddy put down his empty glass and said, 'Good evening. More delightful inhabitants of Turnham Malpas, I assume?' He gave the impression of being about to tug his forelock, which impressed Sheila enormously.

She laughed as she said, 'I don't know about that, but I am here on a mission. Collecting names for the events the W.I. have organized for raising funds for Africa. Can I put you down? But maybe you're a visitor and not here for long?'

Raising funds? Ah! 'Well, I'll be glad to do what I can. I'm here for quite a while.'

So together he and Sheila discussed the various options and he plumped for the midnight skinny-dipping. No, he wouldn't do the race afternoon, no he didn't think so, not gambling, he was a bit strict about that. Sheila, greatly impressed by his moral stance, hurriedly put him down for the swim.

'I may not get many sponsors not knowing many people, but I will make a donation if I don't.'

'Well, that's very kind. I'm going round asking people now.' She surveyed the bar; there wasn't an empty seat and plenty were having to stand by the vast inglenook fireplace, fortunately not lit, otherwise they'd have been burned to a crisp. 'My word, I've chosen a good night. Here's your sponsorship form. Just put your name and address here for me.' She waited while he filled it out, then set off into the crowd, filled with zeal.

By the time she'd returned to Ron's side, Sheila was almost delirious with excitement. 'Look! Just look at these lists. We're going to do so well, we are. I'll have to print out more sponsorship forms and new sheets. Unbelievable. People are so supportive, aren't they?'

She included Paddy in her glance at Ron, and Paddy nodded soulfully. 'If you're down it's amazing how kind people can be.'

Sheila nudged Ron and pointed tactfully at Paddy's empty glass. Ron dutifully rose to the occasion. 'Same again, Paddy?'

'How very thoughtful you are. Very thoughtful. I knew you were nice people the moment I saw you walk through the door.' Conveniently forgetting he was facing the other way when they'd come in.

When Sheila got home she sat down to enjoy counting the names on her lists, and Ron went to make her a cup of tea.

'Ron!' Sheila shouted. 'You'll never guess – that Paddy Cleary is living at the rectory. I'd no idea, I just didn't notice what he'd written down, I was so excited. That can't be right, can it?'

'Rent-free, I've no doubt, judging by his inability to pay for his own drink. You do realize I bought him three pints tonight?'

'Really, and didn't he offer to buy you one?'

Ron shook his head. 'He did not. Too fly by half is that one.'

'That's disgusting. We'll avoid him in future.'

But in the bar there was no avoiding Paddy. Somehow, by what means they never quite knew, just before Dicky called time, Paddy had got a line of five customers going between the tables doing the conga. Before they knew it, the whole bar, including some of the customers eating late in the dining room, had joined on and the line went from the dining room round the bar and then some. They could hardly sing for laughing. Paddy led them all outside as Dicky rang the bell for time and they did one turn right the way around the Green before they dispersed. Windows were opened, curtains drawn back, cheerful shouts were heard – what fun they were all having. It was years and years since they'd had such a laugh. Fancy! All round the Green as well. What a night! All because of Paddy.

That Paddy, he was a laugh, he really was. Good old Paddy. Goodnight!

But no one saw the very satisfied smile on Paddy's face as he got into his bed in the rectory attic. He'd move down to the big bedroom tomorrow, give himself more space. After all, the bathroom up here was very basic, not his style at all.

Chapter 7

Michelle Jones was in one of the hot houses at the Big House examining the peaches to see if they were ready for picking when she heard a voice calling, 'Miss Jones? Miss Jones?' She carefully closed the door behind her and went to find who was looking for her.

'Ah! You're Miss Jones.'

'Indeed I am. Head gardener. What can I do for you?'

'My name's Paddy Cleary. I'm wondering if there's any chance of casual work in the gardens? Haven't done it before but I'm a quick learner.'

'Well, now, you might well have come at a most opportune moment.' Michelle nodded her head at the hot house she'd just left. 'If it's hot all day today, these peaches will be ready for gathering. It's delicate work, not like picking blackberries, and they have to be stored very carefully.'

'I'll do it.'

'Are you living in the village?'

'At the rectory.'

Michelle raised an eyebrow. 'Would Anna give you a reference?'

'I know she would. Can't have much better than living at the rectory, can I?'

'Indeed not.'

'You won't regret taking me on.'

'If I do, believe me, you'll be out on your ear, immediately. I won't tolerate idleness.'

'My sentiments exactly.'

'I only pay for full days. We start at seven-thirty and that doesn't mean seven-fifty nor even seven thirty-five. Five pounds an hour. OK?'

Paddy had to swallow a bit hard when he heard that but outwardly he accepted cheerfully. 'Thanks, that'll be great. And if the peaches are not ready?'

'I'll find other work for you. Right!'

As Paddy Cleary went off, Michelle took her mobile from the pocket in her dungarees and rang the rectory.

'Hello, Anna speaking. How may I help?'

'Michelle Jones from the Big House. I've just had someone called Paddy Cleary come for a temporary job; he said he was staying with you.'

'He is, Michelle. You're Rhett's sister?'

'No. Dean's sister.'

'Sorry, yes, of course. What can I say? He is staying with me and if you can offer him a worthwhile job, I for one shall be delighted. He's had a rough time for years and I'm trying to get him back on his feet. A job will be excellent for his self-esteem.'

'I'm not Social Services and if he doesn't work hard he'll be back down the drive a lot faster than he came up it. Can't afford timewasters. Mr Fitch hasn't got where he is today without hard work and long hours, as he so frequently tells me. Same goes for his workforce. So if Paddy can hack it, fine. Thanks for talking. See you soon. Bye.'

Anna put down the receiver and went to look out of the study window. Poor Paddy. Poor, poor Paddy. What a life he'd had. His father had been a merchant sailor, thankfully away from home a great deal because when he was home he beat his boys mercilessly for the smallest misdemeanour. Then one time he went off to sea again and never came back. At first there was relief and then money began to run out, and in order to keep the family – his mother, himself, two brothers and his two sisters – in the bare necessities, Paddy began stealing. Got more practised, then got under the skin of some of the bigger criminals for his audacity and before he knew it he was being thrashed by them for getting too good at it. As Paddy said, what else could he do but steal to supplement the family income, him being still at school? Wasn't his fault, now was it? It was the cards he'd been dealt. The beatings only made him beat others, then it became a spiral of drugs, drug-dealing and coming close to death.

Anna had met him when she was helping with the doughnut and tea van the Abbey took round every afternoon for the down and outs. One day he'd been alone and they'd talked and the whole sorry tale came out. Admittedly the story he told her could have been found in any magazine or newspaper any day of the week, but Anna had to believe him. She'd taken him to a drug centre where they got him off drugs. She'd cared for him, supported him, and now she'd moved to Turnham Malpas she had the opportunity to give him a home.

But taking a job! That was a definite move forward. She was so pleased. Anna settled down to work at her desk but before she could even check her emails the phone rang again. It was Gilbert.

'Hello, Anna. How are you? Well, I hope? I'm taking the day off, is it possible I could come round for ten minutes to talk about the church music?'

'Of course, be delighted. Coming straight away?'

'I am indeed, if it's not interfering with anything?'

'No, that's fine.'

'Take me ten minutes, OK?'

'Absolutely. Be seeing you.'

Anna took a quick glance in the mirror and decided make-up was called for. So she flung a brush through her hair, applied mascara and lipstick, appraised herself in the mirror and decided her old jeans and the shirt she was wearing were quite satisfactory, and raced back downstairs. As she reached the bottom step the doorbell rang and then the knocker was applied heartily several times.

She opened the door and found Gilbert standing there, looking like something out of a nature film. One of those men of the woods, rough-hewn and splendidly earthy. She caught the sandalwood and lime smell of him and thought: Gorgeous. Does he know the effect he has? No, he doesn't.

'Shall we talk on the doorstep?'

'Oh! Sorry. No, of course, come right in.'

'In here?' Gilbert indicated the study door.

'No, the sitting room.' She led the way. 'You sit on the sofa then you can put all that sheet music on the coffee table.'

Ah, thought Gilbert, none of the cosy camaraderie of the study like he was used to with Peter. He'd shared many a glass of something holed up in there talking music. Gone were the days.

He placed his music on the table and the slenderness of his hands as he did so didn't escape Anna. Into her mind came that picture of him in shorts and sandals in the wood that first Sunday. Today it was a light blue shirt, open almost to the waistband of his trousers, which were corduroy and baggy, but there were the same Jesus sandals.

He was very striking. She realized he was talking and she hadn't heard a word.

'. . . in view of this I thought we'd better get singing from the same hymn sheet, so to speak, so that's why I've come.'

'I see.'

Gilbert waited for her to expand, but instead she said, 'I wish we did sing from the same hymn sheet regarding the choir. All *boys*? Please!' She rolled her eyes heavenwards and awaited his reply.

'The choir has been all boys since it began and I have no intention of changing it, ever. I know lots of the parishioners will be quoting Peter at you, morning noon and night, so I'm not going to apologize for saying that Peter was entirely satisfied with the way I ran the choir. He agreed for it to be entirely male. We have a waiting list for boys wanting to join, we have at least two boys every year who get scholarships to Cathedral choirs and we win county choir competitions very, very frequently. What more can one ask? You know what it would be like if we took in girls?'

'Just as good?'

'It would be "there's more girls than boys", "there's more boys than girls", "it's not fair, it should be fifty-fifty". There'd be no end to the quarrelling about it.'

'It should be fifty-fifty. Are you saying you could tell the difference if you listened to a choir of girls and then a choir of boys on a tape? That you'd know which was which?'

'Very possibly.'

'I bet!' Anna looked her most derisive.

'What matters is the quality of the singing, actually. However, they are all boys and they are staying all boys.'

Anna watched him stroke his pile of sheet music with tender care. Listened to him say, 'I know I'm a traditionalist, I do care deeply for the sanctity and dignity of the contribution music makes to a service and I will not be moved. The odd modern hymn but as for the rest—'

'That's fuddy-duddy, and you know it. If I want modern music, modern music I shall have.'

Gilbert stayed silent.

Anna tried to catch his eye but he didn't look up. 'Hello, there? Anyone at home?'

Gilbert eventually looked up. 'Then we shall have modern hymns but traditional music otherwise. Mrs Peel loved your "Yellow Submarine" that first Sunday. Thought it added something to the service. Quite what, I've no idea, but she did. But if you bypass me and talk to her about the matter, it could be a resignation job.' He picked up the music from the coffee table, tucked it under his arm and said sadly, 'Such beautiful, exquisite music, so uplifting for the soul. It must have its place and I shall fight for it. I brought this for you to see. There's some handwritten stuff, possibly by a past eighteenth-century organist or choirmaster at St Thomas à Becket, which Louise found when she was cataloguing the music cupboard for me years ago. I'd hoped to play some of it for you . . . however, I'll see myself out. Thank heaven's Peter's back in a year; it can't come too soon for me.'

Anna followed him to the door and stood on the step, watching him get into his car. 'Can we still be friends?' she called. In reply she got a weary smile and she could have cried at his sadness. But on the other hand she was also determined to have her own way. Damn and blast the man upsetting her like this.

It felt chilly after Gilbert had gone so Anna ran upstairs

for her cardigan. As she passed the main bedroom she saw the door was open and some of Paddy's things on the bed. She went in and opened the wardrobe door. He'd moved down from the attic. For a second she couldn't believe it, but he had. In the bathroom on the glass shelf were his meagre bits and pieces; toothbrush, comb, deodorant, soap. Wild at his presumption, Anna picked up his holdall, which he'd neatly tucked away in the bottom of the wardrobe, pushed his clothes and his bathroom things in it, and took the whole lot up to the attic where it belonged. She'd made the decision most particularly not to sleep in the main bedroom because she felt it was too much of an invasion of Peter and Caroline's space. In any case, that vast bed was wonderful for two but for one . . . Anna didn't see Paddy for the rest of the day but when he came in at supper-time and went straight to the main bedroom, she heard his explosion from downstairs in the kitchen.

He arrived abruptly at the kitchen door, but she didn't even turn round to face him. Paddy shouted, 'What the hell do you think you're doing?'

'That bedroom is Caroline's and Peter's. I don't sleep in there, and neither do you. No one does.'

'I want to. It's cold in that attic.'

'When I switch the heating on it won't be. Another couple of weeks and then.'

'You've one hell of a cheek.'

'No, Paddy. You've one hell of a cheek. This is not your house, it's not my house, but it is entrusted to my care so I have an absolute right to say what does and does not go on in this house. You sleep in the attic.'

'Who's going to stop me from sleeping where I want to sleep? Huh?'

Anna turned to face him. 'Either you sleep in the attic or you move out.'

'Move out? What's happened to the saintly person I thought you were? What about the dog collar and the cassock, eh?'

'Still there, Paddy.'

'Not as you'd notice.'

'Well, they are, Paddy. I am not obliged by some sort of holy script carved in stone to give you a home. I do it out of the kindness of my heart. But there are limits and this is one of them.'

'Well, too late. I've moved back in.'

Anna realized she had to take a stand. Once he got the master of her there'd be no end to trouble and for his own sake he had to realize she would be the person in charge if they were going to live under the same roof.

'Watch my lips. I shall say this very slowly. So take note. You . . . must . . . move . . . back . . . into . . . the attic. The alternative is moving out. Understand?'

Paddy eyed her up and down. Took in the smell of some sort of delicious thing she was cooking, weighed that up against being top dog at the rectory and decided to disobey. 'I'll move my stuff straight after we've eaten.' He had no intention of ever doing so. She'd never make him leave, Christian conscience and all that. No, she wouldn't see him homeless. Not Anna.

After they'd eaten Paddy went to stretch out on the sofa with the remote control. Anna cleared up the kitchen and then crept quietly upstairs. His bag, still packed, was on the bed in the main bedroom. She picked it up, went downstairs, noiselessly opened the front door and put the bag on the step, but it wasn't balanced and it rolled over on to its side, spilling the contents onto the road. Anna left it just as it was.

With it being one of her rare nights off Anna decided to watch TV herself, and spent the whole evening watching programmes entirely of Paddy's choice. He flicked the remote time after time, finding things he enjoyed without a moment's consideration of how she might feel about watching extreme violence and, on occasion, quite unnecessary sex scenes.

'No porn on this damn thing. I'm off to bed. I'm tired.'

'Goodnight.' Anna sat quite still, waiting for Paddy's outrage when he didn't find his belongings where he'd left them. She heard the thud of his feet as he raced up to the attic, then the long run back down to find her.

'What the hell have you done with my things? This isn't funny.'

'No, it isn't. You were told to move them or you'd be out.'

'So where are my things?'

'Outside.'

'Outside? You've a hell of a cheek. Typical hypocritical Christian. Speaks one thing, does another. Where is it, then? My bag?'

'Outside on the front step.'

Paddy advanced towards her and for a split second she thought he was going to hit her, his fury evidently at boiling point.

'You obey house rules, Paddy. I insist. It's a small thing to ask when you think of the advantages you have of living here.'

'Advantages! It's nothing more than I deserve after the life I've had.'

'There's always some price to pay. By the way, you didn't say you'd got a job.'

'Huh? What?'

'At the Big House. Michelle rang me.'

'She'd the cheek to check up on me, had she?'

'Naturally, it was her right to do so.'

'Well, yes. I have.'

'Then in that case, as soon as you get your wages you can start making a contribution to the household expenses.'

'What?'

'If you're still living here, that is.'

'Pay for my keep? I'm getting little enough as it is.'

'That's what adults do, Paddy.'

Paddy slammed out of the room and Anna heard him open the front door. He bellowed his anger. 'What the hell . . . it's all out in the road!'

In a moment he was back in the sitting room, carrying his bag and pushing its contents in as best he could in his fury.

'By the time you've put your things back in the attic, I shall be making my hot chocolate. Fancy a cup?'

Paddy liked her hot chocolate, it was always so creamy and satisfying. But he wouldn't give her the pleasure of a reconciliation. 'No, thanks, I'm going to bed.'

'Goodnight, then. Don't forget to set your alarm. God bless.'

Paddy looked askance at her and left.

Anna waited to hear his footsteps going up to the attic and they did. She breathed a sigh of relief. They'd come very close to a point where all the improvement Paddy had made would be lost and he'd sink back into that dreadful pit from which she'd rescued him; she just hoped that having won the battle she'd also won the war. As she sipped her chocolate Anna thought about the day she'd had. The one thing she regretted the most was quarrelling with Gilbert. He didn't deserve her saying what she'd said and she wished, how she wished, she could make amends for their disagreement. The only way was to forget about modernizing the services, but that stubborn streak of hers wouldn't allow her to. Somehow she had to persuade him to her way of thinking. She'd talk to Mrs Peel. After all, Mrs Peel was the church organist not Gilbert's organist. Then she remembered he'd said he'd resign if she did. That wouldn't do. What was her next move? She'd pray about it.

In the attic Paddy was also wondering about his next move. But he didn't add anything about praying for guidance. He put on his pyjamas, kindly donated by a volunteer worker at the Abbey crypt but which he suspected had been her recently deceased husband's, and climbed into bed. He snuggled under the duvet and lay until well after midnight, planning his revenge. It had to be something which would strike savagely at the very roots of her existence.

Chapter 8

Dear Friends

Three weeks since I last made contact and we are beginning to settle into a routine. The children are travelling every Sunday evening to the International School and returning home Friday evening. There are children there from European countries as well as America, South America and Russia to name but a few, so Alex and Beth are enjoying meeting them all. Most of their parents are working to improve the lot of these people in all sorts of ways. A wonderful experience for them, though Alex complains about the food and Beth about there being very little provision for games as space is so limited. However, they send their greetings to you and hope everything will be just the same as always when they get back to T.M. They are relying on you, they say, to keep the status quo.

As for my work, I am overwhelmed by the sheer zeal of my congregation. I mention something I would like to have happen and, hey presto, it does. We are short of Bibles (the ones we do have are the very ancient King James version and have been falling apart for many years) and you know I prefer the modern translations. We are short of hymn books and have nothing to print out hymn sheets with. Still, we worship God with blinding faith. How blessed we are.

Winsome, my right-hand woman, is a wonderful Christian despite the difficult life she has led. Her husband Elijah has medical experience and is helping Caroline with the clinic. Their help is invaluable.

I hear you are holding events to raise money for us, though the ways and means appear to be secret! Caroline is battling away with the clinic and achieving real success. Very little in the way of equipment but nevertheless she succeeds.

God bless you all.

Peter, Caroline, Alex and Beth

Sheila Bissett read the email within five minutes of Jimbo pinning it on the Village Voice noticeboard. 'Someone's told them. They have. They've told them and I wanted it to be a secret!' She stamped her feet in annoyance. 'You can't do anything in this village without someone busy-bodying. I wonder who it was?'

Jimbo was tidying the greengrocery and overheard. 'Sorry, Sheila, it was me. I didn't say *how* though, only that he could expect a surprise. When Caroline hears she'll be so envious.'

'Envious?'

'Yes. Missing all the fun. How are the numbers going?'

'Well. At the moment we have twenty-two people for the skinny-dipping and twenty who've promised to dye their hair. They're each paying two pounds to put their names down and then whatever they get in sponsorship. As for the champagne race afternoon, there's ninety-four paid fifteen pounds. That's ten pounds for the buffet and the champagne, and five pounds for their bet. I'm going to have to close the list soon or they won't all fit in at the Big

House. There is a limit. You won't believe it but at the moment there's an English horse expected to run called Major Malpas and forty-seven people have chosen to back that. It'll never win, Colin says, it's one hundred to one at the moment. So that's a bit of a disappointment.'

Jimbo gave her a wink. 'I say, who's down for the skinny-dipping? Anyone . . . you know, a bit . . .' He drew the shape of a buxom woman with his hands and laughed.

'Honestly, Jimbo, I'm ashamed of you. I don't see your name on the list. In any case, we're not having peeping toms. Only those who are sponsored and taking it seriously. Believe me.'

'It's my pool.'

'Oh! Yes. So it is. But you can't just spectate, you've got to do it. Swim, I mean. It's all going to be very tasteful. Beautiful water music, Gilbert's lending *Fingal's Cave* and there will be soft floodlights so it's all nice and select. No leering.'

'So I can't watch from my own window?'

Sheila was nonplussed at this idea. 'No. You have to swim. Though I *shall* need someone to sign the certificates of evidence to say they've actually swum in their birthday suits.'

Almost before she'd finished speaking, Jimbo said, 'I could do that.' But he couldn't keep his face straight any longer, and burst into laughter. 'Only testing, Sheila. I didn't mean it.'

'I'm glad. I'm sure Harriet will be relieved.' Sheila could have bitten her tongue off.

There was something in the tone of her voice that alerted Jimbo. 'Just a minute. Harriet hasn't put her name down, has she? For the swim?'

Sheila's face was angelic when she replied. 'For dyeing her hair, she has.'

'I mean for the swim.'

'Now, do you honestly think she would?'

Jimbo sighed with relief. 'For one dreadful moment . . .' But he didn't notice that Sheila had two fingers crossed behind her back.

'I've opened a special bank account and Ronald is helping me keep an eye on it. I tell you who has put his name down, though: that Paddy Cleary staying at the rectory. I have to admire him; he said his principles wouldn't allow him to go to the race afternoon. Doesn't seem the kind of person to have principles, does he? He let Ron buy him three pints the other night, you know the night they did the conga all the way round the Green, never offered once to buy him one in return. Fair's fair, isn't it?'

'Short of money, you say. I can't understand why she has him there.'

'He is a good laugh.'

'That's about all.'

Sheila, concentrating on her clipboard, which went everywhere with her at the moment, didn't catch the odd tone of his voice and she let it pass. 'I say, Jimbo, if Major Malpas comes in first at one hundred to one, and forty-seven people have five pounds each on it, how much is that?'

In a flash the answer came back. 'Twenty-three thousand, five hundred pounds, but it's a while to the race and the odds could change.'

'Never! I'd no idea! Heavens above. I can't believe it! But still, it won't come in first, will it? Couldn't possibly, not one hundred to one. No. It couldn't, could it?'

'Stranger things have happened, but it's unlikely.'

'Then there's the Pyjama Party on Saturday. I rang Hugh and Guy the other night and they've already sold fifty-five tickets at seven pounds fifty, and someone had just rung to buy twelve tickets for a birthday party to come. So that's twelve on top of the fifty-five. So what's that if they come, too?'

'Five hundred and two pounds and fifty pence.'

'Oh, my word. Then there's drinks; Dicky's doing the bar. I'd really no idea.'

'Don't forget there's the sponsorship money, too.'

Sheila had to sit down for a moment. 'I know Gilbert's been sponsored two hundred pounds from work if he swims naked.' She began to tremble. 'It's much, much more than I ever thought. What a responsibility. I ought never to have taken it on.'

'Here, have a coffee, help get over the shock.' Jimbo handed it to her but her hand was shaking so much she was in danger of scalding herself. 'Steady.'

The coffee, freshly brewed as it was still quite early, calmed her nerves.

Jimbo watched her sympathetically. 'I know we haven't seen eye to eye over the years but I do admire you and the W.I for doing it. It's brilliant. I don't know what could possibly top this. Nothing, I don't think. What about the press, have you informed them?'

But Sheila never got to answer him because at that moment in came Anna followed by a stream of customers, which did Jimbo's heart good. Before they shopped they crowded round Sheila, wanting to pay for the race afternoon, put their names down for hair-dyeing and a few for the skinny-dipping. She gave three customers the names of who to contact for the pyjama party, and in the end completely forgot she'd gone in there to shop and went home to put her paperwork straight.

This was the way to stir everyone up, she thought. As Jimbo had said, what could top it? No one, not no one could think of anything quite so startling. The W.I. were at last on the map! Sheila hugged herself with joy, and then fell in to all kinds of horrors beginning with 'what if'. But she hurriedly put the lid on her fears and kept them all bottled up. If she wasn't careful she'd be having a nervous breakdown, but she'd have to wait until after the race afternoon to have her breakdown, because that was the last event.

The pyjama party was this Saturday but none of that was her responsibility, so she could sit back and let it all pass her by. It had surprisingly mushroomed into being the social event of the season for the younger set in the area. Stuffed-shirt Neville had got quite carried away and had sacrificed his immaculate lawn so they could have a giant bouncy castle. He'd also bought himself a pair of designer pyjamas with matching dressing gown and a red wig so he could get into the spirit of things. The weather forecast promised a fine mild evening so it all looked very promising.

It was an eight-thirty start, and the cars began arriving by eight-twenty. By nine, Church Lane and all Stocks Row were full and the Green had begun to take the overflow. It was no good rushing out to protest at the sacrilege of parking on the Green because it was flooded with cars in no time at all. Hugh and Guy had arranged for the music to be relayed outside, consequently the entire village was enjoying the party. There were some in Little Derehams who swore they could recognize the tunes the music was so loud.

Jimmy Glover had fun looking out from his bedroom window and watching all the cars parking. One was a bit too close to the pond. But never mind, eh! It hadn't rained for days so the ground was firm. He loved the costumes they were wearing. Such ingenuity. The chap who'd got out of the car nearest to his cottage was dressed as Wee Willie Winkie; the fellow with him appeared uncomfortable in his outfit, as though he was regretting his idea of wearing babydoll pyjamas and blond pigtails but was still determined to enjoy himself.

Jimmy spotted Fergus and Finlay Charter-Plackett going over to join in the fun, and surely that was Flick, too. Well, would you believe it. Young Flick old enough for a party. Then he caught a movement by the pond. Was that empty car somehow nearer to the water or was he dreaming? He watched carefully and was sure it was inching, very, very slowly. No, it wasn't, he was going daft in his old age, that was it. Plain daft.

The sound of someone shrieking took his attention for a moment then he looked back and yes! The car *had* moved! No, it wasn't. Honestly! He'd be frightened of his own shadow next. Two party-goers crossing the green between the cars were wearing Victorian nightdresses and carrying lighted candlesticks; they looked good with their hair tied with old-fashioned rags like they used to do to make ringlets. Another glance at the car and Jimmy could swear it had definitely moved again. No, it hadn't. Yes, it had. It was difficult to gauge in the dark. But yes, now it was gathering speed, no, it wasn't, yes . . . yes . . . it was, and before he had time to shout a warning, it sank gracefully into the pond and become submerged almost above its bonnet. He half thought of going to tell someone but decided he was better inside with his windows shut. They'd find out soon enough; no point in spoiling the party.

One person he didn't see arriving for the party was Dean Jones because he'd approached from the Big House and through the churchyard. As soon as he'd heard that Anna was intending to go, Dean made sure he had a ticket. He'd dressed up in his mother's pyjamas, which were much too short in the leg and the arms, a doll's hot water bottle pinned by a ribbon to the right-hand side of his jacket and a giant dummy also pinned by a ribbon to the left-hand side. He waited in the queue to get his hand stamped when he presented his ticket. He'd never been inside Glebe House before and was overwhelmed with the display of good taste coupled with apparently unlimited money. The whole house downstairs was alive with people. The music was throbbing, and the highly charged conversation and the excitement of the crowded rooms added to the buzz. The adrenalin rush he got when he spotted Anna spun him almost out of control. He stuttered and stammered with embarrassment, until Anna said, 'Rhett! You look great.'

'I didn't realize you were coming. You look perfect.'

She did. She was wearing a cream satin nightdress, which reached the floor in a swirl like an evening dress. The straps were thin like shoelaces and sent all Dean's hormones into overdrive. He struggled to control his voice. 'I'm going to get a drink. Can I get you one?'

'Oh, no. Please let me. My turn.'

To Dean's extreme embarrassment, Anna searched for her purse by lifting the hem of her nightdress and exposing her leg well above the knee. Her purse was tucked into a frilly blue garter that secured it to her leg. 'Thought carrying a purse would spoil the effect of the nightdress, so I tucked it into a garter.'

Dean's temperature rocketed and he was glad Michelle had rouged his cheeks before he left otherwise the blushing he was undergoing would have given the game away. Hell's bells! He persuaded himself he was adult and well able to cope but . . . Anna stood in front of him at the bar and asked him what he wanted to drink. He said the first thing that came into his head. 'White wine spritzer.' Then wished he hadn't because it sounded girlie. Too late, she'd ordered the same. Standing close behind Anna because of the crowd, Dean got a close-up view of her neck and he studied the way her dark hair curled itself around her ears. He thought it was beautiful.

What was happening to him? He was behaving like a teenager when in truth he was twenty-two. He and Anna should have a meeting of minds not this base emotion he was experiencing. Did she feel the same? Of course she didn't. Facts were facts: he was a gauche, mumbling idiot, not the bright, debonair, man-of-the-world he imagined himself to be. How could he be debonair wearing his mother's pyjamas?

'Here we are, Rhett, white wine spritzer. I like them; they're so refreshing but you get the alcohol buzz.'

They squeezed their way out of the crowd at the bar and Dean muttered, 'I'm Dean.'

'Of course, I don't know why I keep making that mistake. Of course you're Dean. I do apologize. Let's put our drinks on this window sill behind the curtain and go for a dance. Would you mind? I'll find someone else if you don't want to.'

'Of course I would like to.'

He surreptitiously wiped his sweating palms on the legs of his mother's pyjamas, just in case she fancied him holding her while she danced. He never felt comfortable dancing, those two left feet he felt grow as he took the floor always hampered his performance. Why couldn't he be like Rhett? Laughing and confident and not caring a fig if he stood on his partner's feet or made a fool of himself; now that was something he couldn't bear. But what had he done already? Chosen to wear women's pyjamas? Why hadn't he thought of doing what Neville Neal had done, bought smart men's pyjamas and a matching dressing gown? So much more suave.

The parquet floor in the dining room lent itself beautifully to dancing. The dining table had been pushed to one side, the chairs lined up against the walls, the French windows opened to the autumn sky, the music, slinky kind of, with a hint of the orient in the rhythm. What more could he ask? Anna really threw herself into the dance and some of her enthusiasm rubbed off on him and he began to relax, until Rhett caught his eye and gave him the thumbs up. Immediately he stiffened up and those two left feet came back. He stumbled, causing Anna to say, 'I've had enough. Let's go outside.'

'I'll get our drinks.'

Anna went to stand by the floodlit pond and when Dean joined her she smiled and his heart turned over. God! He'd got it bad. What to talk about?

'Dean, how did you feel about helping at the youth club last Friday night?'

'I quite enjoyed it.'

'Good, you appeared to be quite comfortable with it. Kate and Venetia thought you were splendid.'

'Oh! Thanks.'

'As for your table tennis . . . Well! County standard, I thought.'

'Huh! I don't know about that. It's just one of those things I can do without having to think about it. Always have been able to.'

'Dean, do you know, I wonder why someone with your degree is doing their accountancy qualification in a small town accountant's like Neville's. I don't mean they're a two-bit outfit, they're obviously doing rather well, but you could have got a job with any of the leading companies up in London, couldn't you?'

'Never thought about it actually. Just came home and he offered me the job. Seemed a good idea at the time.'

'I like people to reach their full potential and you could be up there amongst the movers and shakers.'

'I'd miss everyone here though.' Dean thought about her, and how he'd miss . . .

'But they're not all going to disappear, they'll still be here when you come home for a visit. However, I don't know why I'm suggesting it when you're so good with the youth club. They need role models like you.' She grinned at him and if he'd died at that moment he would have gladly gone without a single regret.

'Another drink?' Was that his voice he heard, gruff and croaky?'

'Yes, please. Same again.'

When he came back with their drinks, a crowd of people had come out onto the terrace to dance. Anna thanked him and put her glass on a stone beside a gnome fishing in the pond. 'Here, give me yours; we'll try dancing out here, much more fun than that stiff and starchy dining room.'

'Let's hope the gnome hasn't drunk them before we get back!'

'You never know – he might even fall drunk into the pond.'

So they danced, and it gave him the closeness he wanted. It felt daring and dangerous, but wonderful and satisfying. He threw himself into action.

When the music stopped, Anna said, 'Wow! Thanks for that. Must go get my drink and circulate. See you soon!' And left him standing there.

Dean felt badly let down. He waited a while to give Anna a chance to find her drink, because he couldn't face having to think of something to say to her, then he went into the garden, retrieved his drink from beside the gnome and looked at the empty space where Anna's drink had been. Good at table tennis. God, what a pathetic talent, almost as bad as being good at tiddleywinks. All it was good for was impressing the youth club, nothing more and nothing less. It moved him not one notch closer to Anna. Then the worst of it, he saw Anna was dancing with Rhett and having lots of fun. Blast Rhett! Blast him.

In fact, everyone was having a good time. The party was a brilliant success. Most of them threw any sophistication they might have to the winds and leaped and bounced on the bouncy castle like five-year-olds. But Dean had to draw the line at that. He just wasn't designed for the abandonment a bouncy castle needed. Then he saw Anna having the time of her life. Dean hesitated. Dean prevaricated. Dean half moved towards it, half moved back again. Decided he just couldn't then thought: Damn it! I will. Slipped off his shoes, and hurled himself onto it. In no time at all he and Anna were hand in hand, jumping and laughing, breathless, abandoned, till Anna slipped and hurt her ankle and had to retire.

He sat her down on a fancy garden chair away from the crowd and went to find her another drink. But it was announced over the loudspeaker that the buffet was open and there was a concerted rush to eat, and he lost his chance with Anna and spent the rest of the night watching from the sidelines. She was never without a circle of people interested in chatting with her. He was desolate. He knew them all, Fergus, Finlay and Flick, Hugh and Guy, Rhett and most of the others, but he was too tongue-tied to join them.

It had been decided by Neville that the party must finish at midnight and at five minutes to midnight Wee Willie Winkie put his lighted candlestick on a window sill to free his hands because on Neville's insistence they were all going to join hands to sing 'Auld Lang Syne', much to Hugh and Guy's embarrassment. Why did dads insist on old traditions long abandoned by the young set? they wondered. But no, he wouldn't be denied. Well, he had footed the bill so they'd better humour the old chap.

So they all crowded onto the terrace where there was more room and treated the village to a rather thin wavery rendition of 'Auld Lang Syne' because no one knew the words apart from the first couple of lines. Except for Neville, who sang it lustily if a little drunkenly.

Thank heavens for that, the village thought. Now, at last, we shall be able to sleep. But before a single car door had slammed or engine started up, there was a cry of 'Fire! Fire! Fire!'

With windows and doors open, the wind had blown Wee Willie Winkie's candle flame. It had caught the curtain, then the heavily draped pelmet above, then an oil painting beside it, then the draught had billowed the flames and in a moment the dining room was ablaze. Wee Willie Winkie, returning to retrieve his mother's Victorian candle-holder, fell back at the door shouting, 'Fire!' as loud as he could.

Anna, remembering she'd noticed a reel hose screwed to the outside wall of the house, grabbed Dean by the arm. 'Come with me! We'll get the hose.'

Between them they rolled the hose out to full length, turned the tap and, as the water was released, they both held on tightly and directed the nozzle into an open window. It was a far more powerful hose than they had imagined and it took all their strength to keep it directed onto the flames. There was much shouting and filling of buckets and daring attempts to beat out the flames, but the flames would not be denied their victory.

They'd been fighting it for twenty minutes before the fire engine from Culworth could get there. Hastening along the straight bits, surging round corners, cutting across grass verges, it came hurtling into the village down the Culworth Road, scattering the onlookers. Never had it been more welcome.

Eyes weeping with the effects of the smoke and their skin feeling scorched by the flames, Anna and Dean were glad for Rhett and Guy to take over the hose.

'Where's Michelle? Where's Michelle? Anyone seen Michelle?' Dean rushed about amongst the party-goers searching for her. Then there she was and he flung his arms round her and gave her a big hug. 'All right?'

'While you've been doing your hero bit, I was trapped in the downstairs loo and had to climb out of the window. I've torn this new nightie and I wish I hadn't. I've had such a great time.' Then Michelle burst into tears and Dean had to hug her even harder.

Eventually the fire was extinguished but not before the dining room and part of the hall were gutted.

Liz stood, full of despair, watching the horrific end to their fun evening. 'Neville! I can't believe it. We shall have to begin from scratch. There'll be nothing worth saving.'

Neville said, 'Well, at least everything's insured. And no one was hurt, thank goodness. And we've made over five hundred pounds and that doesn't include the profit on the bar takings. So I call that a successful night. Added to which, we've all had a great time.'

Anna shouted above the hubbub, 'Three cheers for Neville and Liz, everyone. Hip hip hurrah! Hip hip hurrah! Hip hip hurrah! Goodnight. God bless you all.' She found herself being kissed and hugged by everyone for being the heroine of the hour and that included Dean, who, in the excitement of the moment, kissed and hugged her like everyone else. But he wasn't thinking about her quick reaction over the hose, more how much he was enjoying having a reason to kiss and hug her. It ignited Dean's feelings for her all over again, and left him more intent than ever on pursuing her.

Most of the guests stood around in the garden, more out of curiosity than anything, to see the firemen checking the fire was definitely out, making notes, asking if they knew how it started, had everyone been accounted for? They looked at each other in surprise. Had anyone counted? Blank faces all round. No, they hadn't done a count, it never entered their heads.

'Why not?'

Neville became authoritative. 'In the heat of the

moment it never occurred to us. We were all out on the terrace, you see, when we noticed the fire. And certainly no one was in the bedrooms. I'm positive. I was very strict about that.'

The fire officer raised a sceptical eyebrow. 'I'll check.' He disappeared and returned in a few minutes, escorting two friends of Guy's, both laughing their heads off. 'These two were upstairs, sir, in one of the bedrooms. It could have been a tragedy, it could. However . . .'

Neville was speechless. As for the couple, the girl was almost hysterical with amusement when she looked at their faces, and the young man, at first acutely embarrassed, also began to laugh, which infected all the others and soon they were all roaring. How to get your lovelife advertised! Far more effective than sending out emails.

But the village still couldn't sleep because of the party-goer's car that had slid into the pond and had to be pulled out. Neville coerced the firemen to attach ropes to it and pull it out. The wheels had sunk well down into the sludge at the bottom and the car, after a lot of revving on the part of the fire engine, emerged from it with a great sucking noise amidst rousing cheers from the party-goers and half the village, who'd flung on trousers over pyjamas and coats over nightdresses in order to join in the fun.

It was two o'clock in the morning before the village quietened down enough for everyone to get to sleep. What a night! What fun they'd had! And this was only the opening night of their festivities.

A pale moon appeared from behind the clouds, shining on the white painted cottages, highlighting the dark beams and the thatched roofs and the occasional cat out hunting. So peaceful now the village looked, as though it had been forgotten by time. But under the ancient roofs a new spirit beat, a new energy, a feeling of anticipation nothing could dim. If this was what could happen at a pyjama party, what on earth could they expect from the skinny-dipping night and the afternoon at the races? And that pair found upstairs in a bedroom after the fire! Still, you were only young once, and it had happened dozens of times before in this village, except it had been haylofts and barns then, not one of Neville's splendid bedrooms. Time made little change to that kind of hanky-panky. More than one chuckled at the thought as they hunched their duvets a little higher and drifted off to sleep.

Chapter 9

The knocking at the rectory door at nine o'clock on the Monday morning woke Anna with a start. Look at the time! Heavens! She leaped out of bed, opened the bedroom window and looked down to find Sir Ralph on her doorstep. She called out, 'Sorry, slept in. Can you come back, please?'

Ralph looked up. 'Good morning. Of course I can. Back in an hour.'

'Thanks.' Anna closed the window and sat down on the bed a moment to collect her thoughts. How the blazes had she slept in? She picked up her bedside clock to check the time. She'd never set the alarm. For Ralph to catch her oversleeping! Blast it. She dashed out onto the landing and called up, 'Paddy! Are you there? Have you gone?'

She heard a grunting noise and realized he'd slept in, too. Would he lose his job? 'Paddy, it's nine o'clock. You're late.'

'I'll take a sicky. The dragon said I'd be out on my ear if I was late, so I'm sick. Forgot to set the alarm.'

She heard the bed creak as he turned over. 'So did I. I'll ring up for you, then.'

Anna took the briefest of showers, dried herself, omitted the body lotion, flung on the nearest clean things she could find and charged downstairs. She phoned Michelle on Paddy's behalf saying they'd both slept in and he'd be coming in late and sorry. Fingers crossed, she hoped she'd manage to persuade him to do just that. If she couldn't . . . well, she'd have to think of something else. Paddy was like that, though; you found yourself doing things you'd never intended for him, and he didn't give a fig. But lying for him was something she wasn't prepared to do. Anna went into the kitchen to start breakfast.

Paddy came down in a few minutes still in his pyjamas.

'Thought you were taking a sicky?'

'I am. But I need my breakfast and then I'm going back to bed.'

'Don't ask me to phone for you again. Don't mind if it's genuine but not when it's a total fib and all you've done is oversleep.'

'Look who's talking.'

'I'm not going to argue. I've something better to do with my time.' She handed him the cereal packet and watched the flakes pouring into his bowl until it was filled to the brim. He couldn't half eat. 'By the way, you've been paid now. How about something for the house keeping?'

Paddy mumbled a reply through a mouth crammed with cornflakes.

'Mmm?'

'I said all in good time. I'll leave it an hour or two and then I'll wander up there, saying I feel better and thought I wouldn't let her down. Do an extra couple of hours tonight instead.'

'You sound as though you enjoy working up there.'

There was a brief hesitation and then Paddy said, 'Of course not, work's for fools.' But he thought about sitting in the wheelbarrow in the sun, eating his lunch, and how much he enjoyed that blissful hour with his back resting against the brick wall of the potting shed, thinking about life. His life. 'I only work to eat.'

'Then pay me for it, please.'

'OK. OK. Keep your hair on.'

Anna went upstairs to clean her teeth, got nicely into her two-minute cleaning routine and so was unaware that someone had rung the doorbell. Paddy launched himself from the kitchen table and went to answer it.

Ralph, well-schooled in good manners, kept his astonishment to himself and said, 'Ralph Templeton to see Anna.'

'Come in, come in. She's cleaning her teeth, she won't be a minute.'

Paddy showed Ralph into the study.

'You'll excuse me. We overslept, you see. Got to get ready.'

Ralph sat in the comfy armchair, fuming. Just back from holidaying abroad, suffering from jetlag and on top of that kept awake by the pyjama party and then the fire. Ralph was in no mood for finding the rector, apparently, sleeping with some unshaven down-and-out. No, of course not, there must be some other explanation. It wasn't what it looked like. Of course not. She wouldn't, would she? Certainly not, though the evidence pointed to guilt. What were things coming to? A live-in lover in the rectory. But he mustn't judge.

The door burst open and there was Anna. 'Sorry to keep you waiting, Sir Ralph. Slept in. Must be the aftermath of Saturday night. What a successful evening we had, well, apart from the fire and the car in the pond, but even that added to the fun. Have you had a good trip?'

'Yes, thank you. Just a few days but it has perked us both up.'

'Now what can I do for you?'

'An explanation would be welcome.'

'Explanation? Of what?' Anna sat down at her desk, wishing he'd been shown into the sitting room; in the smaller study he was too close.

'I came about parish business only to find you have a lodger.'

'Oh, you mean Paddy.'

'Well?'

'Well, he's a down-and-out I've rescued from the streets in Culworth. He slept under the railway bridge and I felt he needed a leg-up, so I offered him a home.'

'I see.' How to phrase it? thought Ralph. 'Is he purely a lodger?'

Anna was horrified. 'Of course he is. My God, you don't think—'

'It appears that way.'

Anna got to her feet. 'I can assure you that is what he is. He's got a job in the gardens at the Big House. Going every day, well, except today but that was a mistake, sleeping in. I'm surprised at you, Sir Ralph, even thinking on those lines.' She managed to give the impression of an outraged person. Which she was, of course.

'I'm not really into these liberal ideas, all this bending over backwards to be politically correct. PC they call it, don't they? Trying hard to see the other's point of view, instead of standing up for what you know is right. I call a spade a spade and if I thought for one minute that you were co-habiting, I would put a stop to it. It's enough that we tolerate modern hymns and arm-waving but that—'

'Frankly I think it's none of your business, Sir Ralph, none at all, what goes on in my home.'

'In Peter's home.'

'Well then, in Peter's home.'

'He wouldn't allow anything of that nature. Very strict he was.'

'Not strict enough from what I hear.'

Ralph saw he'd stepped straight into a moral abyss. How much did she know? 'Well, he can't help women running after him. He's a very attractive man.'

'Indeed. However, I can assure you . . .'

The door burst open without so much as a knock. It was Paddy. 'Just off to the gardens, Anna. Back tonight. I'll be late, got to catch up. See yer, Ralph.' Paddy left as quickly as he came.

'I can assure you that nothing of an immoral nature is going on in this house. I really shouldn't have to defend myself, you know, you're not being quite fair.'

Ralph got to his feet. 'I'm sorry, of course you shouldn't. I'm at fault, jumped in with both feet. Just back, jetlag and Saturday night, trying to sleep . . . well . . .' He pulled a wry face. 'You must accept my apologies. It went off all right, did it? The pyjama party?'

'Oh, yes! Absolutely fine. Everyone very well behaved, and Neville even wore a red wig!'

'My word! Good for Neville, time he relaxed a little. Stuffed shirt, you know, even by my standards! Must go. I've decided I'm too tired to go through the parish business. I'll delay it for another day. Thank you for being frank with me.'

'He's all right, you know, is Paddy. Hard life. But he's pulling himself up and making great strides. Good morning, Sir Ralph.'

'Good morning to you.'

Anna dashed into the sitting room to pick up her bag and keys before going to Penny Fawcett. For some reason, though, she felt things were not right. She stood gazing round, wondering what had alerted her. Then she realized, checked and checked again. There'd been four of Caroline's Staffordshire figures on each shelf in the left-hand alcove, sixteen all together, but today there were only three on each shelf. The remaining ones had been spread out evenly to disguise the fact that four were missing. The right-hand alcove still had four on each shelf. Damn and blast him. Damn and blast him. She'd throttle Paddy when he got back. Thing was, how long had they been missing? He'd gone into Culworth on Saturday; perhaps he'd sold them there. They were worth a mint.

Anna drove to Penny Fawcett Monday market with her head in a whirl. And she'd defended him too, given him a character reference. It would be impossible to replace them. In any case, she couldn't remember each individual one. They weren't hers but even so, she loved them. Just when she thought he was making good, this happened. One step forward, two steps back.

Penny Fawcett was proving a difficult nut to crack. They were very polite to her, but that was all. She had a suspicion that a woman rector was one step too far. Well, they'd only a year to tolerate her, then their beloved Peter would be back. So with the theft of the figures and the feeling of rejection she suffered about Penny Fawcett, Anna set off home with a heavy heart. Damn that Paddy. He hadn't one single grain of gratitude or he wouldn't have done such a thing. But having done a good deed should one expect gratitude? Was that one's reward?

She ate her evening meal alone. At least he'd not lost his

job. Obviously he'd stayed on to complete a full day, like he'd said. It got to eight o'clock before she heard him at the front door. He sounded cheerful enough, calling out, 'Anna! You haven't waited for me, have you?'

'No. Yours needs two minutes in the microwave.'

'Right.'

Anna put down the book she was reading and listened to him pottering in the kitchen. She'd prepared a big pile of food: lamb chops, peas, new potatoes, courgettes, mint sauce, large helpings of everything. He'd be a while, which gave her time to contemplate how she would phrase her inquisition. In her mind she tried out a few opening questions.

'How much did you get for them?'

Or: 'I'm not a complete fool, I know what you've done.'

Or: 'Can you explain where the figures are?'

Or: 'Why?' with a dramatic finger pointing to the shelves.

She got up and placed the figures in their original position, three and then a space, on each shelf. Picking up her book again, she continued reading.

'Anna, can I finish this pie off?' Paddy shouted from the kitchen.

'Yes, of course.'

He eventually came in, carrying his cup and saucer. He put them on the coffee table and sat himself down on the sofa. Right where Gilbert had sat when they'd had that row. She wished it was him sitting there now and not this betrayer of faith.

'Had a good day, Anna?'

'Not really.'

'Penny Fawcett day? You always come back a misery when you've been there.'

'They refuse to accept me. Polite yes, liking me, no.'

'Never mind, they'll come round. I've had a brilliant day. The Dragon was grateful I'd made the effort. I've won myself some Brownie points there, believe me.'

'I'm glad. So, how much did you get for them?'

'Them? What them?'

'Don't play the innocent with me, Paddy.' She noticed his eyes flick up to the alcove.

'I honestly don't know what you mean.'

Anna could almost believe the innocence of his expression. He was very convincing. 'I mean Caroline's figures in the alcove. There are four missing.'

Paddy looked along the shelves. 'There's always been three on each shelf that side. I remember thinking it looked odd. Expect she was hoping to buy four more to fill the spaces.'

'Paddy, frankly I don't believe you.'

'What the blazes would I want with four Staffordshire figures? I'm not an expert, I wouldn't even know where to go to sell them.'

'I would.'

'Well then, it must be you,' Paddy laughed, 'hoping she wouldn't notice they were missing. You should have organized the shelf better, covered up what you'd done.' He stood up and walked across to the alcove, spaced the remaining figures out more evenly and sat down again. 'There you are, you see. Who'd know? Best if you sold four from the other side then it wouldn't be noticeable at all.' Paddy grinned at her and, picking up his cup, drank down the last of his coffee. 'I'll have another cup. Do you want one?'

'No, thanks.' She'd try again when he came back. He was such a convincing liar. If there was a prize . . .

Paddy came back in with the morning paper in his hand, and settled down to read it.

'You can't fool me, Paddy, I know you've taken them.'

'Why me? You've always got people calling, and you don't like them in the study so they get in here. The temptation must be colossal if they're short of a bob or two.'

'Well, it certainly wasn't Sir Ralph because you showed him into the study. In any case, he's the epitomy of honesty.'

'That's because he speaks with a plum in his mouth and wears good clothes. People who've inherited money are never suspected of anything underhand, oh no! It's poor sods like me who get it in the neck, well before anyone else. Be fair, Anna, you wouldn't dream of asking him, now would you? So why ask me?'

There was a self-righteous, bleating tone in his voice now, which Anna called his 'virtuous bleat'. But she mustn't show such distrust of him. He was right, she'd suspected him first and foremost.

'Please, Paddy, if it is you who's stolen them, be honest with me. Where are they now?'

'I've just said it isn't me. How many different ways are there to say it? I didn't pinch 'em.' He picked up the remote control from the arm of the sofa and switched on the TV. It was a trivial quiz programme but he plainly intended watching it to avoid any more questions.

'I'm sorry, but I sincerely believe it was you who took them and I want them back on these shelves by tomorrow night.'

He didn't answer, so Anna said the same sentence even more loudly. He still didn't answer.

'*Paddy!* Answer me. Do you hear?' Her leaping from her seat and grabbing the control was so sudden Paddy reacted far too late.

'Hey! What do you think you're doing? Give that to me.' He reached up to grab the control back but Anna was too quick for him. She switched it off and then sat down in her chair with it hidden behind her. 'Now, please, answer me. Where are they?'

Paddy was steaming with temper. He wanted the TV on and the TV was going to be on or he'd die in the attempt. He jumped up and tried to pull Anna out of her chair so he could reach the damn thing. But Anna was far tougher than she looked, and she refused to budge. He brought his arm back and prepared to hit her.

Anna said, 'Don't! Or I shall have the police here and tell them what's happened.'

'Ooops! She's getting dangerous.'

'One finger laid on me in anger and so help me I will call the police. You wouldn't want that, would you, Paddy. Twelve months in prison? Think how you suffered before.' His right arm was drawn back once more. 'Out you go if you do, never to come back.'

'Idle threats, my dear, idle threats.' He sat back down, opened his newspaper and left her guarding a TV control he apparently could well manage without now.

'It is you, no matter how vehemently you deny it, and like I said, if they're not back on the shelves by tomorrow night I shall call the police. I don't want to do that, because you'd lose your job, but do it I shall. They're not mine, are they, so they're doubly my responsibility.'

'Damn ugly things, they are. She'd be glad to see the back of them.'

'Only if *she* got the money and not you.'

'I'm really insulted that you see fit to accuse me. Me! Who's led such a hard life, and deserves all he can get. Me!' His eyes opened wide and he sat there for all the world like a genuinely wrongly accused, affronted chap. If it hadn't been such a serious matter, she would have laughed outright. He was an actor. That's what. A top-of-the-range actor.

'You do not *deserve* all you can get by *stealing*, believe me. I shan't say another word on the matter, but they'd better be there tomorrow night or else. I'm going to bed early tonight. Hot chocolate?'

'No, thanks, that face of yours would turn the milk.'

Anna didn't care for this new edge to Paddy's voice. Suddenly he'd decided he was invincible. Well, he wasn't. If necessary, she'd have him forcibly removed. The police would have to be called to achieve that but her heart shied away from calling them because it would mean the end of Paddy's struggle, and hers, to achieve normality. Anna drank her hot chocolate alone in the kitchen, having tired of Paddy's choice of programme. He loved to be in control of the TV. A small thing but it was getting to her. Like the thin edge of the wedge. The bedroom saga was another instance. Blast Paddy.

Next day Anna went into Culworth to attend a meeting in the Abbey. Afterwards she paid a visit to an unreliable jeweller in Abbeygate whom she knew. She scrutinized his window display then opened the door, but before she went in she looked up and saw the iron bracket, which, in the past, had held the sign of the three balls. He no longer professed to be a pawnbroker but in fact he was. She went in to find it dim and sinister, with shadowy corners, and curtains thick with dust. There was a brass bell on the counter to ring for assistance.

Two dings of the bell and from between the dark brown, floor-length curtains behind the counter came the owner, rubbing his hands, but not with the cold, for the shop was steamy with heat. 'What can I do for you, Reverend? Stipend not stretching as far as it should this month?'

He stooped badly, his glasses held together with sticking plaster, a face which hadn't seen a razor in years, and a pointed nose that, without much effort, would be capable of touching his chin. In between was a long, thin-lipped mouth.

'Hello, Mervyn. Long time no see.'

'Exactly. A brooch, wasn't it? For your mother, in the shape of a flower made of pearls with a single diamond in the centre. You got it for a song. I was a mad fool to allow it.'

'You've a long memory.'

'I have. What is it today? I have some good gold necklaces, second-hand, but very good value.'

'I'm not buying. I'm asking.'

His eyes became shifty and his hands were now ceaselessly rubbing each other.

'You've had a man in during the last few days.'

'I've had several.'

'This one was wanting to sell you things. They were stolen, so I've come to take them back.'

Mervyn rubbed his chin. 'Pawned them, did he?'

'I don't know. Sold them for a song, I've no doubt. Come on, Mervyn, that long memory of yours . . .'

He hummed and ha'd for a while, as though he were casting his mind back over the last few days. 'What were they?'

'Some china figures. Four in all.'

He raised a none-too-clean finger and stabbed the air. 'Staffordshire, all genuine. Been left them by his granny.'

'No such thing. Stolen from Turnham Malpas rectory.'

'No! Oh, no. Not from Doctor Harris?'

Anna nodded. She'd got him looking distraught.

'I heard she'd gone to Africa. So you're the Reverend Harris's locum, and a very charming one at that. Who's he then?'

'He's someone I'm trying to get back on his feet.'

'I see. She's a lovely lady, is Doctor Harris. Comes in sometimes with them kids of hers. Beautiful manners, they have, full of questions. As for Doctor Harris, there's no nicer lady this side of the Cul. She's lovely, so genuine and thoughtful. I'm proud to call her my friend. She helped me no end when my dear Rachel died. Kindness itself, she was.' He brought out a handkerchief and dabbed at his eyes.

Breathless with dread, Anna asked, 'Have you sold them? Please say no.'

'You're lucky. I've someone coming in today to look at them.'

Mervyn went in the back, shifting clouds of dust from the curtain as he swept through. He returned after a minute. She didn't need to ask if they were the right ones, because they were carefully wrapped in the evening paper Paddy had been reading the night of the big argument; she recognized a headline.

Mervyn unwrapped them all and stood them up on the

counter. 'She'd be heartbroken if she knew, and I can't have that.' He stroked them with a sensitive finger.

'Did you sell them to her?'

'No, no. This kind of thing isn't my line of business normally, too expensive.' He blew some dust from the head of a child, and smiled.

Anna opened her bag and rooted in it for her purse. 'How much did you give him for them?'

Mervyn, offended, said, 'I don't require any money. It wasn't much and I'm glad to be of service to her. If she comes in when she gets back I shan't say a word, and I hope you won't either. There's no need for her to know they've strayed.' He tapped the side of his nose and winked.

Anna handed him her card. 'I'm grateful for that. That's my phone number. If he comes in again with anything, well, please hang on to whatever it is and give me a ring. I don't expect he'll try this on again, however, not after I've had a word with him tonight.'

Mervyn carefully rewrapped the figures, pausing to caress the head of the child as he did so. 'Lovely stuff. Very precious.' In a dim corner of the shop he found a carrier bag, placed the ornaments in it and handed it to Anna.

'I feel uncomfortable about this. Won't you let me pay you something for them? You must have given him money when he brought them in.'

Mervyn backed off. 'Certainly not. It's a privilege to be able to hand them back to her, safe and in one piece. Good day to you.' There was a flurry of curtain and dust and Mervyn had disappeared.

When she got home, Anna placed the ornaments back in their place in the left-hand alcove and decided to photograph them all so she had a record of exactly what they were.

Then she went out and about with her parish duties and returned home to find messages on her answerphone and emails galore. So she spent a busy twenty minutes answering them all and then began on their evening meal. Paddy was home well before it was ready, due to the heavy rain.

Anna decided not to say a word about the figures, but to wait for his response, if there was one. They ate their meal in the kitchen amicably enough with Paddy entertaining her with tales of the gardens and Michelle's activities.

'I don't care what you say about earning a living, you're actually enjoying being up there, aren't you?' She eyed him over the rim of her glass. 'Well, aren't you?'

Paddy placed two more chips in his mouth before he answered. 'If I have to work then that's the best place to be. Stuck in a factory somewhere would be hell, with all the noise and all the people. That's not for me.'

'Good, I'm glad. Perhaps you could get qualifications.'

'Like hell.'

'OK then, just a thought.' Then Anna couldn't wait any longer. 'By the way, you'll be relieved to know I've got Caroline's figures back.'

Paddy didn't answer but she detected the shockwave that went through him.

'It's not to happen again. Do you hear me? Nothing, but nothing, is to disappear from this house, ever. I'm appalled. It's only because I know the pawnshop owner in Culworth and he thinks the world of Caroline that I've got them back. Maybe I shan't be as lucky another time.

I'm furious, Paddy, absolutely furious. One step forward and two steps back. How can we make progress?'

'You're not my jailer. I'm a free agent.'

'Not for much longer if you do that again. I mean it. All the hard work you've put in to drag yourself back to sanity and yet you allow yourself to steal.'

Paddy glared at her from across the table. 'If I want to slide back down the slippery slope, it's nothing to do with you. If I want to, I shall. See?'

'I don't expect gratitude, but I do expect you to give me the money you got for them.'

Paddy studied this monstrous idea. 'Spent it. All gone.'

'What on?'

'None of your business.'

Anna realized she'd hit a brick wall so far as Paddy was concerned. She was up against a man with few morals. They glared at each other and it was Anna's eyes that fell first.

They both heard the doorbell ring. Neither of them wanted to answer it, but in the end it was Anna who went.

Standing on her doorstep was Gilbert. She was in no mood for him tonight, but she couldn't stop her heart from leaping nor the welcoming smile on her face.

'Hello! Come in.'

'So sorry, are you eating? It's choir practice tonight, and I need to speak.'

'Please don't worry, I shall be glad for a distraction. Come in.'

She took him into the study because she knew Paddy would be wanting the TV on and another altercation with him tonight was more than she could take. In any case, she didn't want Gilbert to know the state of play with her and Paddy.

Gilbert sank down into the squashy armchair, placed his folder on his knee and said, 'I must apologize for being so abrupt last time we talked. Got a lot on at the moment, big dig, TV programme coming up and Louise needing all my support.'

'I've heard, you must be pleased.'

'Normally pregnancy makes no difference to her, but this time she isn't well.'

'I'm sorry. Isn't there something they could do for her?'

'Mainly sickness, you see, and she refuses to take anything for it. Thalidomide, you know. Got to be careful.'

'Of course. What was it you wanted to see me about?'

'Ah! yes. To apologize first and foremost. I'm so sorry. I didn't mean to get off on the wrong foot with you. No, not at all. I'm willing to compromise on the modernization of our services, music-wise. Could be an interesting experiment, so I've brought a few things for you to take a look at.' Gilbert opened the file and handed it to her. 'They're for the boys to practise.'

Anna gravely studied the music, knowing her heart was pounding. She wished Paddy heaven knows where but not sitting down watching TV when she needed more space between her and Gilbert. She could smell that earthy sandalwood scent and was aware of the powerful male vibes which emanated from him and which almost knocked her off-balance. She studiously looked over the music, trying to give it her full concentration but not quite succeeding.

'These appear very suitable, and I'm glad you've had a change of heart.'

'Well, there's absolutely no point in you and me being at loggerheads, is there? It would only involve Mrs Peel too and I don't want that. There can be enough trouble in this village without me contributing to it. Right.' Gilbert got to his feet and took his folder from her. 'Must go. The boys will be waiting.' He put emphasis on the word 'boys' as though saying that was one point he definitely would not be conceding.

An urge to challenge him came over Anna. 'You've not had second thoughts then about having girls in the choir?' She stood up in the hope she'd feel more in charge of herself, and in doing so brought herself within touching distance of Gilbert.

'Absolutely not.' Gilbert smiled down at her, completely unaware that Anna's heart was pumping fast and her insides had turned to jelly.

He drew away and left the study. 'I'll see myself out. Goodnight.'

Anna sat down at her desk, shaking with anger at herself. She must, *must* get these feelings under control, because the only person who would get hurt would be Anna Sanderson. There was no way she could allow herself to be enticed away by a married man with five children and another on the way. Just a minute, he wasn't enticing her, it was she who had the feelings, not him. He was oblivious to how she felt. She knew that deep down, but . . .

Paddy put his head round the door. 'Going to the pub. Are you coming?'

'No. Got a meeting.'

'OK.'

As for Paddy, not even an apology and, only too obviously, she wasn't going to get the money back from him. Apparently he was incapable of feeling. For all Mervyn was a fence and a conniving old rogue who dealt with a rough underworld she could only guess at, he did have feelings, especially about Caroline. Paddy had none. He did all the taking and she was growing mighty tired of it. As for Gilbert, there would be nothing but heartbreak for her there, so Anna clenched her hands together tightly on the desk and willed herself to ignore her feelings for him. But it was easy for the mind to say 'ignore', far harder for her body to comply.

Chapter 10

Just as Anna daren't let Gilbert know how she felt about him, so too Dean didn't dare let Anna know how devastating his feelings for her were. They coloured every waking hour, every thought, each and every dream.

So far as Anna was concerned, his was a teenage crush and he had to be treated with care so as not to cause damage either to him or to her. She saw him on Friday evenings at the youth club, mainly because she was there every Friday night that she could manage and she guessed it was desperately bleak for Dean if she didn't attend. The other two leaders, Kate Fitch and Venetia Mayer, were excellent in their way, Kate for the organization, Venetia for the socializing bit and the ability to draw even the shyest member into participating, and Dean, well, he did the table tennis.

The leaders always had ten minutes' discussion after everyone had left and Dean brought up the matter one evening.

'But it's so valuable,' Venetia protested. 'None of us can play like you can and, like it or not, you're training them even as you play. Haven't you heard yourself giving that commentary? It attracts crowds. They're all eager for a game when they've seen you play; you give them a goal.'

'Yes, but that doesn't seem to make much of a contribution.'

'Yes, it does, Dean. Venetia's right.' Anna, to emphasize her agreement, patted his shoulder and felt him flinch.

Kate agreed. 'Don't for one minute think you're not making a contribution, because you are. See how they flock round you. In fact, why not organize a match? Fifty pence to enter, profit to the New Hope Fund. Every little helps. We'd have to think about a prize.'

Dean heard it all but their approval meant nothing to him, except for that pat on his shoulder. He'd have loved to clasp her hand in his and kiss it. The idea obsessed him. Possessed him. Overpowered him. Then his natural reticence took charge and the emotion was directed that night to writing a poem dedicated to Anna, in the notebook he kept hidden among his papers in his room. If anyone ever found out about this notebook it would be the end of him.

It had a beautiful William Morris design on the cover in gorgeous peacock colours, triumphant and splendid, like his love for her. The leaves of it were made of silky smooth paper, which invited touching, caressing almost. In it were three poems, written with the special pen he kept for it alone. The scraps of paper he'd used for composing the poems were torn to minute shreds before he disposed of them.

If ever Michelle found this book – he smoothed his hand over the cover – he'd die. This last poem was his best so far. Poets were right when they said that their outpourings arose out of their deepest experiences of life. How could anyone write sensitively of emotions they'd never felt? He'd never written a poem in his life until now. Facts. Figures. Calculations. His world had always been governed by rules and constriction, but since Anna his spirit flew free, soaring upwards to the skies, making numbers lose all their magic. And this was he who, for years, had found paradise in page upon page of mathematical formulae.

Having a couple of days' holiday to take, Dean had promised his grandad that he would walk with him around the gardens at the Big House. They were all having to be careful not to make him feel he was 'pensioned off' as he called it. Arthritis brought on by working outside in all weathers had finally taken its toll and he needed two sticks to walk even the shortest distance. So Monday morning found Dean escorting Grandad through his particular paradise. The only comfort he had about the gardens was the fact that his grand-daughter had taken his place as head gardener. His pride shone in his face like a beacon when he inspected the hot houses, the herbacious borders and the neat flowerbeds.

They came across Paddy weeding the winding path through the rhododendron wood. It had been constructed of old bricks and even the least energetic of weeds managed to find a way through the tight cracks.

Paddy got to his feet. 'Morning, Greenwood.'

Grandad Stubbs snapped back, 'Mr Stubbs to you.'

Paddy touched the neb of his cap. 'Sorry, Mr Stubbs.'

'Who are you anyway?'

'I'm temporary help. Name's Paddy Cleary. I do odd jobs for Michelle, that's all.'

'I see.' Grandad glanced down the path that Paddy had already weeded. 'You're doing a good job. Very good, in fact. No point skimping jobs in a garden, they always come back to haunt you. Not used a weed killer, then?'

'No. Michelle, with old Fitch's agreement, tries to stay organic wherever possible, even out here.'

'When did you start this 'ere weeding?'

'Yesterday morning. It's a long job.'

'It is. But take heed of her. She's a clever girl.'

'She is,' Paddy agreed with his tongue in his cheek, and thinking privately that she was a so-and-so nuisance to a self-respecting man.

'Done gardening before?'

'No. It's all new to me.'

'Keep at it.' Grandad walked on, muttering to Dean, 'He's a slimy toad. Tell our Michelle to mind him. He'd slit yer throat as soon as look at yer. During the war I . . .'

Dean sat him down on a seat at the end of the wood and prepared to listen to a monologue about Grandad's war experiences beginning at Dunkirk. He half listened, knowing most of it anyway, until he suddenly heard his grandad say, ' . . . lovely girl she was. Officer's daughter. Slender and pretty with jet-black hair and a lovely fair skin, and eyes that always appeared to be brimming over with laughter.' There was a pause and then Dean heard him speak in a voice he'd never heard him use before, a voice thickened by emotions. 'I loved her. Still do, in fact. Her name was Lorelle. I thought that the loveliest name under the sun. But you see, I couldn't talk on her level at all. Not that she tried to impress me with her education, in fact quite the opposite, but my word we were captivated with each other. Love at first sight.'

Grandad sat dreaming, looking into the distance, his mind and his body elsewhere.

Dean said, 'What happened, then? You didn't marry her, 'cos I remember Grandma had light coloured hair.'

'There was no way a chump from the countryside could

marry her. We wanted to, both of us, but my dad made me see it wasn't right. Eventually the gap between us would have widened and neither of us would have been happy.'

'But if you loved each other . . .'

'We did, but I saw it wouldn't have worked. She was used to far more than I could ever hope to give her, and she'd eventually become unsettled and one thing would lead to another. You see, you've been educated out of your class, you been at Cambridge and that. It might just give you the edge, but at bottom you're still what you are and always will be, a country lad with country morals. They live by a different set of rules, them with education and money. Don't make the mistake of pursuing someone who you know right from the start doesn't quite fit, much as yer love her.'

Startled by his Grandad's homily, Dean stayed silent. My God, did he know? But how could he?

Grandad struggled to his feet. 'Come on, we've a lot to see yet. Have you brought them mint imperials?'

Dean brought out the bag and watched his grandfather's knobbly hand shuffling about in the bag trying to get a grip on an imperial, and imagined what his hands must have been like when he met the love of his life. 'You loved Grandma though?'

'I did that. But it wasn't a love that flew high like a bird with the freedom of the skies, it was more steady and very comfortable but, none the less, worth having. She was a good wife to me.'

'Tell me, did you ever regret not going for that first love, despite the consequences?'

'It would be disloyal to your grandma to say how much I . . .' He swallowed hard. 'She married a major from her dad's battalion and that day I thought I'd never see another dawn. But you do, you know, you do. And time heals. Oh, yes.'

They wandered on slowly at a pace that wearied Dean, then his grandad spotted an untidy corner at the back of the vinery, a mixture of dumped and broken fruit boxes, an old rusting rake with a rotting handle, a bundle of knotted garden twine, yards of old netting from this year's strawberry beds, straw and, worst of all, a box full of perfectly healthy daffodil bulbs, virtually hidden by the netting.

Grandad gave a poke at the netting with his walking stick to move it aside. 'Look at that?' His reverie forgotten, something of the younger man came to the fore. 'See that? I'll have 'em, I will. Someone's about to make off with that lot, and I don't have far to go to know who. You go on and find Michelle, bring her here to me.'

Before Dean had found his sister, Grandad Stubbs heard footsteps. He went to hide in the vinery. It was Paddy Cleary, wheeling his barrow filled with weeds. He stopped by the untidy corner, put down the barrow, moved the pile of weeds to one side, picked up the box of daffodil bulbs, placed it in the barrow, took a sheet of plastic from his pocket, unfolded it, covered the bulbs over, then swished the weeds over the whole lot to disguise the presence of the box, and wheeled innocently on.

Grandad boiled over, but kept a rein on his temper; he was in no state to challenge the man and still less had he the authority to do so. So he quietly slid the vinery door open, closed it firmly behind him and, keeping a safe distance away, followed Paddy.

What Grandad had not bargained for was that Michelle was talking to Mr Fitch close by the estate office, and

Dean was still waiting to speak to her, They were in earnest discussion and merely nodded to Paddy as he wheeled by. So Grandad called out, 'Paddy! Paddy!'

Paddy turned round and waited for Grandad to catch up.

Mr Fitch, who always had time for craftsmen with first-rate skills, shouted, 'Good morning, Greenwood! Nice to see you're still keeping an eye on things.'

Paddy silently picked up the handles of his barrow and began to slip quietly away.

'No, Paddy! I want you to show Mr Fitch those weeds.'

Paddy hastened on but Mr Fitch called out. 'Cleary!'

So Paddy retraced his steps and stood the wheelbarrow down. How the hell was he going to talk himself out of this one?

'See, Mr Fitch,' Grandad Stubbs panted, 'see these weeds, it's a waste of time and money expecting the path through the rhododendron wood to be weeded by hand.'

Mr Fitch raised a protesting hand. 'You know I like to be as organic as possible.'

'I know that, but he's been doing a good job weeding that path for two days now, and still hasn't finished. He could be better occupied, couldn't you, Paddy?'

'I could, Mr Stubbs . . . sir.'

'So I reckon weedkiller in that particular instance. What do you say, Michelle?'

'I agree. It's one hell of a long path, and Paddy's been very patient. I've been thinking on those lines myself. Grandad's quite right, it would save time and money.'

Mr Fitch hesitated and, looking at Grandad, he caught a meaningful glint in his eyes, which quickly flicked down to the wheelbarrow. Mr Fitch dug his hand in the heap of weeds in the barrow and pretended to examine a weed or two. 'They're big weeds. Long roots.'

Paddy sweated relief.

Mr Fitch dug in again and came up with a bulb in his hand. 'What the hell's this?' He briskly dug his hand in a little further and found the box. 'Cleary!'

Mr Fitch's face flushed a dark red and before they knew where they were he had snatched one of Grandad's walking sticks out of his hand and was after striking Paddy with it.

Paddy took to his heels.

The faster Paddy ran, the faster Mr Fitch pursued him. He never actually landed a blow on Paddy's back but he came very close.

Dean, Michelle and Grandad, now clinging for support to his grandchildren, roared with laughter. The faster Paddy went the faster Mr Fitch ran. They'd done two circuits of the hothouses and one of the vinery before Paddy had to call a halt. His breathing laboured, bent over, with his hands resting on his thighs, he rasped. 'Fair does. Can't run no more.'

Mr Fitch on the other hand, though he gasped a little, was far fitter than Paddy and only needed a moment to catch his breath. By now the entire garden staff had downed tools and gathered to watch. They clapped Mr Fitch's performance.

'Stealing! I will not tolerate stealing! I'd whip the hide off you 'cept I've too much to do to spend time serving a prison sentence. You damned thief. You've nothing going for you at all. Even though Michelle's given you a job *I* wouldn't have given you in a month of Sundays, you still can't behave yourself. Where were they going?'

Paddy saw he had met his match, felt that Mr Fitch

himself knew from personal experience the kind of background he came from and he said, 'I'll be honest with you.'

'That's the least you can be. Well, go on. What marvellous altruistic excuse are you going to come up with?'

Paddy cleared his throat, his mind working faster than he thought possible.

Impatient, Mr Fitch said, 'I'm waiting.'

'I do a bit of voluntary work for a children's home in Culworth and these daffodils, well, the kids would love 'em for their garden and I thought, being as you're a generous man, you wouldn't mind if I—'

'You damned liar. You were going to flog 'em.'

This side of Mr Fitch's character rarely put in an appearance and the spectators were astounded. He used a few more explicit phrases to describe what a lowlife Paddy really was, threatened him with Grandad's stick a few more times and then handed it back to its grateful owner.

'Like a fool I'm going to give you a second chance, because I can imagine what it's like being at the bottom of the pile and no one giving you a leg up. But one more, just one more episode like this, even so much as a blade of grass and you're out. You've Michelle to thank for my leniency, because she tells me how hard you work and has nothing but praise for you. Don't break her trust again. Do you hear me?'

Mr Fitch's last few words thundered out across the garden. Paddy had a mind to throw his job in his face there and then, but something, he knew not what, held him back from defying this lunatic. So he ate humble pie and put on his badly-done-to face. 'Very sorry, Mr Fitch, sir. Old habits, *as you well know*. Won't happen again and thank you for giving me another chance, sir. I won't let you down.' He dutifully touched the neb of his cap, then unloaded the box of daffodil bulbs and stood it at Michelle's feet, as though it were an offering to her, and humbly wheeled the barrow away.

Mr Fitch threw a steely glance at the onlookers and they took the hint, leaving himself, Michelle, Dean and Grandad to recover their composure.

'I mean it, Michelle, one more time. These bulbs won't be the first thing he's stolen and they won't be the last, so keep an eager eye.' He patted her arm. 'Don't fret, people like him could steal the communion wine from a priest at the very moment he lifted it to his lips without even a prick of conscience. Just bear it in mind. Good to see you about, Greenwood. Got to rush, but we'll have a talk soon, you and I, seeing as we're both members of the Michelle Jones admiration society.' He strode off towards the house and his waiting car and chauffeur, chuckling with amusement, proud of his fitness and delighted by his own magnanimity.

Michelle kicked the box of bulbs. 'It's not the first thing he's stolen, old Fitch is right.'

Grandad was shocked. 'And you let it go on?'

'Can't help but feel sorry for him. Stealing's such a habit, he almost can't help himself.'

'What's he stolen that you know of?'

'A box of peaches, a tray of bedding plants, some tools . . .'

Grandad almost exploded with wrath. 'Your first loyalty is to them that pay your wages. Do you hear me? He won't stand stealing, won't Mr Fitch, and you know that.'

'But I didn't know for certain it was him. Paddy's such a charmer if I'd tackled him he'd have denied it and I'd have finished up believing him. I don't know which is worst, keeping a blind eye or having it out with him.'

Grandad wagged a finger at her. 'It's old Fitch what pays your wages, remember that. He won't bat an eyelid when he sacks you for allowing it, and we'd all be homeless to boot. Remember that, my girl.' Grandad hobbled off, thanking his lucky stars his stick hadn't broken in half with Mr Fitch's treatment of it. He laughed at the memory of Mr Fitch chasing Paddy. Hell, but the man had a temper.

As for Paddy, he sat in the wheelbarrow, his back resting against the potting shed wall, eating his lunch and thinking. He sensed that old Fitch had had just as bad a start in life as he had. That was why he was so dead against people stealing from him; it was because he knew both sides of the equation. But to think of the success he'd made of his life. Well, well. Something to keep in mind. Still, pity about the bulbs. That chap with the garden stall in Culworth market would be waiting for him in his van down the drive this lunchtime, but he'd have to wait. Pity too about those figures at the rectory. Better apologize about them. Keep Anna sweet.

As for Craddock Fitch he was thankful to sit back and let his chauffeur tackle the driving. It wasn't often the two of them talked. After hours in the car every week together they'd run out of conversation some time ago. This morning, however, it was the chauffeur who opened the conversation. 'Did you know, Mr Fitch, that Paddy Cleary is living with the new rector?'

Craddock, allowing himself time to calm down after that sprint round the hothouses, sat upright, shocked and disbelieving. 'There's living and there's *living*, Spencer. Which do you mean?'

'I mean what they've all started to say, that he's *living* with her. Dropped a hint in the pub the other night and, of course, as you can imagine, it got picked up pretty damn quick.' Spencer stared straight ahead at the road and blanked Craddock when he asked Spencer what exactly Paddy had said. Craddock asked him again.

Spencer carefully phrased his reply. He didn't want his boss to know that Paddy had said it directly to himself, still less did he want old Fitch chasing him round the hothouses wielding a stick. 'What exactly did he say, sir? Don't know, sir, it was about fourth-hand when it got to me.'

Craddock wished he'd actually hit Paddy with Greenwood's stick, brought it down right across his shoulders and his head, good and hard. Rumours like this snowballed till everyone knew and then they all believed it. He got his mobile phone from his briefcase and dialled the rectory. While he waited for his call to be answered, he wished with his whole heart that it would be Peter answering it, but of course it wasn't.

'Turnham Malpas rectory. Anna Sanderson speaking.'

'Anna! Good morning. Craddock Fitch here. I've just heard some gossip about you and I think you ought to know. They're saying in the village that Paddy Cleary is living with you. I mean really living, as in live-in-lover.' He left a pause, didn't get an answer, so continued, 'It needs scotching straight away, it's very damaging gossip. Don't know how, but scotch it otherwise it'll be at the Abbey before nightfall, and the balloon will go up.' Still no reply. 'It's not true, obviously, but it still needs dealing with, as of now. Good morning to you. Sorry to be giving you such bad news.'

Anna put down the receiver, sick at heart.

Chapter 11

Sheila Bissett heard the rumour while talking to Greta Jones by the tinned soups in the Store. Clipboard in hand – she was never without it at the moment – Sheila was shaking her head as Greta was saying, '. . . so he told my Vince, when Vince was in the pub lunchtime Sunday, that he was sleeping in Peter and Caroline's bed. Those were his very words. With a nod and a wink, too, and a nudge with his elbow, which spoke volumes.'

'No! I can't believe it. She wouldn't now, would she? Honestly.'

'Well, that's what he said. I said to Vince, "You must be going deaf." But he said, "I'm neither deaf nor daft", that's what he said. And he isn't, except when there's a job to do in the house and I need help. But that's a man all over.'

'I'm sorry, but I can't believe it. That Paddy and Anna? No, never. Why, he isn't even attractive, is he?'

'He's got something about him though. He can't half make you laugh.'

'Laugh yes, but . . . no, no.' Sheila shook her head. 'There's one thing for certain – he wouldn't get me in his bed.'

'He wouldn't want *you*!'

'Nor *you* come to that!'

They both had to laugh.

Sheila, who was eager to press on with the prime reason for her existence at the moment, said, 'I'm organizing collecting tins for Culworth next Saturday week for all those people who're going to dye their hair. Market day and that. Loads of people about. Thought we'd have an onslaught in Culworth and get some extra money in. The more the better. They've all heard about the pyjama party and the scandal afterwards, so we've kind of got our foot in the door. Invade the place, rattle the tins, just for a couple of hours, start off in the market. We'll make an impact with our dyed hair, don't you think? Can I count you in?'

'You can, seeing as I'm the organizer of it. Good idea. A week Saturday, yes, absolutely. I'd enjoy that.'

Sheila made a note on the appropriate page on her clipboard. 'Gilbert's doing some placard things for us to take. He is a dear, when he's so busy. He's skinny-dipping too. Bless him. Two hundred and twenty pounds he's been sponsored for at the office, would you believe.'

'Your Louise. Saw her the other day. Hasn't long to go?'

'Due February, March time, she's not sure, so there's a good while yet.'

'Oh! She looked sooner than that. Not looking too good either, I thought. Before she's always been blooming all the time, but she looked ill. Maybe she'd had a bad night with the children. It happens.'

'I'm a bit worried about her, actually. You know that she's never had sickness before. Right down in the mouth with it. I'll call round to see her today, just to check. So you're on the bus. That's twelve going, with you and Vince.'

'You dyeing yours?'

'No, I don't think so. Remember. Morning bus, week Saturday.'

'Right. Vince and me'll be there. Must press on, my dinner hour was over five minutes ago. Whoops! Here he is. Just coming, Mr Charter-Plackett,' she called loudly. 'Needed a word about the New Hope Fund with Sheila.' Under her breath she said, 'Slave-driver. He'd have been right handy with a whip in them Roman times, he would. See yer.'

The news about the scandal at the rectory spread like some insidious disease, not just around Turnham Malpas but Little Derehams and Penny Fawcett, too. No one believed it, but they had to because why would he say it if it wasn't true? What possible gain would he get from it? Nothing except derision and disgust. So, it must be true. But him in the rector's bed! And, as Sylvia reminded them, sleeping in Caroline's lovely bed linen. Something had to be done about it.

Ralph shouldered the responsibility and was at the rectory door first thing the very next morning. He didn't relish his self-imposed task but had to for the sake of the village.

Anna opened the door to him and she stood there looking distraught. Instead of her normally welcoming smile and her eagerness to invite visitors in to the house, she waited for him to speak.

'I'm sorry, Anna, obviously you've heard the rumours. Can I come in and we'll have a talk?'

'Yes.' She moved away from the door and made enough space for him to step into the hall. Instead of taking him into the sitting room, however, she gestured towards the study. Somehow she hoped that the strong vibes she felt Peter had left behind in the study might help her through the worst. 'I'd offer you a coffee but I've just had my breakfast.'

'So have I. But thanks for the offer. Now, my dear, tell me all.' He sat on the sofa close to the desk, expecting that she would sit in the desk chair, but she joined him on the sofa. 'Now, start at the beginning. How does Paddy Cleary come to be living here?'

Anna detailed the whole story to Ralph and then said by way of explanation. 'You see, it's very easy for the clergy to deal with the converted, the willing, the nice ones and ignore the rest, but surely it's the rest we should be dealing with? They're the ones who need help. So thinking like that, I took Paddy under my wing. When I had to move here it seemed a golden opportunity to give him a real helping hand. Not just words, but action. Now I realize he's beginning to take over. I've had a fight with him about where he sleeps, insisting he's upstairs in the attic while I sleep in Beth's bedroom. To me it wouldn't be right to use Peter's bed, but he wanted to sleep there and I threatened to throw him out if he did. I won that battle but it's the little things. Always being in charge of what we watch on the TV. Not that I see much of it but when I do I like to watch different things from him. The choice is never mine. And he doesn't help domestically, just expects me to do it all. Cooking, washing, that kind of thing. Maybe I'm getting it all out of proportion but I do know why he's spreading this malicious rumour.'

'You do? He hasn't . . .' Ralph took her hand between his and held it firmly.

'No, of course not. He stole four of Caroline's Staffordshire figures and sold them in Culworth, but I guessed where he might have sold them and I got them back. So basically he's getting at me because of that. Mainly. I think.'

'I see.' Ralph released her hand. 'I see. Is he doing a good job at the Big House?'

'He pretends he doesn't like it, but he's never stuck at a job for as long as two days never mind four weeks. He wouldn't miss it for the world.'

'Good. I like the sound of that. I have an idea. Now he's earning money he could pay his way.'

'He could, but I'm still waiting.'

Ralph raised an eyebrow. 'Expects you to keep him, too. Mmm. I think I know someone who would take him as a lodger. I'm sure Mrs Jones would have him and would be able to knock him into shape. Since her boys left home she's had no one to care for except for Vince and he doesn't want mothering at all. Someone to mother is what she needs, you know. Might be just what he needs, too.'

They sat together, each thinking their own thoughts, and then Ralph stood up. 'He'd have to pay her, but if she can't keep him in order no one can. Leave it with me.'

'I'd be so grateful. You, of all people, know that we're not . . . you know . . .'

'Don't fret, my dear. It's all happened out of the generosity of your spirit, and no one can criticize you for that. It's mean-minded people causing the trouble. Believe me, I'll have this sorted before the day is out.' He took her hand in his and gripped it tightly. 'You're a lovely young woman and I mustn't stand by and see your reputation in ruins. Trust me. I'll see myself out.'

As Ralph set off for the Village Store he phrased and re-phrased the words he would use to reach Greta Jones's heart. It wouldn't be easy; his diplomatic skills would be tried to their limits.

Jimbo was delighted to see him. 'My word, Ralph, it's not often we see you in here. Now what's your pleasure? A few slices of my home-baked ham? More of your special cigars? Muriel's favourite chocolates?'

'None of those, Jimbo. I've just been at the rectory—'

'Ah!' Jimbo interrupted him. 'Sorting out the nasty rumours, then?'

'You've heard?'

'Who hasn't? The news flew round the village with the speed of light.'

'It isn't true, you know.'

'It isn't?'

'Absolutely not.'

'Nothing would surprise me these days.'

'Jimbo! That's just not fair. The girl has a generous heart and it's all turned nasty on her. She isn't at fault, believe me.'

Jimbo eyed Ralph a little sceptically and it angered Ralph.

'I'm not pleased about the modernization of the services, but on this count the rumours are quite untrue. I've set myself the task of putting a stop to it. As of now. So may I have a word with Greta Jones?'

'You may indeed. Good luck.' Jimbo smiled ruefully at Ralph but he ignored it. He had a mission and was determined to achieve his goals.

'Why, Sir Ralph! This is a pleasure.' Mrs Jones stood up, blushing with surprise, and all of a dither.

'Mrs Jones, or may I call you Greta?'

'Well, you've known me long enough so I'm sure I wouldn't mind.'

'Good. Do sit down, Greta. I've come on a mission and

think that you're the only person in the village I could ask.'

He sat on the chair favoured by Jimbo when he and Greta were in discussion. 'I have a problem and when I considered how to solve it I thought: Now, Greta is used to young men, having had three of her own, and she's got empty rooms now her Terry and Kenny are out in Canada and Barry's married. Have you ever thought of taking a gentleman lodger?'

Greta flushed even redder. A lodger. The money would be mighty handy now Vince was retired.

'He's had a bad time as a boy and needs, well, he needs mothering. Where he's staying at the moment it's causing trouble and reflecting on the one who's taken him in. Now how about it? You'd be doing him a good turn, in fact, the whole village a good turn.'

In a flash Mrs Jones guessed who it was. And him thieving like there was no tomorrow. 'You mean that Paddy Cleary?'

'Er . . . well . . . yes, I do. He needs a guiding hand, you see. As I said, mothering really, that's what he needs. Because he's never been mothered. He doesn't realize it but he does.'

'I'd have to ask Vince. You're moving him because of the rumours? They're not true, then? Or are they true and that's why you're moving him?'

'Absolutely not. It's plainly obvious. She wouldn't find him attractive, would she, a charming young woman like her.'

Greta had to say it, bold though she was. 'She's soon convinced you, Sir Ralph. Not two minutes since you were blazing mad about her changes in the church.'

'I know. But I was wrong, I should have said nothing.

147

Her heart's in the right place, you see. Now, what do you think?'

Greta spent a moment pleating the frill round her apron, which was something she did at times of pressure. 'He could come for his tea and I'd show him the bedroom and that. But he'd have to pay. I can't afford—'

'Naturally he'd pay. He's earning up at the Big House so why shouldn't he? It could be a real turning point for him. I'd be very grateful if you could see your way.'

'I'll talk to Vince tonight. They get on all right in the pub on an evening. The money would be useful, too. Be nice to have a young man about the house again and, after all, I'm used to them misbehaving and that, aren't I?' She smiled sadly and apologetically at Ralph.

'Never been to visit them, then?'

'Never. Not got that kind of money. And never will have. Our Terry and Kenny daren't come back home to England just in case.'

'Well, we'll have to see about that. Ring me and let me know your decision. You'd be helping everyone.'

After Ralph had left, Mrs Jones thought about the pleasure of having someone who needed caring for.

She furiously attacked the reel of Sellotape and packaged up all her parcels ready for the post with lightning speed. Yes! She'd do it! She would. Something to get her teeth into. She'd show him what having a mother was all about. That was if he'd come. He must! He really must. She decided not to say a word to Vince tonight, leave it for Sir Ralph to sort out before she said a word to him. Waste of time upsetting Vince if Paddy wouldn't come. He could be awkward, could Vince, no, stubborn was the word. Blinking stubborn.

When Vince set off for the pub that night, Greta went

upstairs to decide which room she could let Paddy have. Their Kenny's had been the smallest one, Terry as usual taking the larger room for himself when Barry left to get married to Pat. Paddy could have the bigger room. The sun came in that window the very first thing each morning, nice for a man who had to be up early for work. Yes, the big room could be his. Before she went to the Store in the morning she'd give it a sort-out and bung all Terry's belongings in the little bedroom wardrobe and put clean sheets on the bed.

While she watched her soaps, Mrs Jones spent a lovely evening thinking about Paddy coming. It would be nice to have someone young about to offset Vince and his non-existent conversation. At least there'd be some life in the place.

As soon as she heard Vince at the door she got up to put the kettle on.

They sat down to drink their bedtime cup of tea and Vince switched on *The Ten O'Clock News* and out of the blue he said, 'Lonely, isn't it?'

'What is?'

'Us at home on our own. Just wish our boys were here. At least they cheered the place up a bit.'

Mrs Jones wondered if this could be her moment to mention Paddy. But she didn't get a chance because Vince said, 'Do you feel it's lonely?'

Cautiously Mrs Jones answered, 'Yes. Thinking about it only today.'

'Well, how about if we take in a lodger?'

'A lodger!' Mrs Jones thought he'd become psychic overnight. Casually she replied, 'Who'd want to lodge with us? I ask yer.'

'There might be someone.'

'Such as?'

'Well, I've been talking in the pub tonight—'

'No change there then.'

'And there's someone . . .'

Mrs Jones held her breath. Surely it wasn't . . .

'Well, it's Paddy Cleary actually. Told him I didn't reckon much to him living at the rectory and he said I could be right and the . . . well, anyway, before I knew where I was, I was suggesting he might come here. We've got two empty bedrooms and—'

Mrs Jones shot out of her chair and shouted, 'You've not said yes without asking me? You have, I can see it in your face. Don't ask me, what's got all the work to do. Oh! No. Not me. What if I say no? Eh!'

Vince began to look concerned. 'He'd be helpful with the garden; you're always complaining about it. He'd be no trouble.'

'He'd need feeding and washing done and that. The very least you could have said was you'd ask me first before you said a definite yes.'

'Come on, Greta love, he's a nice chap.'

'That's not what I've heard from our Barry. Thieving he is, wherever he can. And don't you "Greta love" me just to save your face. I'll think about it.'

'He'd need to know tomorrow.'

'I'm not deciding now, not when you've landed it on me all unawares.' Mrs Jones collected their cups together, clattering them as though she was in high dudgeon, and took them into the kitchen. She ran the tap full on to mask the sound of her laughter and, resting her hands on the edge of the sink, she laughed till she had to stop 'cos she could laugh no more. Talk about Vince playing right into her hands. She couldn't believe her good luck and wondered what on earth had come over him, making dynamic decisions like this. There was life in the old dog yet then. Bless his little cotton socks. She'd never let on, no not she. He'd have to suffer for this, really suffer. The joke nearly overcame her and she almost went into the living room to tell all to that snake-in-the-grass Vince. But no, she wouldn't. It was too good a joke to share with him. She'd wait and see how things turned out.

In the rectory, Paddy thought about moving out to Vince Jones's house and decided it might be a good idea. At least he wouldn't have Goody-two-shoes-Anna-with-the-banner preaching to him. He could do as he liked there, and he'd an idea Mrs Jones would be used to cooking for men, having had three sons. No, things could turn out very well in that direction.

Having given her decision the following morning that yes, all right, then Paddy could come to live with them so long as he paid his way, perhaps even move in at the weekend, Greta decided to take the opportunity to dye her hair as soon as she got home from the Store. She was just towelling it dry and anxiously awaiting the moment when she could admire the effect in the mirror, when the front door opened and a voice shouted out, 'Hello-o-o there, anyone at home?'

Greta stood motionless, feeling ridiculous that what had been going to be a private moment had suddenly become a public spectacle. She raced a comb through her nearly dry hair and walked into the living room. There Paddy stood, a holdall at his feet: her new lodger. Her heart went out to him because he looked so in need of caring for, but she masked that fact by saying, 'I thought you were coming at the weekend.'

He, in turn, was shocked by the brilliant red of her hair, grey with a few mousy brown strands the last time he'd seen her. But he said nothing about it while he got over the surprise. 'Michelle told me to finish early and get myself moved in. I thought no time like the present, though if it's not convenient I'll take my things back to the rectory and come another day.'

Greta looked at the half-empty holdall and said, 'Is that all you have to bring?'

'Yes.'

'Well, you won't take up much room.'

'No. Thank you for taking me in.'

'Thank you for taking pot luck with us. I must come straight out with it, then we both know where we stand. I shall have to charge sixty-five pounds a week.' She'd been going to say £55 but changed her mind just before she said it. 'All in though. Laundry and that. Food.'

'That sounds very reasonable.' Best make a good impression, thought Paddy. 'I was thinking more like seventy pounds. Would that be OK?'

Greta swallowed hard. 'Well, that would be lovely. Seventy it is.' She could see they were going to get on like a house on fire. 'I'll show you your room. Sorry about the hair, by the way. Done it for the New Hope Fund.'

'I think you're very brave.'

'Oh, God. Is it terrible?'

'Well, it's very red.'

'That was the intention.' She took a glimpse at herself in the mirror on the landing wall and nearly fainted. She'd left the stuff on far too long, and her hair grew so slowly. She'd still be bright red at Christmas. What the hell! Time she did something exciting.

★

Paddy sat down on the bed in Terry's old room when she'd gone downstairs to leave him to unpack and looked around him. He heard her call up the stairs, 'Tea and a biscuit?'

'That'll do nicely.'

He looked round the room, seeing the comfort of it all. It wasn't richly furnished, he couldn't expect that, but it was cosy and friendly and homely and welcoming. Everything was as clean and neat as it could possibly be. Even a hot water bottle with a teddy bear cover on it, waiting for him in case of need. Paddy stroked its nose, patted its wobbly tummy and smiled. The mirror on the dressing table was flecked with age and the wardrobe, when he opened the door, smelt of someone else. Now he could make it his.

For whatever reason a kind of peace came over him, a kind of belonging he'd never felt before. He remembered a picture he'd seen on the wall in that blasted Home he'd been sent to one time, of an old sailing ship coming into a peaceful harbour and in the background the wild stormy seas it had struggled through to get to safety, and for one crazy, sentimental moment he felt just like that ship. He heard the front door open and Vince's amazement when he saw Greta's hair, then a silence, perhaps they were whispering, then in a moment Vince shouted upstairs, 'Greta's got the chocolate biscuits out. Come on, Paddy.'

Within two days the entire village knew of Paddy's departure from the rectory, brought about by Sir Ralph. Well, so you see, that proved what they'd all been saying; he *had* been sleeping with her, and her the rector, that was why Sir Ralph had made a point of finding him somewhere else. Whatever would Peter think if he knew, him being that strict? And what's more, what was Greta Jones thinking of, taking in Paddy Cleary? She wouldn't have an ornament left in the place within a week; they'd all be in that dusty pawnshop in Culworth.

'She must have taken leave of her senses,' Sylvia said in the pub the following Saturday night.

'Well,' said Vera, 'I think it's ridiculous. Who'd take a thief on, I ask yer?'

'Exactly. I'm amazed there's anything left in the rectory. Wouldn't surprise me if there's some things missing and Anna hasn't realized.'

'He's a double-dyed villain, he is. Still,' Vera nudged Sylvia, 'she's used to thieves, is Greta, because that's what their Terry and Kenny were, thieves of the highest order.' They both giggled behind their hands.

'Still they were her own two boys and it must hurt never seeing them. Oh good, here's Willie with the drinks.'

Willie put down the tray on the edge of the table. 'Here you are, Don, your orange juice; mind, it's a bit full. Sylvia, your Spritzer. Vera, gin and tonic.' He placed his own beer on the table and sat down to enjoy his first sip.

Willie had just picked up his beer when in walked Mrs Jones, a very rare sight in the bar. Even more startling was her vivid red hair. She was followed by her Vince and, believe it or not, that Paddy Cleary. A quiet hush fell right across the whole bar, broken by a loud voice saying, 'What they brought that idiot in here for? They can't be right in their heads, watch yer money everybody.' It was Don, nowadays always two or three paces out of step with everyone else. Vera gave him a kick under the table. 'Shut up, Don.' She gave Mrs Jones an apologetic smile, and twinkled her fingers at her.

But Greta Jones didn't care. They could say what they liked. She'd had the most brilliant few days since Paddy had moved in. He loved her curd tarts, and the rabbit stew she'd done for the three of them that very day had gone down a treat. Even Vince had woken up after years of stupor, and had stayed up till midnight last night playing cards with her and Paddy.

None of them made a secret of the fact they were all watching poor Paddy as he dug into his trouser pocket. 'Can I buy you a drink, Mrs Jones? What's your tipple?'

'A gin and tonic will suit me nicely, and I did say call me Greta. Thank you, Paddy.'

Someone said, 'He's changed his tune and not half. Cost me a packet last time he was in. He was grateful, but there's a limit.'

Another remarked they didn't think it was fair of Sir Ralph asking in the first place. But then he'd be protecting his church.

'It's not his.'

'Isn't it? You could have fooled me.'

Whispers and confidences flew round the saloon bar faster than light. Paddy sensed the atmosphere and felt uncomfortable. Give a dog a bad name, he thought. Then he spotted someone on the next table had checked their wallet following Don's remark and, in replacing it in his back pocket, not noticed it had actually dropped on the floor. Paddy stretched out a leg and silently hooked it towards him with his foot. He sipped his beer for five minutes then deftly picked it up and slid it into his pocket.

He nodded towards the gents and said, 'Excuse me a minute.' When he returned he bent down to re-tie his shoe lace and pretended to find the wallet. 'Is this someone's? Just found it on the floor by my chair.' He held it up. It was minus a £10 note, but he knew they'd never notice. Which the owner didn't when he counted the money to make sure. 'Well, everything's here. Thanks, Paddy.'

A surprised mutter went round the tables and a kind of acceptance that Paddy must have turned over a new leaf now he was living with the Joneses. But the crisp £10 note, fresh from the cash machine in Culworth, rustled pleasureably in Paddy's trouser pocket. Having rashly promised £70 to Mrs Jones in a gush of enthusiasm for his new quarters, he had to find it from somewhere, and why not from someone who was so well off he hadn't noticed it was missing? A few of the punters raised their glasses to him. More fool them, he thought.

Chapter 12

Sheila had been to see Louise the very day she had promised Mrs Jones she would. Louise and the children had just come back from a walk and Louise was simultaneously helping them remove their coats, hushing the baby, who'd decided it was feeding time, and serving orange juice and biscuits.

By the time she'd got them settled with juice and a biscuit in front of a children's TV programme, Sheila had made a pot of tea and was ready to sit down. She volunteered to give the baby his bottle. 'Isn't he ready for solids? He must be.'

'Yes, but this is the quickest at the moment. Shut him up for a while anyway.'

Louise sank back against the cushions with relief, while her mother fed the baby. Sheila waited until the colour had come back into Louise's face and then said, 'Are you sure this baby isn't due until the spring?'

'Well, the hospital says it's much earlier than that, more like Christmas. Apparently I'd been pregnant for quite a while before I realized. What with feeding the baby myself and being so busy I simply hadn't noticed.'

'That looks more like it. Except it couldn't be more than one, could it?'

Louise smiled at the sound of apprehension in her

mother's voice. 'No, it's not two, I'm sure. Only one, thank God. And the last.'

'Dottie still cleaning for you?'

Louise nodded. Sheila sat the baby up to wind him and, while the children were absorbed in the TV, silence reigned.

When she'd burped the baby and he was feeding again, Sheila asked, 'You're not as well as you usually are. Not like the other times; then you were absolutely blooming. Mrs Jones mentioned it this morning.'

'Mrs Jones is a nosy old gossip.'

'She's taken on that Paddy Cleary from the rectory, gossip or no.'

Louise took a bit of interest in that piece of news. 'More fool her.'

'She's only trying to be kind.'

'Kind! I don't think so.'

'She's right about you, though. You don't look a bit well. It's as though you know there's something wrong but you won't face up to it.'

'There's nothing wrong. Believe me. All I want is for this one to be a boy, then we'll have three boys and three girls. And that's just right.'

'What does Gilbert think about you being under the weather?'

Louise smiled as she always did at the mention of Gilbert's name. 'He's concerned that I feel rotten, but there's nothing he can do about it.'

'Look here, I know money must be tight for the two of you with all these to feed and clothe, but if you want further advice I'm sure your dad and I could stretch to paying a specialist.'

'Absolutely not. There's no need.'

'What about the scan, does that show anything?'

'I don't have scans.'

'Whyever not?'

'On principle. How do we know what damage they might do?'

'What damage?'

'Exactly, we don't know, do we? They bring in all these new inventions without a thought as to what they might be doing to the baby long-term. Look at the problems thalidomide caused and the drug was supposed to be safe. Huh!'

'But, Louise, everyone has them. They're harmless.'

'Did you have scans when you had Brendon and me?'

Sheila hesitated and then admitted that of course she didn't. 'They were only just starting then and the small hospitals didn't have them anyway.'

'Well, then.'

'But if you're worried, it might put your mind at rest.'

'I'm not worried.'

A holy war broke out amongst the children at this precise moment and by the time it was sorted and they were busy playing with toys and making the house look as though a typhoon had blown through only minutes ago, the time had passed to press her point about a scan. But Sheila was determined to have a word with Gilbert and the moment she got home she rang him at the office and talked about it to him.

'Thank you for your concern, Sheila. You're right, she isn't well, but if she had a scan and they found out something was wrong, what would we do? We both feel strongly about abortion. It is murder, whichever way you look at it, and we're not going to have that on our conscience for the rest of our lives.'

'I see what you mean. But I'm so worried about her. She's not well and coping with the five she already has is getting beyond a joke.'

'I know. I know. Got to go. By the way, I've finished the placards for Saturday. Busy, busy. I'll think about what you've said.'

'Would Dottie come more often, perhaps? Do the ironing. Take some of them out for a walk or something?'

'I'll think about it. Thanks for ringing, Sheila.'

Sheila replaced her receiver and went to stand at her window to look out onto Stocks Row and have a think. It really was up to her to do something. If Louise couldn't make a decision – well, she could. In fact, she'd been in decision-making mode ever since she'd encouraged the W.I. to take on the New Hope Fund. Who on earth was this going past? My golly! It was . . . no, it couldn't be. It was! She'd know that figure anywhere, and not only that she recognized the purposeful walk. It was Grandmama Charter-Plackett on her way to the Store. She'd dyed her hair a real, very real orange! Same colour as a Jaffa. Well, I never. If she could dare to do it who couldn't?

Sheila went to assess herself in front of the sitting-room mirror. The years took their toll and not half. Those wrinkles were permanent now, especially the ones round her eyes. God! She peered more closely at herself. When you're twenty wrinkles were something the oldies had. Now *she* was an oldie and not liking it. Where had the years gone? She'd better take a grip or else . . . The hairdresser! Now they'd got the beauty parlour at the back of the salon perhaps she could . . . she'd ring right now. A facial and a manicure, too and – yes, she'd do it – her hair dyed all ready for Saturday! Platinum blonde. This was being decisive and she'd think about Louise tomorrow.

Jimbo took the shock of his mother's dyed hair very stoically indeed as she bounced into the Store, full of get up and go. 'Good morning, Jimbo, my dear. Harriet in?'

'Good morning, Mother.' He kissed her on both cheeks because she preferred that, and then stood back to assess the situation. 'Give us a twirl.'

Tom, behind the Post Office counter, had to turn away to hide his horror. Bel, shelf-filling, lurked behind the birthday cards while she composed her face. A customer, fit to burst with laughter, hid head down in the frozen desserts cabinet, unable to stop herself from looking gobsmacked.

'Well, if this is what being a member of the W.I. does for you—'

'Less of your cheek, Jimbo dear, I thought I'd better make an effort. This is far easier than swimming naked. I didn't want to shock the general populace so I went for dyeing my hair instead, though it wouldn't take much if someone would sponsor me for the swim, too. What do you think?'

Jimbo pursed his lips. 'Brave, that's what, brave.'

'It's permanent. None of this spray stuff. Thought if I was doing it I might as well do it right. Wish I'd done it years ago.'

'Permanent?'

'Yes. Permanent. Greta Jones has gone a vivid red and I thought we'd look good together in Culworth on Saturday with the collecting tins. We shall, shan't we?'

'You'll be the sensation of the day.'

Grandmama Charter-Plackett went across to the mirror Jimbo had strategically placed for keeping an eye on thieves and viewed the magnified image of herself.

Privately thinking she'd gone far too far, she said, 'There you are you see, Jaffa-coloured, just what I wanted. I'll go see Harriet. She'll love it.'

Harriet, concentrating hard on some elaborate decoration on the top of a massive trifle she was doing for a birthday party, looked up and promptly went into shock, which made her hand jerk and the cream burst out from the piping bag she was holding, and straight down her mother-in-law's jacket. 'My God! What have you done?'

'Harriet! Really! I thought you'd love it.'

Harriet pulled a couple of sheets of kitchen roll off the reel and began cleaning her up. 'It was the shock.'

'It's for the New Hope Fund on Saturday in Culworth. Doing it to drag some money out of the pinchpenny residents of Culworth. Will you sponsor me? I should have asked first but I did it on the spur of the moment.'

Harriet stood back to assess her. 'Well, I think you've been exceptionally,' she was going to say 'brave' but changed her mind, 'exceptionally dedicated to the cause. Of course I'll sponsor you.'

'Jimbo's laughing, but I don't care. I didn't really intend being Jaffa-coloured but that hair stylist, well, I daren't think where her brains are. Probably gone down the plughole along with the water. She knew I wanted it subtle. If this is subtle can you imagine what full strength would have been?'

'Some of them are spraying their hair so they can wash it out.'

'I know, but what's the fun in that?'

'None, I suppose. I've always fancied being a redhead. What do you think?'

'Why not? Spray it though. You're a business woman and it would be dreadful if you turned out like Greta

Jones. It's not only the colour of her hair that's gone to her head, either. Taking on Paddy Cleary? She must be mad. Well! I'm just glad Ralph didn't ask me.'

'They say he's turned over a new leaf since going to Mrs Jones's house.'

Mrs Charter-Plackett expressed her derision at such a possibility by saying. 'Hmmm. A leopard doesn't change its spots. Mark my words. Must go.'

As she was leaving – after a word with Tom, and buying a chocolate eclair for her afternoon tea – she spotted Maggie Dobbs talking to Dottie. The two of them burst into raucous giggles when she approached them. Mrs Charter-Plackett responded by looking very annoyed indeed, and then suddenly saw the funny side of it and in moments the three of them were reeling with laughter. Jimbo came out to see what the matter was, saw his mother laughing like he hadn't seen in years and joined in.

Between her gasps for breath Maggie Dobbs struggled to say, 'Oh, dear! Oh, dear. I shall never be the same again. Jaffa, that's what, Jaffa!' Maggie had been deciding which hair colourant to buy but now she couldn't because she kept doubling up with laughter. Dottie, being the kind of person she was, suggested Mrs Charter-Plackett had better not go into Deansgate in Culworth late at night or she might get invited for a ride by the kerb-crawlers!

'Just like you, Dottie, coming out with something like that!' Maggie fell into shrieking with laughter for a third time, leaning against the hair products shelving and holding her handkerchief to her mouth.

When eventually they got themselves under control, they joined Maggie in her decision-making and decided on autumn gold for her. It turned out very brassy indeed, but did Maggie care? Not she. The worst bit was being sponsored for the skinny-dipping. She'd already got £30 promised for that from the dinner ladies at the school, and two of her cousins had sponsored her but threatened to turn up to watch, so perhaps she wouldn't do it if they did come. Though maybe they wouldn't know it was her with this brassy hair. She looked like a tart. But she'd lost half a stone and she did look more sylph-like, so that was a blessing. Still, come Saturday they'd be in the market rattling their tins and what's more, she didn't care a button what people said.

There was a great deal of laughter about the colourful heads of hair gathered at the Women's Institute committee meeting on the Friday night. The first item to be discussed was the success or otherwise of the pyjama party.

'Well,' said Greta, 'I reckon it was a roaring success. Not something you could do every year because it'ud lose its sparkle but definitely, yes, a success. And the fire kind of finished it off with a bang! To say nothing of the firemen finding that young couple in the bedroom. I'm just hoping the skinny-dipping will be as good.'

They all laughed even louder at that.

'It came very close to . . . unwholesomeness and so might the swim if we're not careful.' This from Muriel, who endeavoured to keep the Women's Institute on the straight and narrow and was mindful of Ralph's reaction when he first heard what they had planned. 'Swimming? Naked? Muriel, have you lost your sense of decorum? Whatever next! Surely you protested?'

She'd answered, 'Well, actually, no, I didn't.'

'You didn't?'

'No. They were all so keen and I knew Jimbo wouldn't have anything untoward, you know anything rude . . . or anything . . . happening, so I thought why not? It's all in a good cause.'

Ralph had become enraged at this. 'How about running a brothel in the church hall? Or a gambling saloon in the memorial chapel? Justified, of course, by being all in a good cause. Muriel! I am appalled.'

But Muriel had stuck to her guns when Ralph suggested the naked swim should be cancelled.

'Cancelled?' She was horrified. 'Absolutely not. When I think of Peter's congregation not having Bibles to read, possibly not even being able to read some of them, no organ, no chairs, we have to do something, and some pathetic coffee-and-gateaux evening would bring in zilch in comparison with what they need. No, we certainly shall not cancel it.' Muriel's voice had risen to a crescendo by the end of her declaration so angry was she. She'd almost added, 'And if you protest any more I shall volunteer for the naked swim.' She stopped herself just in time.

Ralph had stood up to enable him to put his point more clearly. 'Muriel! There are times when I really wonder who I've married.'

'Oh! You've married me, a loyal loving wife, but it does not mean that I always have to do as you say. I never promised to "obey" in our marriage service.'

So now here she sat, having to choose her words with care or she'd be in danger of being two-faced. 'You see, we do have to be careful, that incident of those two young people being found in one of the bedrooms at the pyjama party, well . . .'

Her disapproval caused gales of laughter.

Sheila answered. 'Let's face it, Muriel, your Ralph has his so-called cousin Arthur Prior at Wallop Down Farm.

Some cousin indeed, when we all know Arthur's grand-father was born the wrong side of the Templeton blanket. So they were all at it even then.'

'Really!' Muriel went bright red. The rest of the committee didn't know where to look, but Sheila appeared quite unfazed by her outburst.

Harriet was the first to recover. 'I don't think there's any need to bring up matters of that nature a hundred years and more after they occurred.'

Sheila rebelliously remarked, 'But it's a fact, isn't it? It did go on then and always will.'

Rather acidly Greta Jones commented, 'Same as your Louise and Gilbert. She wasn't exactly pure as the driven snow when they marr—'

'Ladies, ladies! This has got to stop. Now, please. It isn't the business of a W.I. committee to trawl through the past like this.' This was Grandmama Charter-Plackett speaking. She brought them to their senses and the uncomfortable moment was passed over. The rest of the meeting was a little fraught but without the venom that had so unexpect-edly surfaced.

The Saturday shopping bus was filled to capacity. The regular driver, dazzled by their dyed hair, gave up checking bus passes and let quite a few others on without paying as well. They rattled their collecting boxes at him, hoping for a contribution, but he ignored it, put the bus in gear and roared off in his usual fashion.

The most spectacular head of hair was Vince's. He'd dyed his sparce tufts in various shades from Greta's gaudy red (she'd saved a few drops of her dye for him) to vivid blue and a sharp acid yellow. My, what a sight he looked, but because Paddy had helped him with it he didn't care about the hysterical laughter he caused. There was Grandmama Charter-Plackett — Jaffa-coloured — and Sheila Bisset — a bold shining platinum at odds with her complexion. Rhett had used sprays to colour his hair as near as he could to a Union Jack flag, Michelle had dyed her blonde hair jet-black. Harriet and her girls, Flick and Fran, had each sprayed their hair a quite splendid matching dayglo pink and they made a spectacular trio: Two of the weekenders had come dyed a riot of multi-colours. They were equipped with a digital camera and intended taking photographs of everyone to take home for their neighbours to see what fun they were having in their weekend cottage.

When they all alighted from the bus in the square, they made a sensational impact on the Culworth residents. Full of delight at their reception, they stood together for the weekenders to take photographs of them and to listen to Sheila's final instructions. There was such a lot of laughing and leg-pulling going on it was difficult for Sheila to make herself heard. Dyeing their hair must have gone to their heads, she thought.

'We'll give it two hours. You don't have to stick here in the market. Go down the precinct or anywhere you fancy. I'll be catching the lunchtime bus home, so bring your tins to me and I'll take them with me so you can stay on to do your shopping. Get plenty of money and don't forget to carry your banners so people know what you're collecting for.'

They all dispersed, shaking their collecting tins at every possible person from old grandads to babes-in-arms, from stallholders to traffic wardens, and scarcely anyone refused them. After an hour their tins were weighing them down. Greta Jones and Grandmama Charter-Plackett made an arresting twosome, and collected as much and more than everyone else. Eventually Greta suggested they went in the pub for a reviving drink.

'They'll have coffee, won't they?' asked Grandmama.

'Coffee! It's not coffee I'm going in for, I need something with a bit more kick in it. Like a whisky. No, I'll have rum and Coke.'

'I miss my morning coffee. But I might just be tempted. I'll pay first time round.'

'How many are you thinking of having, then?'

Grandmama nudged Greta and said, 'I don't know yet. But I shall be glad of a sit-down. This damn tin is weighing heavier by the minute.'

They found a cosy sofa tucked away in a corner and sat down with their drinks, glad for a respite. One rum and Coke led to another, then another, then neat rum. Whether it was dyeing their hair or the sheer euphoria of collecting so much money, they didn't know, but they stayed there drinking until the landlord, tired of their bursts of raucous laughter disturbing his other clients, refused to serve them any more and insisted they left the premises. The two of them staggered out into the sharp air, striving to keep control of their legs and of their silly grins, and immediately collided into two police officers on market duty.

Propping each other up, they laughingly apologized and shook their tins enticingly under the officers' noses. The smell of drink on their breath and the slurring of their voices as they explained what they were collecting for, amused them but not the two officers. Too late it dawned that the officers were not laughing. Drunk in charge of a collecting tin was the charge and they were marched off to the police station.

The others were already gathering in the bus station still shaking their tins. Sheila Bissett, when she felt their combined weight, didn't know how on earth she was going to manage them all back to Turnham Malpas. 'Oh my word, isn't this wonderful! Haven't we done well?'

Maggie Dobbs, in need of the bus station toilets, disappeared into the ticket hall to find them. On her way back she spotted Paddy Cleary. He was standing nonchalantly reading a newspaper; unexpectedly it was *The Times*, Maggie noticed. He was leaning against a carousel next to a woman who was holding copies of various bus timetables and literature about local sightseeing possibilities. She decided to rattle her tin under his nose just to test if there really had been a change in him since he'd moved to Mrs Jones's. She'd also try the woman who was studying the leaflets.

But before she reached him, she saw, without a word of a lie, Paddy slip his hand into the woman's shopping bag, gently extricate her purse, put it into his folded newspaper in a trice and walk slowly away with an unbelievable air of innocence about him. No rushing, just steady walking. Maggie glanced at the woman – who'd by now found the leaflet she needed – then looked back again for Paddy, but he'd disappeared as though he'd never been there. She couldn't believe it. Where the hell had he gone? There one minute, gone the next. The woman rushed outside and leapt on a bus just as it was leaving. So they had both disappeared as though they'd never existed. Maggie stood there vacantly staring into space not noticing that three people had put money in her tin while she was in a trance. She had seen it happen. Definitely she had. No messing. He'd taken the purse from the woman's bag and walked away scot-free. Maggie raced outside, rejoined the others and said breathlessly, 'Seen Paddy Cleary, have yer?'

They all shook their heads.

'Thought I'd seen him in the ticket hall. Must have been mistaken. Where's Greta and Mrs Charter-Plackett?'

'They haven't arrived yet. They're going to miss the bus.'

'It'll be here in a minute. Shall we go without them?'

'Well,' said Sheila, 'I don't want to stand about with all this money; it could get stolen.'

Maggie thought, never a truer word. Out loud she said, 'I'm going straight home. I'll only spend money if I stay here.'

One of the weekenders with red-white-and-blue hair said, 'Me, too. We'll help you with them, Sheila.'

'Thanks. I'm a bit worried about Mrs Jones and Grandmama, though. You don't suppose they've been abducted? With all that money.'

'To say nothing of their hair.' At which they all had a snigger.

Harriet said, 'She'll have her mobile, I'll give her a buzz.'

It was a while before there was an answer. 'Hello, Katherine? Where are you? We're all waiting for the bus . . .'

'Harriet? I'm at the police station. I've been arrested.'

'Arrested? Whatever for?'

The answer was confusing, to say the least. More an incoherent rambling than an explanation. If Harriet didn't know better she'd have thought Grandmama was drunk.

'But why?'

Then her phone went dead.

Harriet said, 'Girls, come on, your grandmama's been arrested. We'll have to go.'

The three of them raced away, leaving everyone else astounded.

'Arrested? What has she been doing?'

'Whatever for?'

'This'll look good in the paper.'

'Any publicity is good publicity,' said Vince.

'It won't really get in the papers, will it?'

'Sheila, you did get permission from the police to hold a collection today?'

'Permission? I didn't know we had to, Vince.'

'Hell's bells. What's more, where's our Greta? They were together.'

Consternation registered on all their faces. The bus roared up to the stop. Late as usual. He wouldn't wait. 'Definitely not. No can do. Get on. And don't rattle your tins on my bus.'

'Harriet will look after them,' Sheila said comfortingly to Vince.

'I'm off to the police station. I can't leave her here. Wish Paddy was about, he'd know what to do.' Vince got off the bus and marched out of the bus station.

Maggie thought that maybe Paddy wouldn't be too keen on a visit to the police station, after what she'd seen him do. She needed to say something to someone about it.

Harriet, the two girls, Mrs Jones, Vince and a distraught Grandmama came home later that afternoon, all squeezed into one taxi. Harriet, having stormed the police station and using her most businesslike and forthright manner, had managed to rescue the two of them without charges being laid. Harriet had a sneaking suspicion that they'd been arrested more as a joke than anything, because she caught a twinkle in the eye of one of the officers, and he gave her a wink.

On the way home to Turnham Malpas, Grandmama complained long and loudly, while Mrs Jones sat mute from the shock. They'd never live it down. Never. The embarrassment! She clutched hold of Vince's hand, wondering just how many people who knew her had witnessed the arrest.

Grandmama suddenly remembered Jimbo. 'Whatever will Jimbo say? Never in all my life have I been arrested. Never.'

Harriet reassured her. 'Most probably he'll roar with laughter and ask why I didn't take a photograph of you being marched off. So I wouldn't worry.'

But Harriet's reassurance did nothing to calm Grandmama's discomfort. Added to which, she had the most horrendous headache coming on and she'd left her tablets at home.

The news of the arrest spread rapidly through the village from the rectory to right down Shepherd's Hill. It also was spread through Penny Fawcett and Little Derehams because the bus went on there after Turnham Malpas and, being the Saturday shopping bus, it was packed to the door.

In the pub that night it was top of the agenda so far as conversation went. Vera, in with Don to give him a bit of a change, laughed herself silly, thinking of the times when Grandmama had made her feel small. Now it was Vera's turn to laugh, and she made the most of it.

What they hadn't bargained for was a photograph of Greta Jones and Grandmama, and a piece about their arrest in the *Culworth Gazette* on the Wednesday of that same week. But who cared? All good for the New Hope Fund.

Mortification was rampant in the cottage on the Green, as Grandmama buried her head in her hands and groaned. Unfortunately Vince and Paddy relished every single inch of column space the arrest had been given, so Greta felt completely humiliated. They would keep howling with laughter and making merry quips, which tore at her heart.

But by Friday night the laughter had died down and Grandmama had begun to go out again and made herself as amused as everyone else about it. She even felt a little pleasure at everyone's interest in her, and actually cut out the article and the picture of her and Greta being marched off by the police officers. Anyhow, she and Greta had collected more than anyone else in their tins. She'd heard it was a dazzling total.

Maggie still had the problem of Paddy stealing that purse in the ticket hall at the bus station. Should she or should she not say what she had seen? Greta ought to know, but she was suffering enough without her landing this thieving story on her. Someone had to be told. Then it dawned on her: Anna. After all, it was Anna who'd brought him to the village in the first place, and wearing a clerical collar she'd know exactly what to say, just like Peter had always known.

So, on the Friday night, she marched across to the rectory and banged the knocker loudly.

Anna came to the door. 'Maggie? How's things? Do come in.'

Maggie followed her into the sitting room. Such a lovely room; it was just as it was when Caroline lived here. Beautifully furnished, in the most pleasant and relaxing way, with subtle colours and cuddling comfort every-where.

'Now, Maggie, do you have a problem? If so, spill the beans.'

Maggie straightened her skirt and coughed to clear her throat. 'I'm not here to tittle-tattle.'

'Of course not.'

'But I am here to tell you something you won't like.'

Immediately Anna thought about the incident with Gilbert in the church the other evening, when she'd got over-animated. Had she been seen holding his arm and talking so intensely to him? That night she could have reached up and kissed him without any encouragement. God! She hoped not.

'You see, you didn't go collecting with us, did you?'

Relief. 'No.'

'Well, we all went to wait for the bus to come back, we had a very successful morning, you know, collected far more than we'd expected. I needed . . . well . . . I needed to spend a penny, as yer might say and – do you know the ticket hall?'

'Well, no, I don't actually.'

'Well, you have to go through there to get to the toilets and on my way back I saw Paddy Cleary steal a woman's purse. It's true, I'm not trying to get him into trouble. Plain as day. It's been worrying me all week, but I can't tell Greta Jones, 'cos she's worried enough about getting arrested and that photo in the paper. So I thought I'd tell you. Is it all right?'

'To tell me? Of course, but I wish you hadn't had to. I thought he'd turned over a new leaf.'

'We all did. We all thought that. But he did. Before my

very eyes, he disappeared with the purse and the woman ran to catch her bus not knowing what had happened.'

'Don't worry, I'll have a word with him.'

'Oh! Thank you. It'll be better coming from you rather than me. Greta Jones can't half take the huff if she's a mind to.'

'I'll tread carefully.'

'Thank you very much indeed. I'm so relieved. Goodnight, Reverend. You're doing very well, you know. Peter was a hard act to follow, but they're all coming round to you.'

'Thank you. I'll attend to this matter as soon as maybe.'

'I'll be off then.'

Anna stood in the window of the sitting room, watching Maggie cross the road to her house and feeling thankful her news wasn't what she thought it was going to be.

That night in the church after choir practice, she'd gone completely over the top talking to Gilbert. He had this strange effect on her, where she lost all common sense and went into overdrive, flirting almost. There'd been other men in her life before she was ordained but none had the capacity to alert her in the same way Gilbert did. He, being a happily married man with a pregnant wife and a large family, made absolutely no overtures to her at all. He treated her like a perfectly normal human being, although there was nothing normal about her when she was with him. She urgently needed to get it under control.

Her other problem was Dean. His kind of calf-love was very flattering but meant nothing to her and everything to him. She sensed it each time he came near her and avoided being alone with him as much as she possibly could. Maybe she was flattering herself but she felt it wouldn't take much for him to kiss her, or at least to hold her. A romance with an inexperienced boy, which he was despite his twenty-two years, would be unkind of her and disastrous for him.

The third man in her life was Paddy. Damn Paddy. Anna glanced at her watch and decided she had time to catch him in the pub if she went right now. But she'd forgotten it was the awards night for the hair-dyeing competition.

Chapter 13

Jimbo was standing on a chair announcing the details. His powerful voice could be heard all round the saloon bar.

'There were three categories of prizes. The most amusing, the most wicked and the most fashionable improvement. Lady Templeton has graciously agreed to present the prizes, which are . . . vouchers for a full treatment at the Misty Blue Unisex Hair and Beauty Salon in Culworth. These vouchers have been kindly donated by the salon, please note, and we are very grateful for their generosity. So . . . prize for the most amusing hair goes to . . . Vince Jones. He gets the full massage treatment as his prize.'

At this announcement great whoops of laughter roared round the bar.

'All right! All right! The prize for the most wicked hair goes to the three Charter-Plackett girls. They'll have to fight that out by themselves. Prize for the most fashionable improvement goes to . . . wait for it . . . Greta Jones! She gets a complete makeover. Give them a big hand for being so sporting.'

The pub was crowded and the applause thunderous. Anna ordered her drink from Georgie and leaned against the counter, watching the presentation.

'OK. OK. Silence please. Thank you. Most important

of all, between them they collected . . . yes, pin back your ears! A wonderful total of six hundred and forty-two pounds, thirty-seven pence, which includes the two pounds they paid to enter the competition. The nearest guess to that was Paddy Cleary's. He guessed six hundred pounds. Come along, Paddy, and collect your prize.'

Lady Templeton handed over to him vouchers for five free drinks in the Royal Oak Bar.

'So those of you who paid fifty pence to wager on the amount they collected and only guessed between twenty and three hundred pounds were way out. But . . . their wagers contributed another twenty pounds to the total. Three cheers for the hair-dyeing competition. Hip hip . . .'

Jimbo led the cheering, then climbed down from his chair and went to kiss his prize-winning family.

Anna caught Paddy in a state of euphoria about his prize.

'I need a word. Outside. Now.'

'But I'm treating Greta and Vince—'

'*Now.*'

'Oh, hell!' Anna-with-the-banner again. He thought he'd got rid of her.

After the fug in the bar, the outside air struck him forcibly. 'Damn blasted cold out here. What do you want? Some more ornaments gone missing, so blame Paddy who hasn't set foot in the rectory since he got kicked out?'

'No. Someone saw you on Saturday.'

'I expect they did, there were dozens of people in Culworth.'

Exasperated, Anna said sharply, 'Stealing a purse?'

Paddy pushed his hands in his jacket pockets. 'Who was stealing a purse?'

'You. In the ticket hall.'

Somehow he wasn't being quite so clever as he had been at persuading others he wasn't a thief. 'All I did in the ticket hall was wait in the warm for the bus.'

'No, Paddy. You stole someone's purse from her shopping bag and don't deny it.'

'You said it, not me.' He glanced towards the lighted window of the pub, the vouchers burning a hole in his pocket.

'What I can't understand is, where is your money going? You're getting paid, you've a roof over your head, why do you need to steal as well? Old habits, is it? You've got a very comfortable home with Greta and Vince, you've done them some good because they enjoy your company, and they've done you some good by providing you with a stable home like you've never had before.'

Paddy looked anywhere but at Anna's face. Why the crusade? he thought. Why the hell did she never leave him alone? 'Look, if Greta and Vince don't know nothing about what I do, that purse and such, what harm is it doing? Just mind your own damn business and let me get on with my life.' He turned to go. 'And you get on with yours.'

'Maggie could report it to the police.'

'Oh! Maggie was it, saw me? A couple of drinks will soon sort that out. She wouldn't dare.'

'I might.'

'And ruin all your good work? All the time you've spent trying to keep me on the straight and narrow. Some Christian you are. Well, I'll tell you something, shall I? Something about you. You're pining for that Gilbert fella. Pining! I can see it in your eyes, and him a married man, for God's sake. And I'm the one to make sure everyone knows.' He stabbed the air with a vicious forefinger. 'So just keep out of my business or I'll start the rumours up, this time about you and Gilbert. He must be a sexy devil, a family the size of his; wouldn't be difficult to get people to believe me. Just a nod and a wink is all it takes in this place and they'd be on to it like a shot.'

Paddy spun on his heel and left Anna standing humiliated and afraid. She'd pray about her feelings for Gilbert and would have to get them under control somehow. She couldn't afford scandal; her position was already precarious enough. What was it about rectors at Turnham Malpas? Were they destined to be the subject of rumours and counter-rumours?

The absent rector of Turnham Malpas had sent an email that had nothing to do with rumours. When Jimbo found it on his computer the following morning, just before he went to Matins, his heart almost burst with the shock of what he read.

To: Everyone at Turnham Malpas
From: New Hope Mission

Dear Friends
Pray for us. Pray for us. Your brother and sister in Christ need your prayers. Our beloved children were ambushed by rebels on their way home from school yesterday. Usually I collect them from school to bring them home for the weekend, but an Anglican missionary we know suggested he drove them home as he was travelling to stay for the weekend with us. The car was attacked and the children are gone. Nothing of them nor their belongings was found at the scene. The missionary was discovered in a storm drain at the side of the

road shot dead. Elijah has gone to search for them. We pray desperately for his safe return and that of the children.

Peter and Caroline

Jimbo felt physically sick. His head pounded with pain, and for a moment his heart felt to have stopped beating. He drew in a huge gasp of air and wondered what use their fundraising was now. He printed out the email, folded it and placed it in his pocket, then went to tell Harriet and the girls what had happened. Fran burst into noisy tears, Flick went drip-white and Harriet clung to him for comfort. He gave the copy of the email to Anna to read in the vestry before the service.

'This has come this morning,' he said to her. 'I thought you ought to know. Read it, please. God in heaven, Anna. We'll have to pray like we've never prayed before.'

Anna's problems faded away. Her hands shook so much she could scarcely read the words. 'Dear God. Why? For heaven's sake, when all they're doing is helping put things right, to give these people the basic needs of a human being, and they do this. What possible good can it do, kidnapping two children? Political opponents perhaps, but *children?*'

Soberly Jimbo said, 'We don't know they were kidnapped, let's hope they're still alive.' He caught sight of Gilbert signalling his readiness from the vestry doorway. 'Gilbert's waiting for you.'

'Gilbert is? Ah! Yes. Tell him I'm ready. Just one minute while I pull myself together.'

Anna held the service, as she was bound to do, but the one she had planned was abandoned and she held an open pulpit for people to speak or pray as they wished. There was not a dry eye in the church that morning. They decided to pray, keeping an all-night vigil, a twenty-four-hour chain of prayer for Beth and Alex. What else could they do? Nothing. It was a last resort.

'Some good us getting money together for such an ungrateful lot.'

'Might as well throw the money down a drain. They'll get no more of mine anyway. That's for certain.'

Anna's reply was, 'We mustn't let this affect us. Those who've done this aren't the ones we're collecting the money for.'

'How d'we know which side they're all on? Could be saying one thing and doing another.'

'You're right there. Blast 'em. Them two poor kids. It's not right.'

Anna broke in to put a stop to the resentment. 'It isn't right, I agree, but we've to maintain our faith and think of Caroline and Peter and support them with our prayers. We must not let the poison of these murderers affect the way *we* think. *We* must behave as Peter would want us to. As I want you to. With courage and steadfastness. With honour and belief. Nothing we do or think must bring us down to the level of these rebels. In the long term the money is obviously desperately needed and we'll see they get it. Bibles to spread the Word, along with medicines and syringes and dressings and drugs. What was it Jesus said? "Turn the other cheek". This is one of those moments to remember that. God bless you all.'

A group gathered around Jimbo to put their names for the prayer vigil and Anna had to leave them to it. She stood in the vestry, alone, overcome by spiritual exhaustion, tears beginning to pour down her face. Unaware that Gilbert was standing in the doorway, his arms full of choir music he was wanting to put away in the choir music cupboard, she let the tears flow.

'Anna!' Gilbert put the sheet music down on the vestry table and opened his arms wide. 'Anna, my dear. What a triumph! There, there, you've done brilliantly and saved the day. It could all have got very nasty in there and understandably so, but you spoke right to their hearts and just how Peter would have done. The thought of a child of mine in those unpredictable, spinechilling circumstances horrifies me. There, there. Come along now, dry your tears.'

Anna loved the comfort his words and his actions brought to her. They eased her soul, strengthened her resolve. He rocked her gently, talking softly to her as he would have done to one of his own children. Thinking that brought her abruptly to her senses. In the shelter of his arms she sniffed back her tears. 'I'm so sorry. Making an exhibition of myself.'

'Not an exhibition. You couldn't have held it all together without some severe emotional drain, it had to come out. Now dry the tears, Anna, my dear, or—'

They heard the vestry door crashing back against the cupboard and before they let go of each other to see who was there, they were violently torn apart. Ashen-faced and breathing fire stood Dean Jones. He thrust Gilbert up against the music cupboard and threatened him with his clenched fist. 'How dare you? How dare you touch Anna in that way!'

Gilbert, sensing he'd been thrust deep into an emotional whirlpool, shrewdly took a deep breath before he spoke. 'Dean! Please. Have some sensitivity. Anna was—'

'Sensitivity! It's you without sensitivity, not I. How

dare you put your arms round her. In public, too. Have you no shame?'

'Look—'

'I did look – and saw *you*.' His face was now flushed and he was beginning to see he was making the most horrendous fool of himself, but his temper got the better of him and he hit out at Gilbert with more power in his punch than he had ever thought himself capable of.

Anna shouted, 'Dean! For heaven's sake!' She shut the vestry door to keep things as private as she could but she guessed she might already be too late. She pushed him away from Gilbert, who now had blood running from his nose and stood, holding up both his hands. 'I'm a pacifist. I can't strike back.' He took his handkerchief out and held it to stem the blood.

'A coward's way out! Huh!'

Anna, boiling with frustration at his idiocy, shouted, 'Dean! I insist you leave the vestry at once. This minute.'

Gilbert shook his head. 'No, I'll leave. You need to talk.' He gestured at the music he'd laid down on the table. 'Please?'

'Of course. I'll put it away.' When Gilbert had left, Anna spoke coldly to Dean. 'You owe both Gilbert and me an apology. It's my turn to say how dare you? Bursting in here when I was talking privately to him, behaving like an angry child, shouting, using your fists. What on earth is the matter with you?'

Her anger mortified Dean. All these beautiful sunlit weeks when he'd longed to tell her, had imagined how delighted she would be when he told her how he felt, fell away from him and he realized so clearly how she viewed him in her mind. A foolish boy with the hots for her. His eyes, shining with his love, slid away from her face and focused on the music laid on the table. Humbly and softly he murmured, 'But he's a married man. With children. How could he?'

'Dean! I'd been crying because of the twins and having to take hold of the service and keep everyone together. I was exhausted, and he comforted me. Believe me, there's nothing between us. It's like you said, he's a married man with children. Full stop.'

Dean's shoulders slumped and a tentative hand went out to her. He touched her cheek and then withdrew his hand immediately. 'I'm sorry to have caused . . . you of all people . . . grief. That was why I came in here because I wanted to help. I knew you'd be exhausted.'

'Well, thank you for thinking of me, thank you very much. But you've to put me out of your mind.' A wry smile crossed her face. 'You deserve someone much more beautiful and exciting than me. I'm much too old for a strapping young chap with prospects like yours. There.' Anna kissed a finger and pressed it to his cheek.

Dean clutched her hand and held it to his lips. 'Anna! Anna!'

There came a hurried tap and an immediate opening of the door and there stood Muriel, flushed and embarrassed.

Anna snatched her hand away, immediately conscious of how things must look. 'Thank you, Dean, for your kindness in thinking of me.'

Dean caught sight of the disgust on Muriel's face and wished himself anywhere but where he was. He managed to control himself long enough to say, 'Think nothing of it. Glad I could be of some use.'

Muriel covered her confusion by saying, 'I've come to see if you're all right. You've done so well this morning. I couldn't have done a quarter of what you've done in such difficult circumstances. Not a quarter. Didn't you think she did well, Dean?'

'She did indeed, Lady Templeton. Must go.'

He nodded to Anna as he squeezed past her on his way out.

Anna rubbed her eyes to make sure there were no tears lingering there, straightened her cassock and looked as brightly as she could at Muriel.

Slowly and deliberately Muriel said, 'I'm glad it was I who came in just then, because I shan't say a word of what I saw.'

'Muriel! He was comforting me because I was crying, that's all. Nothing more.'

'Of course, my dear, I know that, but there are others who would delight in passing on what they'd seen. In your position you can't be too careful.' Oh, dear. Oh, dear. At such a time as this. Poor Dean. Poor Anna.

'Terrible news, isn't it, about the children. Peter and Caroline must be distraught.'

'Anna, my dear, having no children of my own, I can't even begin to understand what the pain must be like for them. We've known the twins since the day they were born, you know, they're both very dear to us all. It's so hard to bear. However, thank you for this morning. You held us together.' She shut the door behind her and slowly made her way up the church and wished, how she wished, Peter and Caroline would be at the door saying good morning to everyone. But they wouldn't be.

Throughout the night, silent figures could be seen making their way to the church to maintain the chain of prayer for Beth and Alex. From down Shepherd's Hill they came, from Penny Fawcett, from Little Derehams, from big houses and tiny cottages, from Church Lane,

Stocks Row and the Culworth Road, an army of sympathizers praying with desperate hope in their hearts for Peter and Caroline and that the children might be recovered safe and sound.

It had a profound effect on the village. What should have been a fun week looking forward to the midnight skinny-dipping event became more sad than they could have ever imagined. Sales in the Store suffered and Jimbo was inundated with people coming to see if there was any more news, standing around and cluttering up the floor space but not spending money. He chided himself for thinking on those terms but his thoughts were really the outcome of his pain. He had two more emails from Peter, each saying nothing more had been heard, not even a ransom note, which might have given a smidgen of hope.

But time moved on, intricate arrangements had been made, and, willy-nilly, the skinny-dipping had to take place as a demonstration of their steadfast faith, if nothing else.

Chapter 14

Early on the Saturday morning, the men installing the temporary lighting arrived to begin work in the back garden of the Store ready for the Sponsored Skinny Dipping at midnight. They arrived with a large van which they parked at the bus stop, an action which rattled the bus driver when he arrived to take everyone into Culworth for their shopping. 'Who's this, then? Making a film are we?' he asked sarcastically as he drew up alongside the van.

There was quite a crowd waiting for the bus and they informed him of the reason for the van.

'A skinny-dipping? Good God! You lot?'

With as much dignity as she could muster given her vivid red hair, Greta Jones said, 'Yes, for charity.'

'What the hell will you get up to next?'

'You never know. We're not some flea-bitten ancient dump like Little Derehams, we have ideas.'

'You can say that again. Get on, then. Sharp's the word this morning.' He took the money for the tickets, meticulously checked each free pass and launched the bus on its journey by stamping on the accelerator before everyone was seated. Those not already sat down lurched and careered about the aisle as though they'd been imbibing since dawn.

'I'm complaining about 'im.'

'It's disgusting, it is.'

'Absolutely disgusting. He isn't fit to be on the road.'

Mrs Jones shouted down the bus, 'You're right there; he isn't fit to drive a horse and cart, never mind a public vehicle.'

Vince, dragged out by Greta and Paddy for a bit of shopping in Culworth, which he hated, gave vent to his spleen by shouting, 'I'm definitely reporting 'im. He'll be injuring someone doing that. He's a maniac.'

At this the driver slapped the brakes on and came to an abrupt halt just as he was turning into the Culworth Road. He stood up, faced the crowded bus and yelled, 'Right, everybody off! I'm not going another inch. Why should I drive you anywhere at all? You do nothing but complain. Come on. All off. I'm taking the bus back to the bus station.'

Complete silence greeted this, until Paddy said with delighted surprise, 'Well, now, would you believe it! In that case you can take us with you, 'cos that's just where we want to go.'

There was an hilarious uproar at this remark.

'It is. It is.'

'Handy that is.'

'Right to the bus station! Good on yer, mate!'

The driver decided to wipe the smiles from their faces. '*Empty*. Not full of you ungrateful, miserable lot. Come on. Off the bus.'

Children began to cry, fearing they were losing their chance of a McDonald's and toys in the market. Mothers remembered all the things they needed and couldn't buy in Turnham Malpas. Older people were disgruntled at missing their weekly trudge round the stalls.

'Here! That won't do! We've paid!'

Vince shouted, 'Listen here, you! Sit down, turn that key and get a move on. The bargains'll all be gone before we get there.'

'Do yer job and do it right. We put up with enough from you week in week out.'

At this, the driver got out and went to sit on the low wall beside the road. He folded his arms and looked very determined. Immovable in fact.

Paddy decided to teach him a lesson. Action was needed and action they'd get. This could be his moment for showing just what he was made of. Could he do it? Yes, he could. There was nothing a Cleary couldn't do once he'd made up his mind. He'd never driven a bus in his life – he didn't even have a driving licence for a car let alone a public transport vehicle – but swift action was required, pronto, and he was just the man for a crisis. He rose nonchalantly to his feet, strolled to the front of the bus as though getting off, but instead nipped swiftly over the barrier around the driver's seat and before you could say Jack Robinson he had turned the ignition key, put the bus in gear with a considerable amount of grinding and grunting, and set off, to gasps of astonishment and loud cheers from the passengers.

As for the driver, he was so astounded by Paddy driving away, almost a whole minute passed before he leaped to his feet and began to run after the bus as it jerked along the road, but he was no match for Paddy's driving. Paddy went off at speed, great gusts of fumes coming from the exhaust, and the driver gave up almost as he started, seeing that catching it was patently impossible. Instead he ran to the phone box outside the Store and rang the bus depot to tell them his bus had been stolen. It took quite five minutes of explanation and protestations before they finally accepted what he told them. They hustled to organize a police reception to wait for Paddy when he turned into the Culworth Bus Station and, when he did, they arrested him immediately.

'You can't arrest him!' Sheila protested. 'He's swimming tonight at our skinny-dipping.'

Greta added, 'He only did it because the driver refused to drive us. It wasn't his fault.'

'Now, come on,' said Vince, hoping to get them to see reason, 'he's a good lad, is Paddy. He doesn't deserve this.'

But it was all to no avail. Paddy was arrested and that was that. Theft. Driving without a licence. In charge of a public vehicle while unauthorized to be so. Reckless driving . . . The list was apparently endless. It was a wonder it didn't include kidnapping, too.

Paddy, considerably concerned about the predicament he was in, nevertheless put on a brave face. 'See yer tonight. Don't fret, Sheila, I'll be there. This won't take long, you'll see.'

'He's a hero he is. A hero.' They all gathered round and cheered and clapped Paddy as he was marched away. Facts were facts though: Paddy was being charged.

The whole incident fired everyone up and they found themselves liking Paddy, forgetting how angry he'd made them and the trouble he'd caused in the past.

By four o'clock in the afternoon Paddy was back in Turnham Malpas, having cadged a lift in Jimmy Glover's taxi.

Greta greeted him with joy. 'You're back! Wonderful. Did they feed you?'

Vince was more concerned about Paddy's fate and asked what had happened.

'Court appearance in a few weeks. They'll let me know. I could eat a horse. Any chance of some food, Ma?'

Greta noticed he'd said 'Ma' and it went right to her heart. 'Of course there is, son. Sit down. It'll be ready in a minute. A doorstep with Jimbo's special smoked ham? Mustard?'

'Just right. Thanks.' Paddy settled comfortably before the fire, him on one side and Vince the other. They smiled at each other and Vince leaned across to pat his knee, glad to have him back.

Sheila had reached an all-time height of panic. What if this skinny-dipping didn't work? What if it rained heavily? What if it was a bitterly cold night? What if the lights didn't work? What if everyone went ultra-modest and daren't, wouldn't, downright refused to swim? The sponsorship money wouldn't come in and they'd be letting Peter and Caroline down so badly.

Ron comforted her as best he could, but everything he said she turned back on itself and moaned louder than ever. Her hands were shaking, her throat as dry as the bottom of a parrot's cage, she started out through the door without her coat, she left her clipboard on the hall table and had to unlock the door again, she left her bag propped on the umbrella stand for some strange reason, which caused utmost confusion as she searched for it, and altogether she was in no fit state to organize a knees-up in a brewery let alone the delicate matter of people stripping to the buff and plunging into a pool on a chilly autumn night.

'Whyever did I suggest this? I must have been mad.'

'Well, you did and you'll have to get on with it. I did

say it was a bit daring but you didn't listen to me, did you?'

'No. Because I never do. Come on, what are you standing about for and holding me up? You're always so slow.'

They left at half past eleven. Jimbo and Harriet had organized several areas at the back of the Store for people to undress in. Everyone had been asked to bring their own bathing towel, to wear it until they stood at the pool edge, then swim two lengths, climb out, pick up their towel, drape it round themselves and go back inside to get dried. It all appeared very simple written on the now well-known clipboard, and Sheila knew nothing could go wrong. But she was horrified when she saw the flood-lights. Surely they were far too bright?

Jimbo agreed, and switched off two very prominent ones, which reduced the lighting to more a modest glow.

Sheila bent down and dipped her hand in the water. 'Jimbo, it's dreadfully cold.'

'Sorry, it's the very best we can do.'

'All right then, but it would have been better just that bit warmer.'

'It's not a bath, Sheila. This is the hottest it gets.'

Ron tried to calm her fears. 'They'll be in and out before they realize how cold it is. Don't worry, old girl.'

She swung round on him saying with gritted teeth. 'Don't call me "old girl" ever again. Not tonight nor any other night. I'm not your old girl.'

'You're right, you're not. Sorry.'

His abject apology did nothing to improve her nerves. She fluttered about with a major hysterical outburst only just below the surface. Gradually the people began to arrive, not just the swimmers but people wanting to watch. A split-second decision had to be made. 'Very well, then, five . . . no ten pounds to watch. OAP's five pounds. Everybody stand this side of the pool so's not to get in the way of the swimmers jumping in. That's right, this side, and you can put your ten-pound notes in this box here look.' She produced a cash box from inside her bag with a flourish rather like a magician and held it under their noses. Inspired, she called out, 'And another five pounds for each camera.'

Things were getting out of hand. There were people all over the place. She couldn't cope. Why had she ever thought of this? She must be the biggest fool. She'd have to move. That's what, she'd move house 'cos she'd never dare show her face again in the village. Ever.

Somehow it all sorted itself out and before she knew it, the church clock had struck twelve, Jimbo had rung a handbell to announce the start of the swim and they were off!

Gilbert jumped in, they just caught a glimpse of his powerful shoulders and his long legs and he was in swimming furiously, he did a very professional turn at the end of the pool, swam a stunning butterfly stroke all the way back, leaped out and grabbed his towel. It was Gilbert they'd all fancied seeing but he'd jumped, swum, turned, swum and got out before they'd had a chance to admire his physique. Bit disappointing that.

Next was Maggie Dobbs wanting to get it over with before she lost her nerve. She'd certainly lost weight and was looking positively sylphlike as she sat on the edge and slipped in. She swam much more slowly than Gilbert but nevertheless put up a good performance – she'd never let on she'd been to Culworth pool to practise – and they clapped her as she got out. In her haste to be decent she dropped the towel as she was putting it round herself and got a cheer and a loud 'Wow!' from someone.

Paddy had had two swift double whiskies in the Store kitchen just before he ventured out, so swam his two lengths in an alcoholic haze. He got thunderous applause for bowing to them all, before he put the towel back on.

By this time there were villagers peering over the hedgerow by standing on chairs they'd dragged out from their homes. It was the best entertainment they'd had in years. All free, too. But not for long. Sheila came round shaking her cash tin and telling them she was disgusted with them for leering over the hedge and they weren't going to escape her tin.

Next to come was Greta Jones. Whether it was on purpose or not – he flatly denied later that it was, but the music which Jimbo played for her appearance was not *Fingal's Cave* as he'd promised but the cancan, so she made her way to the pool kicking her legs as high as she dare, flinging her towel down and leaping into the pool like a twenty-year-old. The crowd roared their approval and those balancing on chairs the other side of the hedge had to hang on to each other for fear of falling off as they cheered and laughed every inch of the way.

There hadn't been a night in the village when everyone had had such fun.

Dean and Rhett followed next, they'd had an argument in the bar and bet each other they wouldn't dare, but they did, and the two of them swam together side by side. Angie Turner came next and she got wolf whistles because her figure was so slim and taut, and altogether delightful. It put the pyjama party right in the shade.

Despite the hour and the cold, they stayed there until the end and no one took fright and wouldn't swim; after all, there was too much money at stake. The last one to go was Harriet Charter-Plackett. She'd just turned to begin her second length when a loud noise, not unlike a police siren, could be heard approaching. At first no one noticed except for Sheila who heard every waver of the siren and went into complete hysteria, though somewhat relieved that Jimbo must have gone to attend to them because he was nowhere to be seen.

Then, before it registered with anyone else, two powerful torches were making their way across the garden and a loud voice said, 'Now then, what's going on here?'

It was the two police officers who had arrested Greta Jones and Grandmama Charter-Plackett that day in the market. Someone snatched up Harriet's towel and held it up so she could climb out of the pool with complete modesty. The main floodlights, which Jimbo had turned off, sprang to life and there they all were, watching in horror. The two police officers took out their notebooks. The larger of the two said, 'Streaking in public, causing a furore, causing a public nuisance − what is going on?'

Jimbo, who had returned, began to explain.

'Who organized this?'

There was a silence and then Jimbo replied, 'The Women's Institute.'

'I need a name.'

What could Sheila do but step forward? 'Me.'

'Name?'

'La . . . Sheila Bissett.' Couldn't say 'Lady', it obviously wasn't a thing a Lady would do.

'What is the purpose of this exhibition?'

'To raise money for the New Hope Fund.'

Greta Jones had appeared in the garden having now dressed herself and was wondering why the music had stopped. When she recognized the two police officers she almost had a heart attack. Thank God she was dressed.

'Names, we need the names of everyone. No one is to leave without giving their name.'

So they went round taking names. Most of the crowd were dreadfully shocked by what was happening. If this turned into a prosecution they might be mentioned in the *Gazette*. Then what would people say? They'd never get over it. It'ud give Turnham Malpas a bad name and not half. So a few gave false names, others were truthful and Jimbo tried to intervene by saying, 'Now, come on, officers, we're doing it for charity, not to leer and to be disgusting. The swimmers are all sponsored, you see.'

'Have you got police permission for this, then?'

Everyone looked at Sheila.

'Police permission? I didn't know we needed it. It's just a private party.'

'Private party you say? Really?' The officer looked sceptical at this and pointed to the frozen figures standing on chairs, though there were fewer than at first as some had taken the chance to scuttle home with their chairs when they realized names were being taken. Then, extra loud unfamiliar music broke the silence; it was certainly stick-your-fingers-in-your-ears kind of volume. The police constable taking the notes suddenly flung his notepad over his shoulder and in time to the music began unbuttoning his jacket. What the . . .

Then the second officer also began stripping off.

They'd all been taken in! It was a joke, a kissogram! But what a finish to a midnight skinny-dipping. Two people laughed so much they fell off their chairs, someone got pushed, fully-clothed, into the pool and the roar of laughter which went up could be heard in Little Derehams as they realized how they'd been fooled.

The policemen stripped with hilarious skill. Slowly the process of undressing reached the climax and, low and behold, under their uniforms the policemen were wearing bikinis with false bosoms and both of them leaped into the pool and swam a couple of lengths to the cheers of the crowd. The crowd clapped louder still as the two policemen clambered out.

So, who's joke was this? Who was the guilty party? Harriet, caught in the nude by this practical joke, had a lot to say to Jimbo after she'd got dressed. Her teeth were chattering with the cold but she managed to splutter out, 'Jimbo! It was you, wasn't it? You organized it? No one else would have the bottle to do it.'

Jimbo tried hard not to let on but the twinkle in his eyes gave the game away. 'It wasn't me, no certainly not, well . . . all right then, it was me.'

'You do realize that I was swimming when they came in?'

'You?!'

'Yes, me. Just starting my second length. If it hadn't been for Gilbert I'd have had to climb out in full view. The water was so damn cold I couldn't have stayed in another minute.'

'What did Gilbert do?'

'He grabbed my towel and held it over the pool so I could get out discreetly underneath it.'

Jimbo clapped a hand to his forehead. 'He saw you . . . you know.'

Harriet primly replied, 'I hope, being a gentleman, he had his eyes closed.'

'I'm sorry.' Someone called his name, he turned to go

but then a thought struck him. 'You never said . . . you rogue. I'd no idea you'd put your name down.'

'As one of the younger members of the Women's Institute I had no alternative. I had to swim.' Harriet pulled her coat more closely around her. 'They were the two who arrested your mother. How did you persuade them?'

'Someone told me they moonlight doing kissograms and such, it didn't take much to get them to do it.' He grinned. 'Thought it would make a good ending to the night's activities.'

'Mmmm. I'm going in to get warm. I'll never let you forget what you've done to me.' But as she hurried away, she looked back at him. 'Brilliant idea, though. Organize the hot toddies for everyone before I strangle you . . . slowly.'

Chapter 15

The Monday morning after the skinny-dipping event, Jimbo found another email from Peter.

To: Everyone at Turnham Malpas
From: New Hope Mission

There is no further news about the children. Caroline and I are shattered. The longer we wait the more likely it seems they have fallen victim to the rebels. It is becoming dangerous here as the rebels are gathering strength by the day. All our outlying villages are subjected to unimaginable savagery. Consequently few of our congregation dare walk to church. All Europeans have been asked to leave the area but we cannot go till we find the children. No news yet from Elijah. We pray that they are hiding in the bush. God bless you all, and we thank you from the bottom of our hearts for your prayers.
Peter and Caroline

Jimbo pinned the email to the Village Voice noticeboard with a heavy heart. He'd been late getting into the Store that morning, leaving Bel and Tom to start the day for him. Consequently the first person he met was Maggie Dobbs.

'You've survived, then?'

Maggie grinned. 'I have indeed. What a challenge! I'd another hot toddy when I got home I was so cold. But well worth it. Just waiting for the dinner ladies to come then I can collect my sponsorship money.'

'Have you seen Sheila yet?'

'No. I understand she's close to total collapse after Saturday night. I think the police arriving was the final straw. I can't make out who did that.'

Jimbo gave her a wicked wink.

'It was you! You devil you. Wait till I tell them at the W.I. meeting tonight, they'll be shocked.'

'A committee that could think up all these devilish fundraising ideas won't be shocked by a couple of police officers.'

Maggie agreed. 'Perhaps you're right. They say it'll be in the *Gazette* this week. Wonder if there'll be any photographs?' She giggled a little then, catching sight of Jimbo endeavouring to look innocent, she began playfully beating him with her umbrella. 'Take that and that! If I'm in one of the photos there'll be trouble and not half. What a trick!'

Maggie was joined by several others coming in for a good gossip about Saturday night and it tuned into an impromptu W.I coffee morning in the Store. Jimbo's coffee pot was refilled before half past nine.

In their usual efficient way they discussed any lessons that needed to be learned. Where had they gone wrong? Would it have been better if . . . How about next time?

'Next time!' Unaware she sounded like Dame Edith Evans saying 'In a handbag?' Grandmama Charter-Plackett added, 'Surely to goodness we're not doing it again. Once is quite enough.'

'Well, perhaps not skinny-dipping but something similar.' Harriet grinned.

'But what?' Greta Jones asked. 'That's the problem. We've been so outrageous it'll be difficult to think up something new. And I'm certainly not doing the cancan like I did, that's definitely off the list.' They all roared with laughter at the memory of Greta dancing towards the pool.

Sylvia, shopping for herself and Willie and wishing she was in there ticking off Caroline's list instead, warned, 'We'll just have to be more strict about police permission. If we're not careful the committee's going to be up in court. We were daft not to think about it. How about the gambling afternoon? That could be a problem.'

Harriet, hoping she was correct, said, 'But we're not actually placing bets *actually* on the afternoon, are we? We've paid for them when we bought our tickets. Anyway it's too late now.'

There was a general murmur of agreement. 'Ah! Right. Yes. Of course.'

Jimbo, enjoying listening to their conversation while concentrating on perking up the cold meat counter, thought then of Peter's email and his heart sank. Poor Peter had an awful lot more on his mind than the whys and wherefores of police regulations. If it were his Flick and Fran missing he'd be frantic and not roaring his head off at the memory of Greta Jones doing the cancan. One felt so helpless.

As Maggie had said, Sheila was still struggling to throw off the effects of Saturday night. She'd spend what was left of the night in restless sleep and all day Sunday she hadn't been worth a row of pins. She'd made up her mind to take Monday very slowly indeed.

'It's no good, Ron, I'm not getting up yet. I still ache and all I want to do is sleep. I'm exhausted and there's the W.I. Committee meeting to chair tonight and I can't cry off that. I feel as if I haven't slept for a week. No, a month.'

'Don't forget it was very successful, one of the most successful efforts we've ever had. Well, since we came to live here anyway.'

'Yes, you're right. That hoax of Jimbo's made for a good ending for the night, didn't it?' She had to smile about it, though at the time she'd thought she would die. 'I've got a good committee, you know, they all support everything we do. I think I'll suggest Maggie Dobbs for the committee when it comes to the year end. There's more to her than I first thought.'

Ron laughed. 'There is! When she dropped her towel . . . Wow!'

'That's not funny.' Sheila lifted her head from the pillow. 'I thought she looked quite good for a woman her age.'

'That's what I meant. She looked good, in fact very good.'

'Ronald Bissett! Do something useful and make me some breakfast. I'll have a croissant out of the freezer with butter and a banana.'

'I don't know what to do with a croissant. Have toast instead.'

'I want a croissant and you know exactly what to do, it's just that you're bone idle.'

The phone rang and Ron went to answer it. He came back upstairs and stood in the bedroom looking at her.

'Well?'

'Sheila . . .'

'That's me.' His demeanour worried her. 'What is it, Ron?'

'Sheila . . .'

He appeared to her to be having difficulty speaking and a terrible fear came over her.

Ron tried again. 'It's Louise.'

'What about her?'

'Gilbert's going to rush her to hospital.'

'I knew it. It's the baby, isn't it?' She sprang out of bed, looking at Ron, waiting for his reply.

'She's gone into premature labour.'

'What! But it's much, much too soon.'

'Exactly. Gilbert wants us to go.'

'Of course. Oh Ron, I've always known there was something wrong with this baby. Things haven't been the same this time. Out of my way.' She pushed him aside and raced for the bathroom.

Ron drove as fast as he dare to Keepers Cottage. But Gilbert and Louise had already left and one of the Bliss twins was standing outside waiting for them.

'Mr Johns says will you have the children? They're all at our house.'

Sheila and Ron turned on their heels and dashed down to the Blisses' cottage. Eleanor had them all eating their breakfast. The baby was in a makeshift high chair and, as she hadn't enough chairs for everyone, the three older ones were standing round her table, eating from cereal bowls.

Sheila called out, 'Children, here's your nana come to love you all. Mrs Bliss, thank you so much. I can't thank you enough. I really can't.' She kissed the baby, hugged the others, smiled at the Bliss family and generally caused confusion.

Eleanor Bliss smiled and restored order, then began calmly toasting bread for them all. 'Have you had breakfast, Lady Bissett?'

'No. We came as soon as we could after Gilbert rang. Please, call me Sheila.'

'I'll get you some then. Tea all right?'

Ron and Sheila nodded. Eleanor put a massive brown glazed teapot on the table and began pouring cups of tea. Weak and sweetened for the children, and unsweetened and stronger for the adults.

'I don't think Louise allows the children—'

Ron gave Sheila a dig. 'I'm sure it won't matter for once, Sheila, in the circumstances. Thank you, Eleanor, for this. You're an angel. Now sit down on the sofa, Sheila, and I'll bring your tea and toast across. Will toast do?'

Sheila nodded. She sat quietly munching her toast and then suddenly burst out, 'Eleanor! I don't think there'll be a baby, do you?'

'I very much doubt it. Poor Louise she will be upset, but perhaps it's for the best. These things happen for a reason sometimes, don't they?'

Sheila looked straight at her and pondered on her wisdom. 'I expect they do. All the time I've known she was expecting, I've felt things weren't right with this one.'

'Louise thought the same, she was very worried.'

Sheila was appalled that Louise could confide in Eleanor and not her own mother. What were mothers for if not for confidences? Still, she seemed an intelligent person, did Eleanor, and had probably said just the right thing, which Sheila knew she most likely wouldn't have done.

When she'd finished her toast and tea, Sheila said

urgently, 'I want to go and see Louise. Right now. She needs her mother. Ron, can we go?'

'There's the children, Sheila.'

Eleanor gave them the answer. 'Never mind about them. It's fine, they can all play in the garden and my girls will be delighted to play with them. Please, just go.'

Ron put £30 in her hand as he was leaving. 'Get one of the boys to cycle to the Store, get some food in. Can't expect you to feed five more children. Here's Louise's spare key. If there's anything you need from the house, nappies and things, feel free. We'll be as quick as we can.'

'Ron! Ron! Come on, please.' Sheila was waiting by the car, cross that Ron was taking so long.

The moment she entered the maternity hospital Sheila became seriously agitated. She knew she wasn't a big enough person to cope with this. She just was not. Then she remembered Saturday night's success and decided maybe she was more capable than she felt.

It was the smell which alarmed her. Disinfectant and polish and cleanliness. At least it all looked very clean, which was more than could . . . The sister came to speak to them.

'Louise Johns's parents? Would you come this way, please?' She took them into a side room and sat them down. 'The baby was almost here when they arrived.'

Sheila blurted out, 'It's come, then. Is it all right?'

'I'm afraid the baby is very ill.'

Ron asked the question Sheila couldn't say for the life of her. 'Are you . . . are you hopeful for it?'

'We're doing our best, but . . .' The sister closed her lips and shook her head. 'I'm sorry.'

Sheila, desperate to know more, managed to say, 'Is it perfect, but come too early?'

'Too early and not perfect.'

Bile rose in Sheila's throat. 'Can you *see* it's not . . . perfect?'

'Yes.'

Ron asked, 'What is it?'

'A boy.'

'Just what she wanted. Can we see her?'

'It'll be a while before you can see her.'

Sheila asked, 'Can we see the baby?'

'Not at the moment. He's being assessed.'

They waited an hour and a half to see Louise. She was whiter than white, if that were possible, all her natural rosy colour hidden by a kind of grey sweat, her hair straggled across the pillow in the most unbecoming way, and she was gripping Gilbert's hand as though her very life depended on it.

'Louise, I'm so sorry. So sorry.' Sheila leaned over and kissed her, then stood back for Ron to do the same.

'We'll get through this. We've to be grateful for the five lovely ones you've already got.' Ron kissed her, too. He then went to the other side of the bed and gripped Gilbert's shoulder. 'I'm very, very sad for you both, Gilbert. Is there anything we can do?'

Gilbert mustered up some courage from somewhere and said cheerfully, 'Would you like to see the baby? We've called him Roderick. He's a grand little chap and fighting hard.'

When Sheila saw the baby she almost cried out in her agony. Grand little chap? Fighting hard? How on earth could Gilbert think for one single moment this tiny scrap of a human being would survive?

He was in an incubator, wired up all over the place, tubes and pipes and plastic this and that, even tubes up his tiny nostrils, and machines whirring away. His little chest was pumping up and down very fast. He was so tiny, there was nothing of him to do any fighting. Gilbert was deluding himself. She couldn't describe all the things that appeared to her to be wrong with him. They were too terrible and too numerous to count. Why couldn't they cover him with a blanket to hide some of his problems? Though he didn't need covering to keep him warm, the temperature in the unit was extremely high. Sheila began to feel faint.

Ron had to take her out. He shook his head at Gilbert, who seemed mesmerized by what had happened. Gilbert followed them out and in answer to the shake of the head Ron gave him said, 'They'll pull him round, don't you worry. They work miracles nowadays. He's got a good team fighting on his side.'

Ron burst out, 'Is that the kindest thing to do? To *fight* for him?'

Gilbert's eyes were cold when he answered. 'Of course. He's our baby and whatever he needs he'll get. *Don't* say a word of how you feel to Louise, I won't have it.'

'Of course not. Of course not.' Ron gripped Sheila's arm even more tightly and placed a finger against her lips. 'Not a word. OK?'

'Does she know?' Sheila whispered to Gilbert.

'Of course she knows. It's going to be a long hard fight, but he has brothers and sisters who'll help him, and parents who want him and love him. He's our flesh and blood, and don't forget he's yours too. He's going to be fine.'

In desperation Sheila gripped his arm and said softly, 'Oh, Gilbert, don't ask it of him, it isn't fair.'

Gilbert brushed her hand from his arm and said emphatically, as though convincing himself as well as them, 'He's ours, and he's going to live. Believe me. Whatever it costs. And don't say that to Louise. Do you hear?'

'He hasn't the will to fight, Gilbert. He's no strength.' She didn't dare mention his disabilities, but in her mind she could see his twisted feet and that appalling harelip.

'He has. I'll go talk to him if you'll stay with Louise.'

Ron and Sheila stayed with Louise until lunch-time and then went home to care for the children. Before he left Ron bent over the bed and whispered in Louise's ear, 'Take care, love. Don't be too disappointed if things don't work out as you'd like. He's very frail. Very frail. Perhaps the good Lord in his wisdom'll take him back for his sake and he'll be one of His angels.'

'Shut up, Dad, you're being ridiculous. Give the children my love.' She took his hand in both of hers and squeezed it in the most loving gesture she'd given him since she was a little girl. Ron went out blowing his nose, and stood in the corridor, hands clenched by his sides, hoping Sheila wouldn't be long.

Sheila wasn't. She gave Louise a peck on the cheek, gripped her hand and said, 'Don't be too disappointed, it might be all for the best. He looks so poorly.'

Louise burst into tears and cried, 'Gilbert! Gilbert!'

So Sheila left the two of them hugging each other, weeping together. She looked back at them from the door and couldn't bear to witness such appalling grief. They didn't deserve it. Ron was waiting; he wouldn't be crying. But he was.

They had to see the children. They'd stay with them in Keepers Cottage; they'd feel safer there with all their own things about them. Someone had to be strong.

Baby Oliver, not yet one year old, missed Louise the most and caused the biggest problem. When it came to putting him in his cot he howled. Missing his nightly routine with Louise, too young to have anything explained to him, he was inconsolable. The older ones seemed to accept her and Ron putting them to bed, despite their ineptitude at coping with so many children. Finally they were all asleep except for young Gilbert. 'Nana, will Mummy be better soon?'

'Yes. She will. She'll be back home in no time taking care of you all.'

'When Daddy spoke on the phone he said the baby was very, very poorly.'

'Yes, he is.'

'Nana, will the baby be coming home?' Young Gilbert pulled the duvet up and snuggled down. 'Do you think, perhaps, he won't ever come home?'

'Well, not yet a while. We'll have to wait and see.'

'I think he's too poorly to come home. He is, isn't he? He's not coming home, is he?'

'We'll have to be patient, but don't build up your hopes just yet.'

'I see. Perhaps he's an angel, come down to earth by mistake. Say it, Nana. Say it.'

Sheila tucked the duvet round his shoulders. 'Sleep tight and mind the bugs don't bite.'

She heaved herself down the stairs and went into Louise's kitchen to make a cup of tea for her and Ron. She stood leaning against the worktop, looking round while she waited for the kettle. This kitchen was only half the size of her own. Same with the living room. She could have sat an army down in her own and here was Louise coping with this little house and five, her mind shied away from saying six, children. The very best thing they could do was swap houses with her and Gilbert. It would be Louise's anyway in time, because her brother never communicated, was wealthy beyond belief and didn't need a thing she and Ron might, in time, leave behind them.

Once all the upset was over, she'd suggest it to Ron. Give Louise something to focus on. Something to think about, because that baby wouldn't survive no matter how much loving attention he got. In fact, he mustn't survive, for his own sake, the poor little scrap. The kettle whistling brought her to her senses and, as she watched the crystal-clear water pouring into the teapot, it brought to mind christening the baby.

'They'll have to get it done, Ron, without a shadow of a doubt. Can't waste any time. Here's your tea.'

Ron sank gratefully down into a chair with his cup. 'We'll have to suggest it very carefully.'

'I know that. But the others were all christened so we've to make things the same, before it's too late.'

'You're right.'

'The other thing is this: how about us and Louise swapping houses?'

'Eh? What?'

'Look here, Ron, we don't need a cottage the size of ours. Your Union speaking jobs and such are coming to a close—'

'Just a minute—'

'Well they are, you know that and so do I. When was the last time we had anybody staying for a meeting or whatever. When did the TV ring up and ask for your opinion? Ages ago! When did the Union last send for you for your advice? Even longer ago. This small house might not have as much style as ours, but it would be enough for the two of us, wouldn't it? And they need it.'

'Well, their garden wouldn't take as much looking after. It would cut down on our heating bills too, and the community charge, wouldn't it?'

'Exactly. Christening first and then moving house.'

'You've missed out a rather important factor there. There's Roderick, remember?'

'I haven't forgotten Roderick, but it will take Louise's mind off things, won't it?'

'You might think it's a good idea but what about Gilbert? He might not.'

'Oh, you and Gilbert. You'll just have to give in and do it. I'm determined. They need our big bedrooms; we certainly don't, now do we?'

Ron thought about how heavy the spade had seemed when he'd sorted out their endless flowerbeds for the winter. Gilbert, with his physique, would have them sorted in no time at all. He was used to digging, being an archaeologist. Perhaps Sheila was right. But he'd put it off for a while. 'All in good time, Sheila. We mustn't rush things. They're very distressed right now.'

'Oh, I know. So am I.' She burst into tears, put down her cup and cried as though her heart was breaking, which it was, for all of them. Herself included. That beautiful picture she always had in her mind of Gilbert and Louise wandering happily through a wood carpeted with blue-bells and the children scattered about playing, with the sun shining through the trees and looking so enviable and perfect, had shattered into fragments. She'd see Anna first thing, then she remembered she was no longer the free agent she'd been for years. First she'd have five children to feed and dress before she went anywhere at all. To say nothing of the daily washing machine routine. As she carried the tea tray back to the kitchen, she thought about Roderick's tiny toes and how sweet those tiny toes would have been if only his feet were perfect . . . Life for the whole family would be a living hell. And for poor little Roderick, a hell he didn't deserve. Years ago he would have died almost immediately and he'd have been back with God where he truly belonged. She mopped her eyes, blew her nose, straightened her shoulders and accepted her burden.

Gilbert had already rung Anna and told her of their situation. 'Could you come? Louise wants the baby baptised as of now, and what she wants she gets at the moment.'

'Gilbert, I'm so sorry, I hadn't heard. Of course I'll come. Today. Lunchtime. Will you want Sheila and Ron there? Of course you will, I shouldn't need to ask. One o'clock?'

'Can I ring you back? We shan't want the children there and Ron and Sheila are caring for them at the moment so I'll have to organize them all. Parcel them out. I'll ring back.'

So when one o'clock came they were gathered at the hospital. Roderick looked so sweet with his tiny blue woollen hat on his tiny head in spite of the machines and the bleeping and the tubes. The unspoken words in everyone's mind were – if only everything was all right. But it wasn't, as they all knew.

Anna conducted a lovely service, so poignant and tender, with soft, loving words, full of meaning, which tore the heart. Ron and Sheila stood in as godparents and though it only lasted a few minutes they felt they'd done the right thing. Ron wheeled Louise back to her room and they all had a glass of champagne and drank a toast.

'To Roderick, our dear little son, God bless him.'

Before she left Anna kissed Louise, then Sheila, then Ron and last of all Gilbert.

She lingered for a moment with her hand on his arm to say, 'Keep strong. They all need someone like you.'

But it was Sheila who kept strong and held them together, not Gilbert. He was too distraught.

Chapter 16

In years past, no one had had much sympathy for Louise and still looked upon her as the troublemaker she'd been when she first came to the village, but the generosity in their hearts overrode that when they heard of little Roderick and all his problems.

'Dottie's working all hours helping Sheila and Ron. I understand there's no improvement in that little babe, poor little mite,' Greta Jones said on the Friday afternoon after Roderick was born.

Angie Turner, leaning against the big desserts freezer in the Store, said, 'Well, Dottie's lining her pockets, I can tell yer. I'm told Ron is paying her in gold bars, that glad they are to have her. Gilbert's got three weeks' leave, saw him getting out of his car at the rectory the other day. He was always lean before, but he's more like a walking skellington now. Looked terrible, he did.'

Greta moved to make way for someone wanting to search the freezer. 'They say he won't live. Well, yer can't win every time and they've had a good run.'

'Doesn't make it hurt less though, does it? You still love 'em, they're still yours.'

'Oh, yes, I'm sure. Oops! Time I wasn't 'ere. Jimbo'll be looking for me anytime. Two minutes past one! Heck! I'm definitely not 'ere.' Greta sped away into the back.

Within minutes she heard Gilbert's voice in the Store. No good, she had to get the latest. She dashed through from the back to offer her sympathy and hope little Roderick was improving. But Gilbert looked at her with eyes that had seen hell. Greta froze. His eyes shocked her to the core and the words died on her lips. 'Oh, Gilbert.' A great lump came in her throat and no more words would come.

In a dry, cracked voice shaking with emotion, Gilbert answered, 'The baby died late last night.' He hunched his shoulders and spread his hands with deepest despair.

It was on the tip of her tongue to say, 'Well, perhaps it's all for the best, with all his problems.' But she remembered what Angie had said about them all being precious no matter how many you had and instead told him how sorry she was and to give her love to Louise.

Gilbert's heart was filled with grief but above all with terror, because he didn't know how he would get through it all. If only he'd been there. Right when he was needed, where was he? Fast asleep in bed. Ron had sent him there at seven o'clock with the children because he hadn't slept since late on Sunday night and he'd shared young Gilbert's bed because his in-laws were in his. Ron and Sheila had gone back to the hospital to keep Louise and the baby company. Gilbert slept like a log until the clock reached midnight and Ron had come to wake him.

'Gilbert. Gilbert. You'll have to wake up. I've come to get you. Louise needs you. Gilbert?'

He'd felt a hand shaking his shoulder, dragging him into consciousness.

'Yes?'

'I'm afraid there's bad news from the hospital.'

Gilbert had sat up. 'Louise?'

'No, not her. It's little Roderick.'

'He's . . .'

'Gone, I'm afraid. I'd just been for a drink from the machine for Sheila and me, and when I came back, well, he'd passed away.' Man to man, Ron dared to speak his thoughts. 'I think perhaps for his sake we'd better be glad. There was too much wrong, Gilbert, the holes in his heart, his hare lip, the cleft palate, his limbs not straight. His life would have been a travesty of what it should be for a little boy. Now get up and go see Louise. I'll stay with the children, and we'll be here all day tomorrow, too.'

Gilbert had dressed in a complete daze and gone back to the hospital.

When he got there, Sheila was standing by the incubator, staring down at the baby. They'd taken all his tubes and machines away and he was laid for all the world as though fast asleep, wrapped in a crocheted shawl all the children had used when they were newborn. All she could say was, 'He's at peace now. He's at peace now.' Time after time, after time. She stood there, rooted to the floor, muttering, 'At peace now.'

'If you'd like to hold Roderick to say goodbye, Mr Johns, please do so.' The ward sister had said this in such a caring tone Gilbert had almost lost control and broken down in tears. So he picked up his son, carrying him for Louise to cuddle in her arms.

Someone came and led Sheila away so they could be on their own.

Standing in the Store, trying to remember all the things they needed, Gilbert couldn't believe that Sheila could be as lively and patient as she was this morning at breakfast. Last night she'd been out of her mind: this morning, it was as if nothing had happened at all. It worried him because it appeared so odd, but he concluded that grief affects people in all sorts of strange ways. He picked up three loaves of Jimbo's special wholemeal bread, two pounds of butter, two dozen eggs, a big pack of cheese, some baby food jars for Oliver to make life a little easier, meat from the fresh meat counter, then he abruptly stopped and stood staring into space again, remembering the feel of tiny Roderick in his arms when he'd carried him for Louise to hold for the first and last time. The child, so tiny, so frail, so without hope. He recalled how his heart broke when he witnessed Louise's painful distress as she cuddled him. Selfishly, the thought occurred to Gilbert that perhaps it was all for the best. Roderick would've needed hours of special care that would have meant the other five not getting the loving attention they needed and which was their right to expect. He berated himself for his thoughts, so dwelt again on the loss of his tiny son who'd had such a fragile hold on life and wept inside himself with grief, then decided there wasn't the remotest possibility that Roderick could have the joys of a carefree childhood, which young Gilbert, Rosalind, Jenna, Emily and little Oliver celebrated every day of their lives. Perhaps it was right what Sheila had said; he was at peace now, free from struggle, free from pain.

Chapter 17

Dean, shaken by witnessing Roderick's tiny coffin being taken into the church for the funeral, went to sit on the seat by the pond to think. Ever since that day in the vestry when he'd pressed Anna's hand to his lips and been observed by Muriel, Dean had been extremely upset. He'd known at that moment, when he'd realized Muriel's face was a curious mixture of sadness and disgust, that he could no longer let his life meander on. It had taken hours of deep thought to come to this decision, hours spent wide awake in bed, doodling on bits of paper at the office, long walks through the woods at night and poems galore. Nothing had stilled the raging passions inside him.

In a desperate attempt to calm his inner turmoil, he'd torn to pieces the beautiful, glossy William Morris cover of his book of poems, shredded the pages and furiously brushed away his tears, as the last few lines of his poetry shrivelled and blackened in the flames of the kitchen Rayburn. That was that. His big romance gone up in flames. Given the chance, he'd have married her tomorrow. But at the same time he knew she would never marry him.

She seemed to think he was capable of being more than an accountant in an insignificant office in sleepy old Culworth. Maybe he was. Just so glad of a job when he'd come down from Cambridge, he'd have taken almost any offer in order to qualify. He'd never rise to giddy heights in Neville's office, though. Comfortably off but nothing more. Besides, both Hugh and Guy Neal would inherit the business and he certainly couldn't work under those two, with their over-inflated self-esteem. He had to strike out alone.

He heard the mourners coming out of the church, so he quickly sprinted away across the Green, squeezed through a gap in the hedge between Glebe House and the brick wall surrounding the Big House estate, and cut across the field to home.

Grandad was dozing in the chair before the sitting-room fire, and his mother was nowhere to be seen. But she had left a note to say a college friend of his had rung. She didn't catch his name but he'd given a number to ring. The number was familiar but Dean couldn't just place it.

When Dean dialled the number he found it was his college friend Rory O'Donoghue on the other end of the line with the offer of a job.

'Chap just left Pa's office without notice and disappeared over the horizon with about a hundred and fifty thousand pounds of clients' money,' said Rory. 'This damned blackguard chose his moment to steal and took off when he knew Pa would be abroad. I'm desperate for a compatible right-hand man, who could sort out, as a matter of extreme urgency, exactly how this chap managed to steal it. Got to close the loophole AI sharp. Be a good chap and come, help me sort out the mess? We always got on well together, didn't we? Will you answer the call to arms?'

Without the slightest hesitation, Dean agreed to go up

to London immediately, and wrote a letter to Neville Neal explaining his hurried departure. Knowing what a stickler Neville was for protocol – and not caring, in fact – he almost smiled at the thought of Neville going ballistic at his lack of notice, and was packing his bag by the time his mother returned. She'd got a car now instead of that wobbly bike his stepfather had bought her years ago and he heard its unique engine noise long before she reached home. Ah! This was going to be hard.

'Dean! Am I glad to be home. Never ever am I going to a child's funeral ever again. It's too harrowing. They were all weeping and Gilbert and Louise looked as though they'll be next in a coffin. Put the kettle on, there's a love. It's been horrific. I stopped long enough for a cup of tea at Sheila's out of respect and then I left. Is Grandad OK? Put out another cup. He always manages to wake up just as the tea's brewed and then grumbles when I 'aven't put out a cup for him. You all right? You're very quiet.'

Pat slipped off her high-heeled shoes and put her house slippers on. 'That's better.' She sat on a kitchen chair and waited for Dean to serve her tea.

'Mum, that phone call was from Rory. Rory O'Donoghue.'

Pat thought for a minute. 'Oh! I remember him. He came here once, didn't he? Plum in his mouth and as ugly as sin.'

Dean had to smile. 'That's the one. He got a double first, he's very clever.'

'What did he want?'

'To offer me a job in London, in his dad's firm. Big accountancy company in the City. Prestige offices, pots of money, first-rate prospects.'

'That's a feather in your cap, then.' She pondered what

he'd said, glad he had a steady job in Culworth, which she was sure he wouldn't want to leave, well in truth *she* didn't want him to leave. 'Pity you can't go.'

The door opened and in ambled Grandad. 'Tea on the go? Good, I'm just in time.' He launched himself into a chair and held out his cup. 'Strong, that's right. Thanks.' He had a drink of his tea and then looked at the two of them. 'Missed something, have I?'

Dean rushed through the story, unable, as yet, to say his case was already packed.

Grandad looked Dean straight in the eye and said, 'Take it, lad. Take it. You'll never get another chance like this. Just go. I'll be glad to see you out of that Neville Neal's clutches. He's a slimy toad.'

'Dad! It's none of your business.' Pat couldn't believe her ears.

'It is. Dean's far too good for that office, and I want him to go. When does he want you to start?'

'Immediately. He says I can have a room in his flat till I find somewhere.'

'Pack yer bags and get off. Don't worry about leaving Neville Neal in the lurch; he wouldn't think twice about sacking you on the spot if he felt like it, believe me. Your horizons won't half be widened. London. Fancy. Never thought I'd have a grandson in a City office. It'll make me right proud, Dean, and not half. As for Mr Fitch! Well, he'll be like a dog with two tails, when he finds the money he gave you for university has brought such dividends.'

'I think, Dad, you'd do best to keep your mouth shut. I don't want him to go.'

'Don't hold him back, Pat. He needs to go. Spread his wings a bit.'

Dean stood up. 'Right, I will.'

'Stay where you are, Dean, please.' Pat banged her fist on the table and looked defiant. But Dean left to go upstairs to make a pretence of packing his case.

Quietly, so his voice wouldn't carry up the stairs, Grandad said, 'Listen to me, Pat. I don't think you've realized that he's been pining for Anna Sanderson. He's been in love with her since the day she came. What do you suppose all the new clothes were about? And borrowing your pyjamas for that party? He'd never have made such a fool of himself wearing them if it hadn't been for how he felt about her.'

Pat was astounded. 'Anna? Carrying a torch for Anna? For heaven's sake, Dad, you must be going senile if you think that. Our Dean? I don't believe it.'

'It's true. I know what I'm talking about. It's been making him ill. He needs to go away to get her out of his system. So untie the apron strings and send him off with a smile. He's going to a job, he's got somewhere to live till he finds his feet, he'll be OK. You see, Pat, we all have to fly the nest sometime, don't we?'

'How do you know about Anna? Has our Dean told you?'

'No, but I have got eyes. Never looked at his face when we've been talking about her?'

'Well, no.'

'If you had, you'd have seen the glow, but just recently the light's gone out, so he must have realized it was hopeless. I'm damned sorry for him.'

'I'd no idea. Anna? But she's years older than him. Years. What did he think would come out of that? Mmmm?'

'The love story of the century, I expect.'

Pat drew a pattern on the kitchen table with her finger and eventually said, 'If that's the case he's better out of it. You're right. I'll smile. But it'll break my heart. I wonder, did she encourage him, do you think?'

'I think she might have been just as friendly and open as she is with everyone else, and that Dean made no progress at all. Anyway, he won't have to see her now, will he?'

The doorbell rang and a voice called out, 'Pat? It's Anna from the rectory. Can I come in?'

Grandad and Pat looked at each other in horror. Eventually Pat shouted back, 'Of course, you're welcome. We're in the kitchen.'

Anna came in. She was wearing the clerical collar with the thigh-length black jacket and narrow black trousers that she'd worn for the funeral. 'Good morning, Mr Stubbs. How's the rheumatism? Better, I hope? Morning, Pat.' She shook hands with them both.

Pat offered her a cup of tea.

'Wonderful, I'm absolutely parched. It's been one of the most difficult mornings of my life. Funerals are never easy but this one . . . the poor little mite, we shouldn't question the wisdom of God, but my word I came close this morning.'

'The service was beautiful, all credit to you. You were wonderfully understanding.'

Rather ruefully Anna replied, 'I expect Peter would have done it better.'

Pat smiled. 'Perhaps he would, but you came a very, very close second. Sugar?'

'No, thanks, I've come about the lunch we're doing for the Senior Citizens' Club. Is it possible you could organize it, Pat? I've got a good team of volunteers but what they need is a well-qualified organizer, and I thought you'd be just the one.'

Pat was having difficulty in concentrating on what Anna was saying due to her shock about Dean, but said, 'Give me the date and I'll check I'm not working for Jimbo that day.'

'Of course.' Anna dug about in her briefcase and brought out her sizeable diary. 'It's the twenty-fifth of next month, quarter to one for one o'clock. The new dishwasher will be installed by then so that'll be a help.'

'We need it. Glad you persisted. I did notice that those who said it was all too much expense were the very ones who're never seen washing up, ever.' She flicked through her diary and agreed she was free that day. 'I'll do it. Thanks for asking me.'

'Not at all. I'm the one who should be doing the thanking. It'll be a full house, you know what they're like when there's food supplied. But it's a new venture and I want it to work out very well indeed, which I'm sure it will now you're on board. Now . . .'

Dean walked into the kitchen case in hand. Anna had deliberately called when she thought he would be working and had to swiftly change the expression of surprise on her face. 'Hello, Dean. Going on holiday?'

Dean's face flushed and his throat clammed up, but he managed to apologize for not being at the Youth Club on Friday. 'I've got the offer of a job in the City, you see, right out of the blue, and I've taken it. Leaving right now.'

Anna got to her feet and went to shake his hand. 'What did I say? You've done the right thing, I'm absolutely positive. I admire you for striking out, it's not easy. Isn't it brilliant, Pat?'

'It is. I'm very proud. A really good chance.' Pat

succeeded in sounding pleased but it was extremely hard to put the right amount of enthusiasm in her voice. 'Very proud. We won't know him when he comes back.'

Dean went even redder because Anna was still holding his hand. She let it go and patted his arm. 'Well done. Must be off.' She picked up her gloves and bag and made for the door. 'Ring me, Pat, if need be. Run an eye over the menu, tell me if you want any changes. I'll leave it here on the table for you. Bye, everyone.' She gave a careless wave in their direction and left, but not before she'd heard Dean say he'd put his case in the car.

So he followed her out and they stood talking. 'It's a wonderful opportunity. I'm glad you're going. Well, I mean—'

'Glad I'll have something else to think about other than you?'

'No, no, I didn't mean that.'

Dean drew in a long breath to brace himself to say, 'I realize nothing between you and me is possible, we're worlds apart. But I love you very much, more than ever if that counts for anything. It hurts badly.' He smiled ruefully. 'At least you remember my name now, I suppose that's progress. If ever you're in London . . . I'll let you have my address and phone number.'

'Of course it hurts, and in many ways I'm proud someone worthwhile like you chose me to love. Certainly, if ever I'm in London, I'll look you up. We could go for a meal, couldn't we? But you do see . . .'

'Yes, I do see, I'm not stupid. Best wishes for the rest of your stay here.' Vowing not to return until the end of July when Peter would be back, he took hold of her free hand and pressed it to his lips, and continued to grip it tightly.

Then he couldn't resist saying, 'And Gilbert. How do you stand there?'

'Today, I only have feelings of deepest sympathy for Gilbert after what he and Louise are going through. It's unbearable. Totally unbearable what they are having to face. They need each other more than they have ever done.'

Dean could have kicked himself for being so insensitive. 'Of course, I'm so sorry. Forget I said that.' He was still gripping her hand, then leaned forward, as though he might kiss her on the lips for the very first and last time.

'Dean, please, no!'

Reluctantly he let go her hand and turned to go into the house to say goodbye to his mother.

Anna called after him, 'Take care, Dean!'

Pat had watched him kiss her hand and her heart ached for him. Her Dean. He'd always been so sensible all his life and now this. The pain which showed in his face broke her heart. 'Oh, Dean! I wish—'

Dean cut her short, not able to bear her sympathy. 'Bye, Mum. I'll ring when I get there and bring you up to speed.'

'Yes, of course, love.'

'Tell Barry . . . tell him I couldn't wait to go, I'll speak to him tonight. Can you tell Michelle? She'll be gob-smacked at the way I'm stepping out of line.'

'She'll be proud of you. Barry will be, too; he's always thought the world of you. Don't forget to say goodbye to yer grandad.' Pat gave him a huge big hug and managed to hold back the tears until she'd waved him off. So that was the end of another chapter, and she found it hard to take. Still, Michelle hadn't left yet, and didn't look like doing so. That was a comfort.

Comfort was not something Jimbo found when he read the latest email from Peter and Caroline.

To: Everyone at Turnham Malpas
From: New Hope Mission

We have been asked to move away from this area with the greatest speed. The rebels are becoming ever more confident. They now have control of the local radio so none of the news we are getting can be relied upon. All we know is that our dear children are still missing. We can hear guns firing quite close now, and have about thirty of our congregation living in the church in the hope they will be safer there than in their own homes. Winsome is doing the best she can to feed everyone but food is scarce as holding the daily market in the nearest township is impossible. Pray for us.
Peter and Caroline

Jimbo had never felt more useless in all his life. All those miles away and nothing he could do about it. Of course they couldn't leave. Save their own skins when their children were missing? Impossible. He dreaded to think what might have happened to them; in fact, his mind refused to contemplate their fate. He had to talk to someone about it. But who? Who had any influence? He clapped a hand to his forehead when he remembered Ralph. Of course, late of the diplomatic service, he'd be the very one. He might still know people who could help.

Knocking on Ralph's door at nine prompt, he found both Muriel and Ralph ready for visitors.

'I've come to show you this.' Jimbo said, and gave them the email to read.

Muriel blanched and Ralph, well, Ralph, even the least

perceptive person would have been able to see the ghastly distress on his face.

'Dear Lord, whatever next.' Ralph read the message again and then once more and then again. 'This is dreadful. If they don't get shot it sounds as though they might starve to death.'

'Is there anyone in the Foreign Office you might know who could help? Someone has to step in. They can't leave, you see, because of the children, though heaven knows they might not even be alive.'

Horrified at hearing her own thoughts spoken aloud, Muriel sat down on a chair with a handkerchief to her lips. 'Poor Caroline, poor Peter. Do something, Ralph, my dear.'

'I am. I'm going up to London. I'll pack a case, go there and cause a shindy. It's no good being politically correct and all stiff upper-lipped in circumstances like these. Positive action is needed. I'd no idea it was so bad out there. Things have definitely escalated these last few days.'

'It's not getting much attention from the media, is it, you see? Too many wars and things going on, for them to take interest in what appears to be a very local situation. I don't suppose we'd be taking much interest in it if it wasn't for Peter being out there.'

'That's the other point of attack, of course. The media! Muriel, organize me.'

Jimbo made to leave. 'I'll go and let you get started. If there's anything you need, just ring and I'll attend to it, only too glad to help. Petition or whatever. Good luck, Ralph. I'll leave it in your capable hands.'

To Jimbo's and everyone else's surprise, Ralph was featured on the national news the following day. He gave an intense and passionate run-down of Caroline and

Peter's situation, and even managed to slip in the fundraising efforts of the Turnham Malpas Women's Institute and how much they'd already raised towards helping the New Hope Mission and the medical clinic Caroline ran. Everyone in the village was glued to the TV waiting for a repeat on *The Ten O'Clock News* and spontaneous applause broke out when Ralph's piece finished.

In the Royal Oak, Dicky and Georgie decided on a free drink for everyone to toast Ralph, and Peter and Caroline.

Ron had taken Sheila in there to give her a break, but she couldn't bring herself to cheer when Dicky asked for three cheers for Ralph. She was too exhausted. OK, they'd got Louise home so Sheila and Ron were sleeping in their own bed, but the strain of caring for them all without Louise organizing everything was too much. Ron swore he'd lost half a stone these last two weeks; as for Sheila, she'd always wanted to be thin, now she'd no need to try, because her clothes were hanging loose on her.

'Ron,' she said, 'I want to go home. I'm so tired.'

'Stay a bit longer and then we'll be off. It'll look unfriendly if we leave now.'

'I am unfriendly. I don't want to speak to anyone. I just want to go home.'

But then Jimmy Glover called across, 'Sheila! About the afternoon at the races. Is it right that it's black and white? What yer wear, I mean?'

'That's right. All the tickets are sold, the champagne's bought and you should have chosen your horse by Tuesday. Write it on the form and give it to Colin Turner. Five of your fifteen pounds is for the bet. Colin's advising if you need any help, and if you don't choose, then he will choose a horse for you.'

'Right. Just wanted to make sure. I fancy Major Malpas. Seems like fate, yer know, Major Malpas.'

Someone else scoffed at his sentimental idea. 'It's one hundred to one, a rank outsider.'

'Not today he isn't. Latest is he's fifty to one, Major Malpas is, so he's got a better chance than we thought. I have a feeling in my guts that I'm right. I'm wearing my dinner suit and a white shirt.'

There was a burst of laughter at the thought of Jimmy in a dinner jacket. Paddy called out, 'You, in a dinner suit? It'll be worth going just for that.'

'Less of your cheek, Paddy Cleary. I could do a pretty smart tango at one time wearing my dinner suit. Competitions and that.'

More laughter.

'Tango? What's a tango?' Paddy asked, just to taunt him.

Jimmy had to laugh at himself. 'You haven't lived, you haven't. It's Latin American. Just you wait till the day. You'll see. I haven't put a pound on since I was twenty-one. It'll fit, believe me.'

'I fancy La Belle Royale,' said Vince Jones. 'She's a beauty, been winning or placed all season.'

There followed an in-depth discussion as to which horse they all fancied and what they were going to wear.

'You'd better make up your mind – there's only two weeks to go,' someone said.

Only two weeks to go, thought Sheila. However shall I manage? Heaven help me. She checked her diary. They were right, it was two weeks. 'Ron. I want to go home.'

Ron looked at her and saw the exhaustion and worry in the dark shadows under her eyes. This business of the baby had hit her hard. 'Come on, then, we'll go. Goodnight, everybody. Be seeing you.'

Sheila called out, 'Goodnight!' as they reached the door and as it closed behind them, Ron said, 'Let's have a walk before we go to bed, blow the cobwebs away.'

'Where to?'

'Just onto the spare land, have a look at the beck. It must be in flood with the rain we've had lately.'

So Sheila took his arm and they went off past their house and down the footpath behind Hipkin Gardens. Ron always took a torch with him when they went out at night. Sheila thought he was crackers for doing it, and said so frequently.

'We'll be glad of this some night. Believe me.'

'I've been waiting almost forty years for something to happen that made us need it and it hasn't happened yet.'

Ron tightened his arm to squeeze the hand tucked comfortingly into the crook of his elbow. He chuckled and then said, 'I've been meaning to say you're right about swapping houses with Louise. It's a sensible thing to do.'

'At last you've seen sense! Mind where you walk – I'm nearly in the long grass this side.'

They could hear the water rushing along under the footbridge even before they got there. It was pleasant to stand in the dark on the bridge, leaning over watching the beck rushing and pushing its way through the narrow gap and then on towards the river somewhere.

'Where does it go, Ron?'

'Finds its way to the River Cul, surely.'

'It doesn't matter what we do or don't do, it keeps going, doesn't it? On and on and on through the centuries. I wonder how long it's been running like this? It makes me feel very small and useless. It didn't even dry up in the summer when we had all that dry weather.'

Ron took her hand. 'You're very thoughtful tonight.'

'I feel all philosophic. If that's the right word. But most of all, I wish there wasn't the race meeting afternoon to organize. I've had enough.'

'Well, there is and we can't let everyone down. They're all looking forward to it. You can tell that from the way they were talking in the bar. I'll help as much as I can.'

'Thanks. It's knocked me sideways, what's happened.'

'It's knocked all of us sideways, most of all Louise and Gilbert. It'll be at least a year before—'

'They'll never forget. Never. It'll always be there, buried deep. You don't think they'll try for another one? Gilbert's always said they wanted six.'

'That's not for us to decide, is it?'

'No.' Sheila paused for a moment and then said, 'It isn't. It's for them and we shouldn't interfere. No, we shouldn't. We should never interfere. Never ever.' She gripped Ron's hand and continued staring at the water. 'I wonder if anyone has ever stared at this water and thought about ending it all?'

'Sheila! Don't talk rubbish! Of all things, saying that. Anyway, it's too shallow even when it's in spate, so you can cross that off for an idea.'

But Sheila didn't reply. Ron took her hand and urged her to set off for home.

Sheila remarked, 'Won't be our home much longer, will it?'

'We haven't mentioned it to them as yet, so we can always change our minds. We can do exactly as we wish.'

'We could always move somewhere entirely different. Leave it all behind us. I know what people think about you and me. They laugh at me. Not you. Me. They scoff because they think I'm an uneducated fool, that I always miss the beat with the way I dress, but I do try. And I behave like an idiot when I meet people like Sir Ralph, I get so het up.'

'I don't know what you're talking about. They all think you've done wonders with the fundraising for the New Hope Fund. No one, and I mean no one, can beat you at doing the flowers, there's something inside you that's very artistic and it comes out in flower-arranging. What's more, you're free to dress as you like, you know. What to wear isn't carved in stone.'

'Think so?'

'And with the W.I. You've really stirred them up, not that they needed much stirring up, but you know what I mean. One final effort and you can resign or whatever you want to do.'

'Ron, I know I don't treat you as I should. Is it possible to make up for past nastinesses, do you think?'

'I should imagine so, but you've always treated me just right.'

She was furious that he denied her her confession. 'You're lying. I haven't. I've been rotten to you. I wish Peter was here. He'd help me.'

'I expect he's having to do a lot of helping himself right now, poor chap. Come on, Sheila, let's go home.'

'I'll stay here a bit longer.'

'You won't. It's cold and looking like rain.' He took her hand and pulled her off the footbridge, switched on his torch and propelled her along the path. 'We're going home. Straight to bed with Horlicks and a hot water bottle and a couple of tablets for your bad head.'

'I haven't got a bad head.'

'Well, I say you have.'

When Ron had finally got Sheila to bed, he sat downstairs drinking a whisky, thinking. Ron wasn't given to thinking about anything much. Mostly he ambled on, doing as Sheila told him to do, and letting life pass him by. But tonight he was feeling strangely troubled. She'd had a terrible shock when little Roderick died, so had they all, but she didn't seem to be coming to terms with it.

It was worrying and he'd have liked to confide his worries to someone, but he couldn't think of anyone to turn to. Peter would have been the person with the right answer. Peter, poor chap. What a state of affairs that was. His children missing. Poor Caroline.

Ron went into the kitchen to rinse out his glass because Sheila hated going into the kitchen in the morning to find it smelling of an unwashed whisky glass. When he thought about it, like he was doing right now, she ruled every little corner of his life, and it was time he took charge. Maybe that was what she'd needed all these years, for Ronald Gladstone Bissett to take charge. Had he always been too soft? Too eager to please her right from the start? He stared out through the kitchen window into the dark of the night and remembered how he'd once said in the very early days he'd have liked to have been called Gladstone Bissett, it sounded so much more distinguished than Ronald, he thought, and much more heroic when he was up-and-coming in the TUC, but Sheila had laughed her head off, and when she could speak she'd said, 'You'd be nick-named Gladys and that would never do.'

He wasn't half the man that Gilbert was, with his gentle manners and his compassionate outlook on life, and his big family. He was a pillar of strength for Louise to lean on. Maybe he'd better be someone for Sheila to lean on.

When he went into the bedroom Sheila was whimpering in her sleep like a small child in the midst of a bad dream. Must be that dream she's been having about that lost child, thought Ron. He got into his pyjamas, lifted the goose-and-duck-down duvet Sheila had insisted upon, even when she knew he preferred blankets – 'Everyone who is anyone has duvets these days,' she'd protested – slid into bed as gently as possible so as not to wake her, scooped her up into his arms and held her close.

Chapter 18

The fact that no more had been heard from Peter and Caroline for several days was a matter of considerable concern for everyone. Was there any point in going ahead with the New Hope Fund race afternoon?

It fell to Anna to convince everyone that they must hold it. 'After all, the money is needed more than ever, surely? If Peter isn't there, someone will be and the congregation'll still need Bibles and church furniture, won't they?'

She felt certain, deep inside herself, that they would come home, all four of them, shattered by their experiences but safe. The mind, though, with the knowledge gained by the sort of intimate insight one got through viewing uprisings worldwide on the television thought differently. Just one small outburst, one wrong word, and they could all be shot dead or worse. She prayed earnestly every day for their safety. Surely the potential they both had for doing good wouldn't be cut short, would it? That would be too cruel.

Anna decided to go see Gilbert and Louise, one of the neediest of families in her care. Even before she got out of her car she could hear the noise they were making. Obviously they were out in the back garden, so she unlatched the gate, and went through to the back. Louise, holding Oliver in her arms, was watching the other children chasing Gilbert round the garden, trying to beat him with the sticks they were holding. There was a lot of laughter and shrieking and the children kept almost catching him but still he got away.

'Hi, there!' The chasing game abruptly stopped and they all turned to look at her. 'I came through, hope you don't mind. I thought perhaps you wouldn't hear the doorbell.'

Anna was horrified when Louise turned to greet her. She'd lost weight, a lot of weight, her hair hung lifelessly around her shoulders, and the worst of it was her face had grown old in a matter of weeks. All the happy content-ment in her marriage, her husband and her children had disappeared, to be replaced by total dejection and despair.

Gilbert looked scarcely any better than Louise. He had had no weight to lose but he had lost it anyway. His shoulder blades were evident, his back hunched, his eyes distraught. So the chasing and the laughter were put on for the sake of the children.

'Hi! What fun. Come and introduce yourselves, chil-dren. My name's Anna.' She pointed to young Gilbert. 'And you're Gilbert, and I know Baby Oliver,' he got a tickled tummy and she got a smile from him, 'but I'm afraid I don't know you girls.'

Louise helped her out. 'This one in blue is Rosalind, the one in red is Emily and this one here hiding behind me is Jenna. Say hello, girls.'

They did. Gilbert said nothing. It was left to Louise to invite her in. 'Please, we were just about to go inside for a drink. Shall you have one with us?'

'I'd be delighted, if it isn't too much trouble.' She followed Louise into the kitchen.

'One more won't make a big difference.' She started to

smile and then wiped it off. 'Sorry. I keep saying such stupid things. I have to keep going for the children, you see. I'm *compelled* to keep going for the children. After all, they still need feeding and dressing and taking to playgroup and ballet and things . . . I have to get up in the morning whether I want to or not.'

'It must be very difficult. I think you're doing marvellously well, considering.'

'Considering we've lost one of our babies?' Louise ran the tap and held the kettle under it.

Anna nodded. 'Well, yes, I did mean that, of course. What else could I mean?'

'I feel guilty, you see.'

'About what?'

'About not having scans and tests.'

'Are you saying you'd have had an abortion if you'd known?'

Louise turned off the tap and switched the kettle on. 'No, we wouldn't, we consider that murder.'

'Well, then. You did the only thing you could do, you waited to see.'

'We did. Yes. But why did he die?'

'Because he was too frail. He was much too early. He just didn't make it. You've nothing to blame yourself for. Nothing at all. Nature doesn't always behave perfectly as any wild animal could tell you . . . should they be able to speak.'

'Was it a punishment?'

'For what?'

'For Gilbert and I loving each other too much. Because we do. In the dark hours of the night I'm so glad it was Roderick and not Gilbert who died. Isn't that dreadful of me?'

'No, it's understandable. Very understandable in the circumstances. Every woman feels vulnerable when she has small children to bring up. It's only natural you should feel like that.'

'Since the first day I met Gilbert our lives have been so beautiful. We wanted children and we've got them. We wanted a rural life and we've got it. Now, out of the blue, this terrible blow, everything shattered into fragments. It's hard to understand and even harder to bear.' Louise began putting out cups and mugs. 'Mother's suggested that we change houses with her and Dad.'

'Now that is a good idea; hers is so much bigger.'

'I know it is, but this is *home*.'

'Yes, it is, but think of the convenience of two bathrooms and bigger rooms and a huge garden. I imagine your dad is well past keeping it in order, he'll be secretly relieved to hand it over.'

Louise agreed with her. 'Yes, but the upheaval. It's all too much.'

'It will give you something to focus on, won't it?'

Anna didn't get an answer for a moment and then Louise said after a deep breath, 'I need that. Something to focus on. I'm so frightened we'll never pull through this.' She stared out of the window, watching Gilbert brushing Emily down after a fall.

'Here, let me.' Anna made the tea, put out the children's orange juice, poured the tea and carried the tray into the dining room so the children could sit up to the table, leaving Louise to cry by the kitchen sink.

Anna went back into the kitchen to pick up Oliver out of the pan cupboard, where he was merrily dragging the pans out and banging them with a wooden spoon, and to put him in his high chair by the dining table. Gilbert came in with the other children, settled them down with their drinks and biscuits, accepted his cup of tea from Anna and sat at the head of the table. Anna sat at the other end and endeavoured to involve the children in conversation.

But Gilbert interrupted before she'd even begun. 'Anna, is Louise all right?'

'Having a good cry, it'll do her good.'

'I don't know what to say or do next.'

'Take it one day at a time.'

Rosalind began kicking young Gilbert under the table. 'Easier said than done. Rosalind! That will do, thank you very much. The slightest thing upsets her.'

Rosalind looked suitably chastened.

Anna marvelled at the calm way Gilbert kept the children in order. She didn't envy them coping with such a large family when both of them were in such depths of despair.

'I'm sure that must be so. But eventually you'll catch a glimpse of the light at the end of the tunnel and you'll start to get there before long. You won't forget what has happened but the pain will recede and you'll be able to look to the future.'

Gilbert rewarded her sympathy with a faint smile. 'Are you happy here?'

'I'd be much happier if we knew what was happening to Peter and Caroline and the twins. Sir Ralph had that brief moment in the spotlight and then it's all gone dead again. I only hope we hear good news before the race afternoon. Everyone is losing interest, but they mustn't.' She banged her fist on the dining table, which made the children jump. They all laughed and so did she. Louise came in, having obviously given her face a good rinse under the kitchen tap to wash away the tears, and asked what the joke was.

Gilbert explained, as Anna stood up to make room for Louise. 'I'd best be going. Sit here, Louise, where you belong.' At the door she turned back to look at them all and thought how wonderfully lucky they were. They didn't feel that at the moment but they would in time. 'Bye, children. Take care, all of you.'

On her way back to the rectory, Anna spotted Greta Jones walking up Shepherd's Hill towards the village and stopped to offer her a lift.

'Are you out for the exercise or would you care for a lift?'

Greta turned to see who was offering. She was in two minds. Accept or not? Give herself more time to think or . . . she made up her mind. 'Thanks.'

'Sit in the front, I'll just move my bag.'

'Before we drive off, can I have a word?'

Anna switched off the ignition and sat back. But Greta didn't say anything at all at first. She simply sat looking out of the window, pondering.

'Is it something I can help you with?' Greta still didn't speak. 'Just take your time, Greta.'

'Well, I don't know if you can. Help, I mean. I'm so disappointed.'

'What about?'

'Paddy.'

'Isn't it working out then, him lodging with you?'

'That bit's OK. Vince enjoys his company and Paddy's done loads in the garden, it looks really good now. He's strong, you see, and can dig like a navvy. He's made me a bigger vegetable patch out of some rough ground I'd never bothered with. One minute I looked out and he'd just started; next minute, it seemed, it was double dug and waiting to be planted. He's been a real tonic for Vince and me. Someone to look after, yer know what I mean. But . . .'

'Is he thieving still? Is that it?'

Greta turned a concerned face towards Anna and said quietly, 'Well, yes, that's it. He is. Damn and blast him. Oh! Sorry, I didn't mean to say that.'

'Don't worry, I've heard far worse on the Bun run in Culworth. There's not much can shock me. How do you know he's stealing?'

'He's started bringing home fruit from the hot houses, and vegetables I don't grow, from the kitchen garden. *Says* he's paid for 'em but I'm sorry, I don't think he has. But we're eating 'em 'cos we don't like to tell him we think he's stealing 'em. Sounds like we don't trust him, which we did, except now we don't. He doesn't need to, we manage very nicely with his money. And what if Mr Fitch finds out? Someone what works in the estate maintenance told our Barry he has no more chances left since Mr Fitch caught him with a box of daffodil bulbs he was going to sell to a chap on the market. Can't tell Michelle because she'll lose her job for letting it go on, and they'll all be homeless. I can't have that on my conscience. What's worse, Vince and me's eating the stuff so we're a party to the act of stealing. Puts us in a very difficult position.'

'Would you like me to have a word?'

'But how can you? He'll know I've told you and then he won't trust me no more. He feels like a son to me.' Greta dabbed her eyes with a tissue. 'Then . . . I haven't told Vince this . . . yesterday I was doing his bedroom and putting his laundry away for 'im and I found something in his drawer what I think's come from the Big House.'

Anna's heart jumped. 'What was it?'

'A little silver dish, like a bon-bon dish, kind of old, yer know. I don't understand hallmarks but it's got some and it's very elegant, so it's not rubbish. That's the worst thing. Old Fitch'ull have him in prison in a jiffy. He's told him so. Why does he do it? Can you tell me? He's got a home and a job. Why?'

'Since he was a boy he's been out in the big bad world, fending for himself and his family, and he can't seem to stop it. It's like an addiction, like smoking or drinking or gambling. We've got to do something though.'

'Yes, but what?'

'I'll think about it. Where's the dish now?'

'I left it where it was . . . here, look at the time. I promised Jimbo I'd work this afternoon extra. We've got so many orders in. I'll have to go.' Greta tried opening the door.

'Don't get out. I'm driving you there, remember?' So they charged up Church Hill like bats out of hell and roared up to the Store. Greta got out, saying before she put her feet on the ground, 'Don't let on, will you?'

'Of course not. I'll be in touch.'

Anna found Paddy sitting in the wheelbarrow in the sun eating a late lunch and leaning against the brick wall of the potting shed.

He appeared very nonchalant but she caught a flicker of wariness in his eyes as he greeted her. 'Hello! To what do I owe this honour? Don't usually get company in my lunch hour.'

She stood quite still looking at him and not speaking.

He didn't attempt to fill the silence and neither did she. His ham and salad sandwich looked gorgeously tempting, with its homemade crusty brown bread and the mayonnaise squeezing out of it at each bite and the ham hanging out over the edges. When you haven't yet had your lunch . . . So she reached across and took the other half from his lunchbox and began eating it.

Paddy looked startled. 'Eh! That's mine, I've been working hard all morning and looking forward to that. Give it me back.' He was squinting into the sun when he looked up at her and it made him look like a particularly unpleasant garden gnome.

'I wanted it.'

'But it's not for you to just take it, without so much as a by-your-leave. Give it back.'

'No, I want it. Just like when you want things and take them. I'm doing the same.'

Paddy peeled himself out of the wheelbarrow and stood looking at her, the corners of his mouth oozing mayonnaise. 'What's that meant to mean?'

'You know what it means. You're stealing from Mr Fitch, aren't you?'

Paddy had to wet his lips before he answered. 'What makes you think that?'

'It's a wild guess, because I know you can't resist when there's easy pickings available. Garden produce, I bet. Mr Fitch will sack you when he finds out, and also Michelle. All her family will lose the house they live in. Will that please you? Will you be satisfied then? Eh? Will you be pleased with yourself? Real feather in your cap, won't it be?'

Paddy looked panicky and tried to bluster his way out of it. 'I wouldn't do a thing like that, knowingly.' He became quite indignant at this slight on his character and was amazed to hear himself say, 'I'm not that kind of person.'

'She gave you a job when you needed it and you're taking a risk with *her* job, to say nothing of your own. Whether you admit to it or not, you enjoy this gardening lark, I can tell.'

'Mind-reader are you now, as well as saintly?'

'Oh, you'd be surprised. By the way, I've heard on the village grapevine that there's things going missing from the Big House. What do you know about that?'

'Nothing. Give me my sandwich back.'

'No, I shan't. Haven't had my lunch yet, so I need it. You don't like a dose of your own medicine, do you?'

Paddy began to lose his temper. 'I insist you give me my sandwich back.'

Anna took another bite of Paddy's sandwich before she answered. 'What was it you took, then?'

Paddy pressed his lips together in a thin line and declined to answer.

'You've made such a good start to creating a proper life for yourself, I can't believe you'll throw it all away because you can't keep your hands to yourself. It's such a pity, just when you've won everyone's admiration for your stance about the bus.'

'Huh.'

'You have, you know. They're all on your side and willing to act as witnesses if it comes to a court case. Please, Paddy, think long-term. It's like giving up smoking, I expect, so very hard but with just that little bit more effort—'

'Mmm.' He sounded almost convinced.

'If you've taken it, couldn't you put it back? Without anyone knowing, like when you took it?'

'Suppose.'

'No suppose about it. Think of Greta, how upset she'll be. She really cares about you, you know. So does Vince. She says you're like a son to her.'

Paddy frowned, a nasty suspicion had come into his mind. 'When did you last speak to her?'

She had to lie. 'Last Sunday after Church.' There was no alternative. It was surprising how often she was able to justify lying for Paddy's sake. It was becoming a habit.

'I'll put it back.'

'Put what back?'

'All right, then, the silver dish I nicked.'

'Pity you can't do the same with the—'

'All right, all right, I won't pinch any more vegetables either.'

'Good chap. Come for Sunday lunch, in exchange for your sandwich.'

'OK, then. Thanks.'

'Being trusted, that's the thing. Remember. One o'clock sharp, Sunday. Be seeing you.'

Paddy watched her leave, realizing the truth of what she said. He was on to a good thing here. A good home where, for the first time in his life, he was appreciated, and a job which he loved. The thought of prison after all this freedom in this beautiful fresh air! Hell! Standing on a chair, peering at the sun through a barred window wasn't to be compared to standing out in it with the breeze ruffling yer hair like it was doing today. In prison there wasn't no wheelbarrow to sit in and no sun shining on you while eating yer lunch. He thought about that hell hole he'd been sent to as a kid and the picture of the roaring sea and the peace of the harbour where the sailing ship had found sanctuary, which had come so vividly to mind on that first day at Greta's. He was definitely in that safe harbour now. No, he'd too much to lose. That blasted dish 'ud have to go back. Somehow.

Chapter 19

Almost before they knew it, the day of the race afternoon was on them. The excitement had been mounting all week and there'd been a lot of trying on of outfits, discarding of the impossibly tight, getting into Culworth to buy new shirts, new skirts, for hairdos and facials at Misty Blue's, and a general surge of anticipation, which had put a spring in everyone's step. In Turnham Malpas there was nothing they liked better than a good knees-up, as Angie Turner would say.

Jimbo and Harriet were taking Flick but not Fran; she was being left at home with Fergus, who was recovering from an appendicitis operation and didn't feel up to standing around for hours and socializing. Fran objected strongly but Jimbo had decreed she was too young for such an event and would only be bored and very likely irritating to her parents, who intended enjoying themselves to the hilt. 'Considering your appalling behaviour at my cousin's wedding a few weeks ago, we certainly are not taking you. It will be a long time before I recover from that appallingly disgraceful exhibition by a spoiled brat called Fran.' Fran had the grace to blush with embarrassment.

Harriet had supervised the provision of the food and was on tenterhooks in case it didn't work out as she'd hoped. She was dressing in their bedroom when she said to Jimbo, 'I just wish we'd heard from Peter and Caroline. That would have made me feel so much happier about this afternoon. It feels dreadfully selfish to be looking forward to enjoying ourselves when they're living through such horrors.'

'Believe it or not, it's now two weeks since we last heard. I feel really fearful for them.'

'It's not two weeks, it's at least four.'

Jimbo, knotting his tie in front of the mirror on the wardrobe door said, 'Never! Is it really? Of course you're right it is.'

'What on earth can possibly have happened?'

'I've stopped thinking about that, it's too scary. Absolutely anything could have happened to them. They could all be dead. Those kind of situations are so unpredictable. All normal standards are thrown to the wind.'

Harriet shuddered. 'Don't, I can't bear it. Is this suit OK, do you think?'

Jimbo turned to look at her. 'That's new. I like it. Style's a bit funky though.'

'It's all the rage.'

Jimbo chuckled and said in fun, 'Oh, well then . . . '

'Sometimes . . . '

'Yes?'

'I could strangle you.'

'Not your Jimbo. Come here and give me a kiss.'

She did. And held him tight, thinking how glad she was he was here in this house, safe and comforting and hers. What's more *she* knew where all *her* children were. 'I'm so glad I'm yours and you are mine. So glad.'

'Ditto. Love you for ever.'

'We are lucky.'

Jimbo released her, glanced at his watch, and called out to tell Flick they were about to leave and would she ever be ready? Finlay was downstairs having his first drink of the afternoon. Flick was proud to be going with him. He looked so handsome now he'd got past the spotty youth stage. He'd inherited Harriet's lean figure and not the slightly portly one that Fergus had inherited from his father. Flick looked delightful. She was wearing a short white dress, too short in Jimbo's opinion, with black spots, made of georgette. The dress was floaty at the hem but close-fitting, too close in Jimbo's opinion, everywhere else, and she was lit up by the anticipation she felt for this swish afternoon at the races.

She wasn't the only excited one. Everybody was looking forward to the event, including the two Senior sisters, who had squeezed the money for the tickets out of their meagre income, on the strength that they'd be able to steal enough food – well, steal wasn't the word they used, they said 'procure' – to last the week. They got out their capacious bags and their ten-year-old best frocks, washed each other's hair, snipped a bit off here and there to straighten their respective bobs, put on the shoes they'd worn first at Muriel and Ralph's wedding, even though they pinched unbearably, and began the trek up the long drive to the Big House.

They were passed by car after car, including Jimbo's but he couldn't pick them up as the car was full now Grandmama had joined them. She was wearing a sharply styled black suit and a white blouse with a waterfall collar that softened the severity of her suit. She also wore a tiny black hat perched on top of her Jaffa-coloured hair, its starkness softened by veiling. Finlay gave her a wolf whistle when she got in the car and he received a steely glare from his Grandmama for his vulgarity.

Close upon their heels came two of the weekenders accompanied by their snivelling son, Merlin, who rarely came to the village at the weekend, his parents having found his grandparents loved having him for the weekend. They went up the drive in their classic Cortina at a stately pace, arguing fiercely. Merlin was already crying.

'It's all in the upbringing,' said Sylvia Biggs to Willie as they wended their way up to the Big House. Sylvia's car had finally packed up and they'd decided not to replace it, so Sylvia had her strappy, high-heeled sandals in a bag and was wearing her flatties she used for the house, as she could hardly walk at all in the sandals. 'That Merlin snivels all the time. I can't understand it. And thin! Heaven help us. He looks as though he lives on carrots with that sandy hair and his strange complexion. Mind you, when you look at his parents ... there's no wonder he's odd-looking. Uriah Heep, he reminds me of. I bet he cried all the time when he was little.'

Willie could tell Sylvia was put out, and he racked his brains to think what might have caused it. 'Now, my Sylvia, what's the matter?'

She stopped and turned to look at him. 'You ask me what's the matter? You ask me that?'

Willie apologized. 'I'm sorry. Of course I know what's the matter, just didn't think.'

'Here we are going to this thingy,' she waved her hands about, 'you know this event ... and the people it's for ... we don't know if they're alive or dead. It's terrible.'

Trying to take her mind off things, Willie said thoughtlessly, 'Don't cry, you'll spoil your make-up.'

'What does make-up matter at a time like this? Tell me that.'

Humbled, Willie answered, 'It doesn't matter one iota.'

'What if they're dead? Whatever shall I do?'

'Keep going bravely forward like you've done all your life. With me.'

'Oh, Willie. I'm heartbroken.'

'We haven't heard they're dead, have we?'

'No, but they must be. Oh, look, there's the other weekenders. They do wear the strangest things. Hello!' She twinkled her fingers at them as they sailed by in their huge 4×4, looking for all the world as though they owned the estate. 'They'll have got that on the never-never, I bet.'

'Sylvia, it's not like you to be so critical. I just hope you cheer up before we get there. It won't do, won't this.'

He sounded so desperately disappointed with her that Sylvia decided to cheer up. 'Maybe we'll hear today they're all safe and sound and on their way home.'

Willie patted the hand she'd slipped into his. 'I've no doubt that they will be. Absolutely safe and coming home before we know it. Though, knowing the rector like I do, he won't want to come if it means leaving his work undone.'

'He'll have to come home if it's not safe.'

'We're here now. Shoulders back and be determined to enjoy yourself. Ready?'

They had thought they'd arrived early, but as with all Turnham Malpas do's everyone had arrived well before the time. The hall was filled to capacity already. No sign of food though, which the Senior sisters found disconcerting.

A huge screen had been erected at one end of the hall, and the race meeting at Longchamp was already in progress. But it was scarcely worth looking at the screen because all the excitement was with the people attending. There were tables all down the longer side of the hall covered with white damask cloths, holding battalions of glasses, silver trays, canapés, with smart stainless-steel refrigerators at intervals, from which seemingly endless magnums of champagne were being removed. There was a positive chorus of champagne corks being pulled and the smaller children were running about among the guests collecting them all. The photographer from the *Gazette* was hopping and skipping about, taking pictures of the guests, till they all became quite blasé about posing with bright smiles on their faces.

The black-and-white outfits were stunning. Dottie Foskett, who'd had her ticket paid for by Ronald Bissett in gratitude for her help during little Roderick's short life, was dressed from head to foot in white, with a white feather boa around her skinny shoulders.

Grandmama Charter-Plackett muttered to Harriet, 'All white? For Dottie Foskett? It's the most inappropriate colour for *her* to have chosen.'

'Katherine, really!'

'It is. We all know what she is. I'm amazed Louise and Gilbert are willing to employ her. Still, they say she was trained to clean in a convent so her house-cleaning skills are beyond reproach apparently, which can't be said of her occupation.'

Dottie suddenly and unexpectedly materialized in front of them, beaming from ear to ear. 'Good afternoon!'

'Hello, Dottie. Lovely to see you,' said Grandmama, quickly reversing her tone of voice. 'You're looking dazzling.'

Harriet tried hard to cover up their embarrassment. 'You certainly are, you look altogether splendid.'

'Thought I'd get in the spirit of things.' She nonchalantly flung the feather boa over her left shoulder then smoothed her hands over her narrow hips. 'Bought this years ago. Never thought I'd wear it again, but it's quite appropriate today, isn't it?'

'Absolutely,' said Harriet. 'Absolutely appropriate.'

'I'm glad to get a chance to enjoy myself. It's been hard these last few weeks, you know, the baby and what not.'

Harriet nodded her agreement. 'It must have been very difficult. I'm just glad they had someone like you they could rely on. Are they feeling any better about it?'

'Not much. I was glad to help 'em. They haven't come. Not ready for jollification yet. They will be ready, in a while. They've taken it very badly.' She shook her head.

'Of course they have. Takes time. Which horse have you chosen?' Grandmama asked. She needed a chance to air her views on horse-racing, having secretly checked the racing pages in her daily newspaper for weeks.

'No contest, I've chosen Major Malpas. It's sure to win.'

Grandmama nodded sagely. 'He's got quite a good record this season, but there's a lot of excellent competition: Le Petit Trianon; Masquerade; Beau George; Myladymelody; Carnival Queen.'

'I looked at them and I've still decided to back Major Malpas. He's in with a chance.'

'No contest. It's Le Petit Trianon. Five to one. Sure to win.' Grandmama said this with such authority she sounded as though she were privy to inside information straight from the stable yards.

Harriet and Dottie burst into scathing laughter.

Grandmama took umbrage and declared fiercely, 'You've wasted your five pounds. Sorry, but you have.'

'Wait and see.'

Dottie wandered off to find her cousin Pat while Harriet surveyed the crowd. There was Jimmy in his dinner jacket, two of the weekenders knocking back the drinks at a phenomenal speed, Greta Jones with Vince but no Paddy – he'd said he didn't bet and wouldn't be coming – Sheila and Ron, neither of whom looked particularly happy, and yes, Ralph and Muriel. Just emerging out of his office was Craddock Fitch.

Harriet drew Jimbo's attention. 'Oh, look! There's Craddock.'

'I can't see the old goat. Oh, there he is. Let's go and thank him, you know how pleased he is when his generosity is recognized.' They pushed their way across the hall.

'Jimbo! Harriet, my dear.' Craddock Fitch held Harriet's shoulders and kissed her effusively. 'My dear, I've taken a peep at the food and it all looks very splendid indeed. What a clever wife you have, Jimbo.'

Mockingly, Jimbo replied, 'I don't need telling, Craddock, she reminds me every day.'

'Quite right. She should. Isn't this magnificent? It does us all good to get together from time to time. Now. Have you got your champagne?'

'Not yet. We were going to head for the kitchens just to check.'

'Believe me, there's no need, Pat Jones is in there and it's all going with a swing. She's excellent, you know, really excellent. Such an unexpected talent.'

Jimbo agreed. 'We're very lucky. She's found her niche, you know.'

'Worth her weight in gold. I hope you pay her accordingly.'

'Of course.' Jimbo reminded himself to give her that rise he'd been intending to award her and never got round to. 'She's a mainstay of the organization.'

'Ever thought of branching out now you've got everything here doing so well?'

Jimbo was too much of a business man to declare his plans for the future to anyone, so he passed it off by saying, 'A few irons in the fire, so to speak.'

'That's what I like to hear. Never stop the ideas coming. If you do it's the end.'

'True. True.'

Harriet grew restless, she hadn't come for a fun afternoon only to find herself pinned down by talking business. That was the trouble with successful entrepreneurs, they had no other subject of conversation. She wondered exactly what ideas Jimbo had up his sleeve for expanding the business; he certainly hadn't discussed them with her. If it was another fancy restaurant like his previous one in Turnham Malpas . . . its failure had gone deep with her and she dreaded it happening all over again.

Jimbo, sensing her restlessness, excused himself and took Harriet's arm. They melted away into the crowd. 'Hells bells, but he's splashed out on the champagne. He definitely won't meet his costs, at ten pounds a nob.'

'Honestly, Jimbo, you can do nothing but talk business.'

'I wasn't, I was only saying—'

'He doesn't care about the cost, he only cares about making a success and being admired for it.'

'He'll never change, not now. Wonder if Kate still feels the same about him?'

Harriet nudged Jimbo's arm and said softly, 'Look at the

expression on her face, there's your answer.' He looked up and saw a genuine deeply loving smile on Kate's face as she met up with Craddock. A smile so obviously full of such deep love that Harriet and Jimbo almost blushed at having been privy to it. 'There you see, you old sceptic, it is working out well, isn't it?'

Jimbo denied ever doubting the fact and they squabbled pleasureably while deciding which one of them it was who'd said the marriage wouldn't survive.

When they'd stopped scrutinizing tickets at the door because it was obvious to them all that every guest must have arrived, Paddy quietly slipped in through the back door and found himself immediately in the kitchen. He'd decided to come today when the house was swarming with villagers because he thought it might be rather easier to be found wandering about, but he hadn't expected the back door to lead him straight into the kitchen. There was a lull in the frantic activity, the staff were quietly standing about and waiting for the off. Someone had a portable TV on and a few were gathered round enjoying the build-up to the big race. Paddy spotted Pat Jones checking through her lists, and decided he'd better not get into her line of vision or she might question what he was doing; creeping in through the back door for a free champagne buffet perhaps? His heart was thumping so strongly for a split second he imagined everyone could hear it. It had never been like this before when he was thieving. He'd always been icy calm. But this time . . .

He felt his inside pocket to check the silver dish was still there. It was. Why the hell he'd pinched it he didn't know. Old habits perhaps. He'd negotiated the kitchen and was now standing in the passageway that led to the hall and the dining room. He touched the old wall panelling, appreciating the feel of the ancient wood, enjoying the sensation of touching something as old as it must be. It occurred to him that it was a miracle it had been saved from old man Fitch's passion for everything being bang up to date. This deserved to be nurtured and cared for, it was beautiful.

He looked down the passageway at the crowded hall. My, what a crowd! Were they enjoying themselves! He wished he'd bought a ticket. Everyone was so happy, so full of joie de vivre, he regretted not being part of the excitement. Paddy's hand closed on the knob of the library door. He entered, closed the door softly behind him and went straight to the huge glass-fronted display cabinet at the side of the fireplace. A low fire burned in the grate. Two vast leather armchairs with high backs and wings stood in front of it, nice idea that, read a book all quiet like, shut out from the rest of the world. He reached out to open the glass door. It creaked slightly, and he held his breath for a moment. Hell! The dish safely returned, polished perfectly and without any incriminating finger marks on it, Paddy closed the glass door and . . .

'It was you!'

He spun round. Seated in one of the big leather chairs, which appeared much too large for him, was old man Fitch. Sweat broke out on Paddy's forehead, his knees trembled. He couldn't even run. He was frozen to the spot.

'Well?'

Paddy was so frightened his tongue was stuck to the roof of his mouth. He couldn't face prison again. Oh, God no! Please, no.

'I guessed it might be you who'd taken it.'

Still Paddy couldn't speak.

'I thought I'd have a minute's peace and quiet before the big race.' Mr Fitch looked immaculate in a dove-grey tailcoat, the whitest of white shirts, a tie in the best of taste, a gold tie pin, which shouted 22 carat gold, and highly polished shoes. You could have sworn he was born to it.

'I was putting it back. I promised Anna I would.'

'Drink whiskey?'

'Not usually.'

'Share one with me.' Mr Fitch reached across to the small table beside his chair. He poured out a second glass and handed it to Paddy. 'Sit in the other chair. I'd expected my wife coming to join me but she's obviously found something needing her attention.'

Paddy's glass was shaking so much he was sure the whiskey would be jumping straight out of it before he'd taken a sip. He used two hands to hold it and still it shook.

'You've reformed, then? Putting it back.'

Paddy rather thought he must have done. 'Yes, I suppose so.'

'I'm glad to hear it. What does it feel like?'

'Funny peculiar.'

'I can imagine. What brought it on? This reform?'

There wasn't an explanation really, it just happened. He couldn't explain.

Mr Fitch gave him several good reasons for his change of heart. 'Someone caring about you? Good food? A job you enjoy?'

'You're right about the job. I'm sorry to've . . . let you down. I suppose you could say a sandwich brought it on.'

Mr Fitch grinned. 'Tell me.' So he got the story of the ham and salad sandwich and how hurt he'd been, and how it had got him thinking.

After Mr Fitch had taken time to light a cigar he

replied, 'I'm always thought of as a hard man, which I am, always, and I should order you out, lock, stock and barrel, never to return, as I promised I would the next time I caught you. But a certain mellowness comes with a happy marriage, so in a sense you've got my wife to thank for me not giving you the sack. Also, I know from personal experience where you're coming from, and I know it's damned hard to rise above our kind of childhood. But rise above it we must. I'll pay for you to go to agricultural college to learn horticulture and whatever. If you like the idea, that is.'

Paddy panicked and thought his heart would leap from his chest. 'I'd like the chance. But I can't leave home though, just got settled.' He surprised himself with his use of the word 'home', first time he'd used that word and really meant it.

'No need to. Go on day release on the morning bus to Culworth. That's where the college is, that's where Michelle went. Easy as that.'

Relieved, Paddy studied the fire burning brighter now in the grate. 'I might just do that.' He got to his feet, put his now empty glass on the table, its unfamiliar contents warming his insides and giving him courage. 'In fact, yes, I think I will.'

'Better take the chance with both hands, I shan't offer it twice. You've caught me on a good day. Must return to my guests. Are you coming?'

'I haven't got a ticket.'

'Never mind, be my guest. After all, I'm footing the bill.'

Paddy hadn't dressed for going racing, but when he looked down at himself he realized he'd had a stroke of luck for he was all in black – black polo-neck, black trousers, black denim jacket – so he wouldn't look too out of place. Then he gave himself another surprise when he said, 'It's for charity. I'd feel better if I paid my way.'

Expecting a refusal, Paddy had another surprise when Mr Fitch held out his hand. 'Very well, I'll accept.' So Paddy dug out a £10 note from his pocket to give him and instantly felt all the better for doing so.

'Thank you. Go on, help yourself to the champagne. Enjoy.'

Paddy didn't need to appear humbly grateful; he was. 'I want to thank you for your generosity. It's greatly appreciated. I can't ever thank you enough for being so understanding. Wait till I tell Greta Jones.'

But Mrs Jones was in conference with members of the W.I. committee and things were not going well. If there was anything they all hated it was a mix-up in their meticulous arrangements, for they prided themselves on Women's Institute efficiency. And here it was, a monumental mistake. Who should present the bouquet of flowers and to whom should they present it? And were flowers appropriate? They'd got together in a corner of the hall to decide.

Harriet declared she thought flowers to Kate would be appropriate.

'But it's Mr Fitch's money that paid for all this,' Greta Jones said. 'I don't even know if giving a man flowers is the right thing anyway. We should have thought about this before today. What do you think, Lady Templeton?'

Muriel knew the answer without having to deliberate. 'I think a bottle of really, really fine Irish whiskey would have been far better than flowers. I know he prefers Irish.'

'But where would we get a bottle of really, really fine

whiskey on a Sunday afternoon in Turnham Malpas? We've been very remiss in not giving more thought to this,' said Grandmama in high dudgeon about the matter.

Sheila felt hurt. There'd been something nagging her for days and she hadn't been able to home in on what it was. Now, of course, at this most important moment, she'd realized it was Mr Fitch's gift. 'I've done my very best, you know. My very best. It simply slipped my mind, there's been so much to think of. I've slaved over this New Hope Fund. I just hope you're not blaming me.'

'Well,' said Greta Jones, 'you are in charge what with your lists and that blessed clipboard you've taken every-where for months . . . and—'

'Just a minute,' Angie Turner interrupted, 'that's not fair. Sheila's had a terrible lot of things on her mind with the . . . baby . . . and that.'

But Greta Jones would not be persuaded that it was anything less than criminal that Sheila had not remem-bered.

'Far be it from me to criticize, but she is in charge and it didn't take much doing just to write down on one of her lists "thank you present for Mr Fitch". He's a very generous benefactor. We need to keep him sweet.'

Harriet had an inspiration. 'Jimbo had a bottle of Irish whiskey given to him by a grateful client. It's very special and he enthused over it for days. It's never been opened, as he was saving it for a special occasion. But I'm sure he wouldn't mind if we—'

They all leaped on this with enthusiasm.

'Are you sure?'

'It would save us extreme embarrassment.'

'Won't he be upset?' This from Muriel who hated the idea of hurting Jimbo; he'd always been so kind to her.

Harriet shook her head. 'Don't you worry about Jimbo. I shall go out and buy him another bottle and he'll never know.'

'Harriet, my dear, is this wise? You know how particular he is about his whiskey. He takes after his father for that. Fortunately, for Jimbo, not in anything else, thank heavens,' said Grandmama Charter-Plackett with a wry smile.

Harriet calmed their fears. 'Don't you worry, he's no intention of drinking any of it unless there's something really special to celebrate.'

'Yes, but where would you buy a replacement bottle for him? In this neck of the woods?' asked Sheila.

'His wine merchant in Culworth. He's ghastly expensive but he'll have a bottle, and if he hasn't he'll get one, and that way we save our bacon. Flowers for Kate and very special Irish whiskey for Mr Fitch. Absolutely perfect.'

'Well, that sorts it then. That's what we'll do.'

'Well, I'm off home to get the whiskey. The race will be starting soon. I'll put it with the flowers, right?'

They all nodded their agreement, thankful that a very thoughtless omission on their part had been remedied.

When their impromptu meeting broke up, Greta Jones found Paddy at her elbow.

'Got a minute?'

Greta beamed, 'Of course I have, son, what is it? I thought you weren't coming?'

'Changed my mind. Been talking to Mr Fitch.'

Greta was amazed. 'You have?'

Paddy nodded. 'Yes. He's asked me if I'd like to go to college to do gardening like Michelle did.'

'You!'

'Yes, and he's paying for it.'

'What did you say?'

'Yes.'

'Paddy! I'm delighted.' She daringly kissed his cheek she was so pleased and hugged him for good measure.

'He even gave me a whiskey.'

'I didn't see no whiskey being served, it's all champagne or soft drinks. Where's the whiskey, then? Vince loves a drop of good whiskey.'

Paddy stepped carefully with his reply. 'We had it in his library, he asked me.'

'Oh, right!' She took a deep breath. 'What you doing there in the first place? Have you paid for a ticket? You're not sneaking in? It is for charity and I'm on the committee and I'm not having you—'

Self-righteously Paddy replied, 'I've paid for my ticket, honest to God.'

'Oh! Right. Just a bit surprised, that's all. Anyway I'm right glad for you. Eh! Just a minute, does that mean you going away from home? I hope it doesn't. I really do.' She looked shattered by the prospect of him leaving.

'No, don't fret, it's only in Culworth at the agricultural college.'

'Oh, well! That's all right, then. I'll let you go.' She smiled fondly at him. 'Tell Vince, he'll be very pleased. Mr Fitch's had a change of heart about you, hasn't he?'

'Yes. I told him how much I appreciated it.'

Greta tapped his chest with her finger. 'No more pinching, then?'

'No more pinching.'

'Not from nobody.'

'Not from nobody.'

'Good lad. You've turned a corner. I told the rector

you were like a son of mine, and you are.' She gave him another smacking kiss, hooked her arm in his and they went off to find Vince to tell him the good news.

The main race of the afternoon was about to begin, so everyone's attention was focused on the screen. Colin Turner, a sheaf of papers in his hand and a Biro lodged behind his ear, was beginning to feel very sick. He always did whenever he bet on a big race, but today he felt ten, no, twenty times worse. Most of the money was on Major Malpas and he quaked in his trainers at the thought. He'd told them it was unlikely to be a winner, but the coincidence of the name had persuaded most of the villagers that it would win. He'd worked out that at current prices if the next favourite horse of their choice, Myladymelody at 25–1, won they only stood to make . . . help! Six thousand two hundred and fifty pounds, plus what they'd put on. Now he really did begin to sweat, because they'd put far more on Major Malpas and his mind being in such a whirl he couldn't work out what they'd make on him. He just had to hope that Major Malpas was the three-year-old of three-year-olds. With the favourite Le Petit Trianon now at 3–1 and no one had bet on that except Jimbo and Grandmama Charter-Plackett, he felt certain in his heart that the massive money they'd hoped to win for the Fund would not be forthcoming. He'd been careful not to recommend any horse for fear of being blamed if it all went pear-shaped, so they couldn't blame him for undue influence, all the same he felt desperate as he watched the runners parading.

It was a magnificent collection of classic horseflesh going round in that ring. They pranced, they skittered, they reared, they tossed their heads and played up for all they were worth, seemingly filled to the brim with the excitement of the day. A fortune in horseflesh.

He caught sight of number six, Major Malpas. Now he was in fine fettle, his proud head turning this way and that observing the crowd, apparently loving the attention, ears pricked, hooves a-dancing and bright, intelligent eyes glowing with curiosity. His jet-black mane was sleekly groomed, his black coat was gleaming and the white diamond mark on his forehead was perfectly shaped. It occurred to Colin that Major Malpas matched all the guests because he was the only true black and white horse in the race. Was that a good omen? He laughed at himself for clutching at straws! Then the sickly feeling returned and he found himself overcome with the responsibility of it all. If only you knew, thought Colin, if only you knew, Major Malpas. Go for it, boy. Go for it.

Everyone in the hall was waiting with baited breath for the off. When the signal was given it was hard to know whether it was the roar of the crowd on the race course or the roar of the crowd in the hall they heard, because the explosion of excitement was so great. The horses were bunched together going up that first gentle slope, but descending down to the long right-hand bend, the field spread out with Le Petit Trianon and Myladymelody in the lead. Then La Belle Epoque took the lead but fell back and Carnival Queen took the lead, then Beau George. Where was Major Malpas? Nowhere near the front. Then someone spotted Major Malpas coming up the outside. The excitement level in the hall began to increase, if it were possible, as their favourite horse began to creep resolutely forward, tail flying, hooves flashing, his jockey urging him on. The Major gradually used the descent to catch up with the front runners and as the racetrack levelled out to the last straight 500 metres he gained ground in a spectacular manner. Then he stumbled and vital seconds were lost as the jockey struggled to keep his seat and regain control. A great groan of disappointment filled the hall.

But within seconds he was in the running again and everyone hollered their support. Wild with delight, people were throwing things in the air, clapping, cheering him on, shouting, 'Come on, boy, come on!' and shrieking, 'That's it. Yes!' Then, from nowhere at all, Carnival Queen appeared alongside Major Malpas, 'Ohhhh!' A shattering wave of disappointment flew around the hall. It looked as though she was getting ahead, but Major Malpas . . . yes, the Major was . . . yes, he was, he'd caught sight of Carnival Queen. They were now neck and neck, pressing on to the finishing post. As it came into focus Major Malpas dug deep and went belting first past the post with great elan. He'd won by a head, that was all. Carnival Queen was second, and Myladymelody third, leaving the rest of the field several lengths behind.

In the past there'd been excitement in this hall – moments in centuries gone by when the rafters rang with exhultations – but none more so than today. Champagne corks were popping, glasses were topped up, people were hugging each other, shouting for joy, thrilled that their daring gamble had paid off. It was really only at that moment that they realized the risk they had taken: it could have been such a bitter let-down.

Jimbo climbed up on a chair, champagne flute in hand, and for a brief moment made himself heard. 'Charge your glasses. We drink a toast to Major Malpas and the New Hope Fund. Three cheers. Hip hip hurray! Hip hip hurray!' The third cheer was lost in the tumultuous cheering and clapping. Fabulous. Couldn't have been better. The money they'd got for Peter's church was absolutely unbelievable. They'd pulled off the most colossal gamble.

While Jimbo had been up on the chair, he'd felt his mobile vibrating in his pocket. Amidst the hullabaloo, he looked at the phone and found a brief text message: '*We are all safe. Peter.*'

Jimbo stared at the message. It must be a hoax. Some foul trickster playing a joke on him. It couldn't be true. Not possible. 'Harriet!'

Harriet was right beside him and when she looked at him and saw his face was white as a sheet and pinched-looking she was filled with dread. In a whisper she said, 'Oh, Jimbo, what on earth's happened? What is it?'

'Look. Read this.'

He felt her body jolt with the shock.

Taking his hand, Harriet opened the dining-room door and they slipped away from the noise. 'Well, it says so. But is it from Peter?'

'Exactly. Is it some dreadful joke? I daren't tell anyone until we're sure.'

'It must be true. It says *all* safe so they must have found the children. Who'd be cruel enough to send a message like that when it wasn't true?'

'But if it isn't true and it's some ghastly trick and we say they're safe when they're not at all, that would be terrible.'

'Jimbo, it must be true. We should be celebrating. We could tell everyone right now, what a finish to the afternoon!'

'Darling, I think we'll wait until we hear more. Perhaps he'll ring properly later. Then we could announce it.'

'But everyone should know. Immediately.'

Jimbo tried to text back, but to no avail. He put his phone away in his pocket and said firmly, 'We'll not say a word. One more day, even two more days will make no difference, let's wait and see. There's been enough heartbreak over this business.'

'Perhaps it's wise to do that.'

'If it is true and they are all safe I shall open that bottle of Irish whiskey, because what with Major Malpas coming up trumps and all the Harrises safe, that will be *the* moment to open it. Don't you think so?'

'Absolutely.'

Harriet thanked her lucky stars Jimbo had decided to say nothing about the text message thus giving her the time to replace his precious whiskey. If he'd known what she'd done . . .

Chapter 20

Harriet hurtled into Culworth the following morning on the flimsy excuse that she needed a haircut. She didn't, but anything was better than Jimbo finding out what she'd done with his whiskey. He clearly hadn't made the connection when Mr Fitch was presented with his bottle, his mind being so full of the text message he'd received. She paused at that difficult crossroads where it was impossible to see if anything was approaching from either left or right, and as she raced over the junction with her fingers crossed, a bright red taxi also raced across heading for Turnham Malpas. For one brief silly moment she was convinced she'd seen Caroline sitting in the back. But not the Caroline she remembered, this woman looked about twenty years older.

Therefore it couldn't be Caroline, of course not. It was someone else, a weekender perhaps. They were always on the verge of retirement, if not already retired when they bought a cottage, so it could possibly be one of them. By the time she was leaving Culworth, with the bottle of whiskey safely cradled in a wooden box packed with bubble wrap, she'd entirely convinced herself it wasn't Caroline.

However, as she paused to turn right down Stocks Row, out of the corner of her eye she spotted two big backpacks and a suitcase standing outside the rectory. The door was wide open. She pulled up beside Jimmy Glover's garden fence, leaped out of her car and ran round to see for herself. Peter! He was just coming out to attend to the luggage.

'Peter! You've come home!' Harriet flung her arms round him and hugged him. He smelled different and he was thinner, much thinner. She looked up into his face. His eyes were still strong, and penetrating, but there was a deep sadness behind them she hadn't seen before.

'Peter! You're all here? The children?'

'All present and correct.' He managed to smile but it appeared to be a strain to do so. 'Go in. Caroline will be delighted.'

Harriet said. 'Let me give you a kiss first.' He bent his head and she kissed his cheek. Never before had she been so glad to kiss anyone.

The twins were nowhere to be seen, but Caroline was sitting at the kitchen table and Anna was fussing over cups and saucers. Harriet said, 'Caroline! Am I glad to see you.' They embraced again and again, and then they both wept with relief, hardly able to find any words that would express their feelings.

'The children? Where are they?'

Caroline wiped her eyes. 'They've gone next door to see Sylvia and Willie. They've inspected every inch of the rectory to check everything is in order.'

'Of course. I can understand that. Look, let me ring Jimbo so he can put a notice up that you're home. Please.'

'We don't know if we can cope with visitors just yet.'

'Please. It'll help you, I'm sure, to know how we've missed you. We've all missed you so much. You've no idea. Needed Peter to talk to us, you know.' Harriet immediately realized that Anna was listening as Peter came in with the backpacks and dumped them in the hall. She apologized. 'I'm sorry, Anna, I've made it sound as though you've not been welcome, but you have, believe me. Very welcome. You've been brilliant.'

Anna nodded. 'Of course I understand. I was only a stand-in after all. There's no need to apologize.' All the same she felt a little let-down by Harriet's declaration. 'Here's a cup of good old English tea. Would you like a cup, Harriet?'

'No, thanks. I'm going home to spread the news.' Harriet got to her feet and disappeared out of the door before she broke down in front of them. She was so horrified by Peter's and Caroline's appearance: they were barely recognizable as the two vigorous people who'd embarked on their mission only a matter of months ago. Anxiety and terror had all left their mark on the two of them.

Harriet dashed into the Store shouting, 'Peter and Caroline are back! It's true. I've been talking to them!'

Excitement broke out like a rash. Tom emerged from the Post Office 'cage', Bel from behind the till, Jimbo from his office, Greta Jones from the mail order office and the kitchen staff carrying whatever piece of kitchen equipment they'd been using when they heard Harriet's voice. All gathered round to hear the news.

'It's true! They are. They've just arrived.'

Jimbo took off his straw boater, smoothed his bald head and said, 'Thank God for that. Are they back for good?'

Harriet thought for a moment and then said, 'I don't know.'

Bel asked, 'And the children? Are they back, too?'

'Yes, but I haven't seen them. I'll go ask.' She ran all the way back to the rectory, charged in through the front door and asked. Peter was sitting in his usual place at the head of the kitchen table, cradling his cup of tea in his hands. Caroline was facing him sipping her tea.

Her question was received in silence. Harriet looked from one to the other, and eventually Peter answered. 'Yes. We are.'

'Good.' Harriet raced back to the Store and called out from the door, 'They're here for good.'

'Thank God for that,' was Tom's heartfelt reply.

Breathless with all her running back and forth, Harriet said, 'They both look terrible.'

Jimbo put an arm round her shoulders and gave her a squeeze. 'That's likely with the things they've had to face. I expect we'd look terrible, too. But they are back safe and sound. This moment is the time for a toast. We'll all share that whiskey of mine I've been keeping.'

Remembering where she'd left the car and that the whiskey was still wrapped up on her back seat, Harriet, thinking quickly, said, 'I think it would be better if Caroline and Peter are with us when we toast them, don't you?'

'Of course, of course, you're absolutely right.'

'Don't rush over there now, they seem to be in shock at the moment. I think we'll have to keep our pleasure on the back burner for the moment.

Then Tom said, 'What about Anna?'

'Ah, yes. What about Anna?'

Anna was having to do a serious readjustment of her life. She couldn't stay in the rectory – she felt they would need their own space – but on the other hand Peter would need time to recuperate before he returned to doing a full day's work. So what should she do? Her own flat at the Abbey was let out so there was no room for her there. She knew Peter and Caroline would say they didn't mind if she stayed, but that would never do, because deep down they would mind.

There came an imperious ringing of the doorbell, so Anna went to answer it.

It was Grandmama Charter-Plackett. 'Harriet's told me. I haven't come to visit, but I did think about you and the difficult position you're in.'

'Actually, I am in a difficult position, yes.' Anna stood out on the step, closing the front door behind her. 'I can't stay here, they need their space.'

'Exactly. Well, if nothing springs to mind, come and live with me. I have a lovely second bedroom, all mod cons as they say, and I'd love to have your company. For as long as it takes. Right! Tonight if you'd prefer.'

'Really? You don't know how grateful I am. They've let my flat to a Bible student for a year so there's no way I can go back there, and if I did we'd have to take it in turns. It's so small.'

'Give them all my love, my dear. And you're not to feel as though we don't want you, it's just that . . . we all rely so deeply on Peter's spiritual wisdom. Bit nearer to God than the rest of us, don't you know. We love him dearly . . . and the children of course . . . and Caroline.'

'Thank you for saying that. I'll give them your love, and thank you for the offer.'

'I mean it. Just give me a buzz. I always have clean sheets on the bed so it's no trouble at all.'

'Thank you, I'm so grateful.'

Anna closed the front door and as she did so, the phone began to ring. Out of habit Anna went to answer it. It was the first of many callers that day asking if it was true that the Harrises were back.

At two o'clock it was Miss Gotobed's funeral. Question was, would she be doing Peter a good turn by taking it herself or would he prefer to be there himself?

When Anna returned to the kitchen, Peter was pouring himself a second cup of tea. 'Who was that at the door, Anna?'

'Mrs Charter-Plackett checking the rumours were right. She sends you her love and will be seeing you whenever. The phone was someone from Culworth asking if it was true you were home safely.'

'They must have seen us at the station.'

'I have a funeral today, Peter. It's Miss Lavender Gotobed. Would you prefer to take it?'

Peter didn't answer.

'Obviously, I don't mind. I've been seeing quite a bit of her these last few weeks. She's missed her one hundredth birthday by four weeks. Bright as a button, planning to write to the council about the drains in Little Derehams, then all of a sudden, as she said, her body gave up the ghost and she was gone inside a week. What do you think?'

'What time?'

'Two o'clock.'

Peter hesitated. 'I should, but I can't cope, I'm afraid. I really need you here for a while to keep the parish ticking over. You're welcome to stay.'

'No problem. Mrs Charter-Plackett has offered me her spare bedroom and I shall take her up on that. You need your space.'

Caroline, struggling to be charitable, said, 'Oh! But we would be glad for you to stay.'

Anna shook her head. 'No, I shall begin moving my things when I get back from the funeral. This is your home and you need to have it to yourselves. I mean it. And Sylvia can't wait to get back in to look after you all. I'm quite sure about that.'

Peter began to protest but Anna would have none of it. 'I didn't want her to clean for me as I'm perfectly capable of cleaning for myself, and she's been itching all this time to get back to the rectory. I think she has suspicions that I haven't been dusting properly.' She smiled. 'I've no doubt she'll be reporting for duty first thing tomorrow.'

She'd no sooner said that than there was a knock at the door and a voice calling out as though they'd never been away, 'It's only me.' And there Sylvia stood in the kitchen doorway, her face alight with pleasure. She managed to hide the shock she felt on seeing them and walked straight across the kitchen to hug Caroline. 'I'm so glad you're all safe. It's been terrible. I thought I'd never see you again. Never ever. But here you are.' She stood back to study Caroline and saw without a shadow of doubt the anguish not yet gone from her face. 'And you, sir, so glad you're back.' She shook Peter's hand with both her hands and then couldn't restrain herself from hugging him, too. 'We've needed you these last few months.'

When Sylvia released him, Peter answered, 'Sylvia! Lovely to be back. The children, where are they?'

'Don't you fret. They're just finishing a game of snakes and ladders with Willie. Strange really, they haven't asked to play it for years and here they haven't been back two minutes and they were asking for a game.'

'Do them good.'

Sylvia couldn't resist her need to know where they'd

been all these weeks and asked straight out. 'So where were they when they were missing?'

Caroline cleared her throat. 'We can't bear to talk about it just yet.' There was a finality in her voice, which didn't allow for anyone persuading them otherwise. So one of those strange silences fell where everyone present was thinking their own thoughts, but not for long because Beth and Alex returned. They stood in the hall, looking at them from the kitchen doorway and then went upstairs together without speaking.

Anna jumped up from her chair. 'I've been sleeping in Beth's bedroom. I'll go get my things out, don't want to upset her.' She raced up the stairs to find Beth standing in her room looking out of the window.

'I'm so sorry. If I'd known you were coming . . . I've been sleeping in here, you see. It's been a lovely, welcoming bedroom. Thank you for the use of it. I've slept very well in here, but now I'm going to take all my bits and pieces out.' Anna began by stripping the bed, and Beth didn't answer her.

While Anna was clearing some books from the shelves, Beth said, 'I never thought I'd stand here looking out at our garden ever again. I love this view. Mum's flowers in our garden and then Pipe and Nook Lane and the ancient hedgerow. Lady Templeton once threatened to lie down in front of the tractor that was coming to pull it up, you know. And she did do it. Mr Fitch was horrified when he saw her. She won though. Most daring thing she's ever done. Funny name, isn't it, Pipe and Nook Lane? No one seems to know how it came about. Then Rector's Meadow and then the Big House Wood the far side of it; it's so beautiful in autumn. This was the view I thought about so often, it was all I had to hang on to.' Beth fell silent.

'I'm sorry for what you've been through. I can't begin to imagine—'

'Alex was so brave. If it hadn't been for him—'

'Well, you can put it all behind you now.'

'Think so?'

'If you get back to school . . .'

But Beth walked out of her room and up the attic stairs and left Anna to finish clearing out. Anna could have kicked herself for so thoughtlessly trying to encourage Beth to look forward to normality so soon. Of all the ridiculous things to have said. The sooner she was out of here the better, before she made any more stupid remarks. The child looked tortured beyond belief. Not perhaps physically but certainly mentally, and far too thin for a girl of fourteen. So what had Alex done that had somehow saved her sanity?

Anna left for Grandmama's cottage immediately, but Sylvia stayed and shopped and put things where they belonged, and couldn't wait to have a good clean-through, but not today. The rectory was far too fragile a place just now. It was in the air, in every room, a heavy cloud of distress, and the Harrises were almost speechless with a mixture of relief and terror. Sylvia was longing to know, but she had a feeling they wouldn't be telling her because the pain was still too close, the wounds as yet too raw to touch.

She cooked them one of their favourite meals. Caroline protested but she insisted that was what she was going to do. That pecan pie they all loved to finish and before that a glorious beef casserole with mushrooms and lashings of wine, and those lovely floury jacket potatoes, which Sylvia was a genius at. Then she left, reluctantly, saying, 'It's Tuesday tomorrow so I shall be in as usual, to *clean*.'

It was only when she had left and got home that she cried. 'It's destroyed those two children. Destroyed them. They ought never to have gone.'

As soon as the door closed on Sylvia, Peter said he was going to the church. He'd wanted to go ever since they'd got home but the phone had rung constantly and he hadn't known how to cope with the silence of the twins and he felt so dreadfully concerned about Caroline that he daren't leave her. But Caroline urged him to go while he had the chance; she'd be OK and the children were watching TV. She knew the guilt he felt at having suggested going to Africa and bringing about this near catastrophe.

Peter went to the old familiar drawer in his desk and took out the keys to the church. He cradled the huge key to the main door in his hand, feeling it might hold the answer to his torment.

The church had been locked at five o'clock by Zack the verger, so when Peter entered it felt chilling. He looked straight to the altar where the small light was burning as always. Slowly Peter walked down the aisle, savouring every pew, every echo of his footsteps, every flagstone under his feet, every kneeler so lovingly restored by the W.I. embroiderers, every rafter above his head, every ancient tattered flag hanging from them.

When he arrived at the altar steps, he smiled at Sheila's small weekday flower arrangement on the table. To him it represented the whole village welcoming him home, and there he knelt, hands together in prayer, feeling like a lost soul finally, despite all his tribulations, arriving home where he belonged.

He'd knelt there praying for more than an hour when he sensed the door open and footsteps, his darling Caroline's footsteps, coming towards him. She didn't interrupt him, just stood with a hand on his shoulder, waiting. Peter bowed his head, indicating he'd finished and Caroline said softly, 'Darling, you'll catch your death in here. Come home. Jimbo and Harriet have come, and they've got big news for you. You can always come back tomorrow.'

He got to his feet, stiff and aching with kneeling so long. When she looked in his face she thought she caught a tiny glimmer of his enduring inner light, and she was glad.

'Are they jolly?'

'Of course. What else? They're so glad we're home.'

'And the children?'

'It's really time they were in bed after such a long day, but I'm saying nothing at all. They sleep so little at the moment, for now it's best to leave it to them.'

Peter locked the main door and paused to look up at the sky. 'Remember those fantastic sunsets we used to see?'

'Of course.'

'But . . . other things . . . crowded out the pleasure.'

'You have to remember the wonderful support your congregation gave you. Remember Elijah and how hard he tried to find Alex and Beth; it was his clues that helped us find them. The children owe their lives to our neighbours and friends. Remember what a tower of strength Winsome was. Don't forget the triumphs we had, the joy of such enthusiastic Christians.'

'Of course. But whyever I felt the need to drag my family into such hell I shall never know.'

'We all went willingly, and we didn't know it would turn into hell. What's more, we needed to go. It's been a kind of cleansing for me. I've seen what other people's lives can be like and it's taught me to be grateful for the peace we enjoy, and the security and love that surrounds us. You know, ever since the twins were born, I've been carrying a load of emotional baggage, which I've never been able to rid myself of. The children meeting their real mother for the first time was almost unendurable for me. I was glad to go away and get some perspective on it. But here I am, I've survived and I'm stronger for it. And much happier. So let's wipe the slate clean. Make a new start.'

Peter smiled at Caroline, took her hand and said, 'Thank you for saying that.'

Patiently waiting for them were Harriet and Jimbo watching TV in the sitting room with Alex and Beth.

Jimbo had his bottle of Irish whiskey prominently on display. He got to his feet to shake hands with Peter saying, 'My God, man. Am I glad to have you back.' Then he took Caroline into his arms and hugged and kissed her. 'We've waited for this day. Believe me. Anna's been brilliant in the circumstances but it was the two of you we wanted back. As for you, Alex, I swear you've grown at least a foot since we saw you last. And Beth, I think you get prettier by the day.'

Alex turned off the TV and they all sat down again.

Peter said, 'It's great to be back. We feel as though we've been away for years, and it's only a matter of months.'

'Well now, I've brought this very precious bottle of Irish whiskey I was given and I intend that we all drink a toast to friends and home. It's a very special malt, rarely obtainable. How about it?'

Peter got the glasses out of the dining-room sideboard and carried them in on a tray with a jug of water. There were six whiskey glasses.

Caroline protested, 'Peter, surely not for Alex and Beth.'

'Just for the toast, I insist.'

Beth declared she doubted if she would like it.

Alex said, 'Am I grown up, then?'

Peter studied him. 'Judging by what you've done this last few weeks, I think you must be.'

Harriet longed to ask what had Alex done, but daren't. There felt to be a complete embargo on mentioning the Africa question.

Jimbo proposed the toast. 'To all of us, glad to be reunited, to Turnham Malpas for being so stout-hearted in the absence of their rector and his wife, and to Anna Sanderson who has so manfully held us together.'

Caroline asked, 'Did you need to be held together?'

'Oh yes, at times. My mother, bless her dear heart, got arrested when she got drunk in Culworth, in the middle of the day too, which seemed to make it worse, and—'

Caroline almost choked on her drink with surprise. 'Your mother! What on earth for?'

So gradually all the stories came out: Neville Neal in a red wig and smart dressing gown at the pyjama party; Greta Jones doing the cancan; Grandmama Charter-Plack-ett's Jaffa-coloured hair; Paddy Cleary driving the bus into Culworth – Paddy Cleary? Who's he?; the fire at Glebe House; the car in the pond; the two policemen at the skinny-dipping in Jimbo's pool – You mean, naked? And so it went on. Both Caroline and Peter, to say nothing of the twins, were totally amazed.

Peter wanted to know who had organized it all and Harriet had to confess it was the W.I.

At this everyone by the name of Harris went into explosions of laughter. It was a few minutes before they could speak.

'All this going on when we were away. What we missed! Oh my word.' Peter couldn't help himself, he had to ask. 'Tell me, why was your mother drunk with Jaffa-coloured hair?'

So the sponsored hair-dyeing competition was brought to light. The thought of dignified Mrs Charter-Plackett with orange hair was almost too much for Alex and Beth, and they reeled about on the sofa, helpless with laughter.

Jimbo refilled glasses, intending to relax everyone even more.

'All this to raise money for the mission?'

Harriet answered. 'Oh yes. Sheila Bissett has been an absolute gem. Everything meticulously organized except . . .'

Caroline prompted her. 'Yes?'

'Except when . . . Oh, well, never mind, another time.'

'I insist.' Caroline patted Harriet's knee. 'Come on.'

Harriet glanced briefly at Jimbo and decided confession time had arrived. 'This whiskey you are drinking is not the bottle Jimbo was given.'

Jimbo grabbed the bottle to read the label. 'It is.'

'No, darling, it isn't. We found ourselves yesterday with no thank you gift for Craddock Fitch for the champagne race party so I gave him yours.'

Jimbo got to his feet, shocked. 'What? But that was only yesterday. Where's this come from?'

'Culworth this morning. That high-priced wine merchant, fortunately for me, had a couple of bottles in. I didn't need a haircut at all, I was going for the whiskey. So pour us another one and we'll toast wives, ever the deceivers.'

So they toasted wives and then had another toast to the race afternoon, when it had been explained.

'So these were all the charity events you mentioned?'

'That's right.'

Alex interrupted their conversation saying, 'Mum, I'm taking Beth upstairs, I think she's drunk.'

'Good idea. She very probably is. Mind she doesn't fall. Oh dear, no more whiskey for her for a while. Whoops! Night-night, darlings, sleep tight.'

'Goodnight.'

'Goodnight.'

Caroline watched them leave and as soon as she knew they couldn't hear what she was saying she explained, 'Hoped the whiskey might help them sleep. They're so uptight over it all. They haven't had a full night's sleep for weeks.'

After the children had gone Jimbo said, 'One day perhaps you'll be able to tell us all about it. I did think a couple of whiskies might just help, but perhaps another time, eh?'

Glass in hand, Peter replied, 'Another time. Suffice to say for the moment that the children were hidden for weeks in a wood by some of our congregation. They were fed as best the people could, seeing as they themselves were starving because of the fighting. The whole situation was horrifying. We didn't know whether the children were alive or dead. They'd escaped the attack on the car and managed to run away in the dark. Eventually Caroline and I set off with backpacks to hunt for them, found them and then we too couldn't get away. Two soldiers who'd been in our congregation came across us quite by chance and where we'd expected instant death we found ourselves being cared for and helped to get away. They took terrible risks on our behalf. We can never repay them for what they did.'

'Well,' said Jimbo, 'what we've done while you've been away might just perhaps help you to repay them in some way. We've managed to raise over twenty-seven thousand pounds for that congregation. Mostly because of gambling on a horse.'

Caroline and Peter were astounded. 'Gambling on a horse! And twenty-seven thousand pounds. We can't believe it! That's amazing. They do so need every single penny.'

Jimbo checked the time. 'Sorry, got to go. Things to do. Stay here, Harriet.'

'Where are you—?'

'You'll see. It's Anna. She's organized things. Be back.'

It was ten o'clock when Jimbo disappeared. The three left behind chatted about the village and what had been happening, when their conversation was interrupted by the church bells. Peal after peal, following one on another, till the very earth seemed to tremble with the resonance of it all. They were ringing out a gloriously triumphant statement of thanksgiving for the safe return of their rector. Peter's spirits, so long in turmoil over recent happenings in his life, rose to unaccustomed heights: he had to open the front door to listen. He was joined by the twins and Caroline, who came to stand beside them, an arm around each of her children.

Outside in the road were a host of villagers holding aloft

lanterns or lighted torches and Peter's heart almost burst. Everyone listened until the last peal had drifted away into the night, their faces alight with pleasure.

Anna was standing at the front of the crowd. When the final peal had died away, she and Sheila Bissett, each of them holding a corner of the cheque, handed the money they had raised to Peter.

'Delighted to have you back,' Anna said. 'Please accept this on behalf of the church but, most of all, on behalf of the Women's Institute because they did all the hard work. God bless you, so glad you're home where you belong. Three cheers for Peter and Caroline and Alex and Beth.'

The cheers echoed round the village. There hadn't been a time when they had cheered more earnestly than they did this night. The moon was up, the stars were out and the village resounded with happiness and heartfelt relief at the safe return of their best-beloved rector.

When they all went to their homes, Peter sat down in the kitchen while Caroline tidied the glasses. He was looking at the cheque, lost in thought.

Caroline interrupted his thoughts. 'I'm done. Cats in bed, doors locked. Ready for bed?'

She didn't get an answer immediately so she sat down at the table opposite him and waited.

Peter cleared his throat and looked up at her, his eyes brimming with tears. 'This cheque.'

'Yes.' Caroline's heart beat a little faster.

'This cheque. Aren't they kind? So kind.'

'Yes.' A powerful feeling of foreboding took possession of Caroline. She waited for the words she guessed intuitively might be coming.

Slowly and deliberately Peter said, 'I truly believe I

cannot abandon these people for the sake of my own safety.'

Caroline swallowed hard. Surely he wasn't going to say . . . but in her heart of hearts she knew he would . . .

Peter took a deep breath and said quietly but yet very firmly, 'I must go back. This money has to be used wisely, and who better than myself to do that? They were so brave caring for our children like they did. They don't deserve for me to walk away and abandon them.'

'I see. And what about me? What about the children? Do you want them to go back?'

'They must not go back.'

'Then neither must I. I'm not abandoning them, not right now. They're far too fragile.'

Peter nodded. 'That's what I had in mind. I'll go back by myself. Leave you and Beth and Alex safe at home, picking up the threads. I'll come back when the twelve months are up, as we promised.'

It had never entered Caroline's head that he might want to go back, but she realized he must, and she dreaded him leaving her. She got to her feet, trembling with a mixture of fear and bitter disappointment. Peter stood up, held wide his arms and she went gratefully into them. He held her close without speaking.

Eventually Caroline stirred and reached up gently to kiss his lips. 'Of course I ought to have guessed you would. I was so glad to be safe I didn't think beyond getting home. This money will make such a difference to them. Running water, endless improvements, chairs in the church, a school to open. Of course you must go back.' She gripped tight hold of him and added, 'You take my love with you. I knew when we married I'd bound myself to a courageous, honest, upright man and now I've to pay the price. *I love you!* So very much.'

That night Anna slept the sleep of the just in her cosy bedroom under the eaves at Grandmama Charter-Plackett's. Before she fell asleep she dwelt on the happenings since she'd come to Turnham Malpas only a handful of months ago. It had been a much happier experience than she'd imagined it would be, except for Gilbert. His effect on her had gone deep and she could still feel the powerful stirrings of longing for him in her heart. But without a shadow of a doubt that had to be scotched. Then memories of all the events for the New Hope Fund filled her mind. They were worthy, these people she'd been directed to shepherd for a while. In fact, they couldn't be better, not a single one of them, and if she'd done nothing else she'd got Paddy settled. She turned over, pulled the sweet-smelling sheets and blankets more closely round her shoulders, and was grateful for good friends and kindly neighbours in a village which had not been left behind by the centuries as she'd first thought, but was up there in the vanguard of things, leading the way. Goodnight, Turnham Malpas. Goodnight! She suspected they'd all sleep easier in their beds tonight now their very own rector was home. She hoped, one day, that she too might be revered by her congregation in the same way as Peter, and then she fell asleep, blissfully unaware of Peter's decision.

All Orion/Phoenix titles are available at your local bookshop or from the following address:

> Mail Order Department
> Littlehampton Book Services
> FREEPOST BR535
> Worthing, West Sussex, BN13 3BR
> *telephone* 01903 828503, *facsimile* 01903 828802
> *e-mail* MailOrders@lbsltd.co.uk
> (Please ensure that you include full postal address details)

Payment can be made either by credit/debit card (Visa, Mastercard, Access and Switch accepted) or by sending a £ Sterling cheque or postal order made payable to *Littlehampton Book Services*.
DO NOT SEND CASH OR CURRENCY

Please add the following to cover postage and packing

UK and BFPO:
£1.50 for the first book, and 50p for each additional book to a maximum of £3.50

Overseas and Eire:
£2.50 for the first book plus £1.00 for the second book and 50p for each additional book ordered

---

BLOCK CAPITALS PLEASE

name of cardholder ....

....

address of cardholder ....

....

....

postcode ....

delivery address
(if different from cardholder)

....

....

....

postcode ....

☐ I enclose my remittance for £ ....

☐ please debit my Mastercard/Visa/Access/Switch (delete as appropriate)

card number ⬚⬚⬚⬚⬚⬚⬚⬚⬚⬚⬚⬚⬚⬚⬚⬚

expiry date ⬚⬚⬚⬚ Switch issue no. ⬚⬚

signature ....

prices and availability are subject to change without notice